HIGH STRIKER

by

G.T. RIGDON

Cover Design: Rebecca Swift, rebeccaswift@yahoo.com

Editor: Autumn J. Conley, autiej@gmail.com

Printed in the United States of America

ISBN: 0615638880

ISBN 13:   9780615638881

Acknowledgements

I would like to thank the following people for patiently reading very early, raw manuscripts and providing constructive feedback:

The Idiot Girls' Book Club of Woodbury, MN

My sister Janet Rigdon

My friend Xin Zheng

Acknowledgements to my early editors, Edit911 and Cindy Davis, and special thanks to Autumn J. Conley, Book Editor for helping me polish the final draft.

Dedication

This book is dedicated to my two children, Forrest and Jaxon. After years of thinking about writing this story, in the spring of 2009, they inspired me to finally "Go for it!"

CHAPTER 1

AMOS KONKLIN'S FINAL KILLINGS

Dr. Amos Konklin departed the intensive care unit at 11:15 p.m. on a seemingly typical Wednesday at the hospital. While late evenings were commonplace, Wednesdays were planned neurosurgery days and traditionally busy. He often spent those nights on his office couch. Nevertheless, this particular Wednesday was different, for its dawn gave birth to a murder plot that commenced at home, when Amos awoke from one of his routine nightmares. While his wife Cynthia lay asleep, Amos arose and made his way to the garage. There, in the quiet lull of privacy, he placed a sledgehammer in the trunk of his car. The garage was a repository for many of his tools, but the twelve-pound sledge occupied a place all its own in the corner. He kept it in a hard plastic case, the type in which one might store a billiard stick. It was not the first time such an early morning event had occurred.

Much of Amos's day was occupied by two planned brain surgeries that required his attention and focus. His patients, Vicky Moore and Dorothy Woolf were strangers in life, but they shared a common disease. Now, both women were surgical patients of Dr. Amos Konklin, a capable and caring healer, a man consumed by matters of life and death. This Wednesday was far more meaningful, though, than just the day Vicky and Dorothy would be healed.

Thoughts of vengeance flooded his mind, and Amos deliberately chose Wednesday night for the trip to the Old Wilderness Campground; it was a good night for an alibi, assuming he would ever need one. The campground was in Orange County, New York, about fifty miles northwest of Times Square. The reference to the campground had become a hospital joke, as doctors often spoke of getting away from it all by taking a quick trip to "The Wilderness," a whopping one-hour drive from their beeping machines and whining patients. Cabin 326 at Old Wilderness was actually hospital property, donated years earlier by a former chief of staff at the time of his death as a shared resource for the senior doctors, a hideaway where one could take off their scrubs and stethoscopes and relax. Amos had frequented the campground on several occasions and was confident he could be back at the hospital within a three-hour window, a reasonable amount of time, he believed, considering the stability of his patients in recovery. The safety of his patients was always at the forefront of his mind, though admittedly, on this night, his professional concerns competed against a strong personal urge, one that demanded his attention.

He walked from the I.C.U. up a flight of stairs and past Nurse Hadley's station, which was always vacant at that time of night. From there, a side door took him within fifty feet of his reserved space in the hospital parking garage. Seconds later, he was exiting the parking facility and on his way to another operation, one for which he preferred a sledgehammer instead of a scalpel. His skilled surgical hands had given new life to Vicky Moore and Dorothy Woolf, and now those same hands steadily maneuvered the jet-black Mercedes onto the New York State Thruway. On this night, however, Amos was experiencing an unfamiliar emotion. He was anxious, for his actions were not driven by a dream—this mission was personal.

Amos arrived at the road leading into the campsites at exactly 12:19 a.m. He took the next road, which went behind the campground and down to the lake. Old Wilderness offered a mix of accommodations, both cabins and tent sites. Back at the hospital, it was rumored that Dave Garth was screwing Lois Winston in Cabin 326 every weekend. In the absence of other reservations among the doctors, Garth took advantage of the circumstances, and the secluded cabin seemed to be the perfect place to carry on his torrid relationship with Lois.

About a quarter-mile out from the lake, Amos drove into the woods and shut off the engine. He sat for a moment with his hands clasping the steering wheel, then uttered to himself the passage he'd memorized from the Bible book bearing his name, Amos 9:1-4:

> *"Strike the tops of the pillars,*
> *so that the thresholds shake.*
> *Bring them down on the heads of all the people,*
> *those who are left I will kill by the sword.*
> *Not one will get away,*

none will escape.
Though they dig down to the depths of the grave,
from there my hand will take them;
Though they climb up to the heavens,
from there I will bring them down.
Though they hide themselves on the top of Carmel,
there I will hunt them down and seize them.
Though they hide from me at the bottom of the sea,
there I will command the serpent to bite them.
Though they are driven into exile by their enemies,
there I will command the sword to slay them.
I will fix my eyes upon them,
for evil and not for good."

Amos got out of the car and quietly shut the door as he scanned the area. He walked to the rear of the car and popped the trunk, revealing the case that concealed the sledgehammer and an oversized physician's bag. He bent over, removed the items from the trunk, and then, exercising the same notable caution he had taken with the car door, he closed the trunk. Amos let the heavy head of the hammer down on the ground with the handle on his left thigh, then tied his surgical mask over his face. Although it was a dark night, there was enough moonlight to capture the silhouette of a man, draped in surgical greens, prepping for an operation.

Amos took one final look at his watch: Everything was on schedule. About seventy paces from the car, he emerged onto a trail that was often used by the campers walking toward the lake. In fact, it was on that very trail that he had made love to Cynthia one night during a weekend excursion—a fond memory that faded as quickly as it had entered his mind. The cabins were in separate areas from the tents, and Cabin 326 was isolated from the others. It was the most luxurious, in the most favorable location, and—perhaps best of all—it was the most private.

By the time Amos reached the cabin, it was dark and silent. He tiptoed toward the master bedroom window and knelt. It was a warm August night, and the perspiration dripped from his forehead onto the dirt as he strained to hear any activity inside the cabin. Amos crouched, completely still, until his watch indicated that two full minutes had passed. He was convinced the couple was either sleeping or preoccupied with something else he'd rather not see. In either case, he didn't mind interrupting the occasion, considering his physician's bag was equipped with all the proper tools. He could even put on his anesthesiologist's hat if necessary.

From there, he crept toward the front door, with the heavy end of the sledgehammer clutched firmly in his right hand and the strap of the physician's bag flung over his shoulder. At the door, he took a key from his pocket—a key he'd had made while the original was in his possession during one of his frequent visits to the cabin. Then he stood upright and shifted the sledgehammer into his left hand in order to insert the key with his right. The key slipped in easily and unlocked the door with a slight turn of his wrist. He twisted the doorknob and inched the door open to avoid making any sound. Once inside, he again turned his careful attention to the door, making sure it closed without a *creak* and locking it without so much as the faintest *click*. Turning back, he stood completely still for a few seconds to allow his eyes to adjust to the dark.

To the left of the foyer was the kitchen. Amos squinted, making the best use he could of the dim moonlight coming through the small window over the sink. There were dishes on the eat-in table and leftovers that weren't considered worthy enough to be properly put away; it appeared spaghetti had been the supper selection. At that moment, another fond memory raced through his mind: His friend Becky, who had lived near him in Canada while he was a teenager, had once told him during a casual conversation that if she were ever on death row, she'd request spaghetti as her last meal. He smiled briefly, thinking how ironic that little piece of nostalgia was at the moment, then walked into the hallway.

The master bedroom was quiet, and the door was open, as if offering an invitation. When he reached the entrance to the bedroom, he saw the two lovers wrapped in each other's arms, asleep, relieving him of the need for the bag hanging on his shoulder. The image made him think of his friend Kevin Winston, who now lay lifeless in a coffin six feet underground. Kevin was a good man who had been betrayed, and he'd paid dearly for it. As Amos looked at Dave Garth, he felt nothing but disgust for the man. It wasn't the first time Garth had bedded a woman from a broken marriage in which he'd played a key role, and he often bragged about his exploits openly. However, this was the first time his sexual exploits had carried him into the path of Amos Konklin. It was a precarious collision indeed, for the path of Amos Konklin burned with the zeal of righteous vengeance.

Amos went first to the right side, to the place where Garth lay on his back with his lover's head resting on his chest. Amos paused only briefly before he took advantage of the vaulted ceiling, which enabled him to get a full, extended, unencumbered swing. The impact was tremendous, and—much like a peanut splitting under the crushing force of the index finger and thumb—Garth's skull cracked wide open beneath the hammerhead. The blood spurted upward and outward, like a high-pressure stream of water bursting out from a broken pipe, covering Amos's surgical greens with those familiar crimson splatters. The thumping sound of the sledgehammer impact startled Lois, but before she was able to fully wake or utter a single syllable of protest, confusion, or terror, a second swing caved in her right temple. It was a bloodbath, accentuated by the sound of gurgles and gasps for breath. Amos knew death was certain; he did not need to strike each person more than once.

He left the room, grabbed the bag he had dropped in the entrance, and walked down the hallway to the bathroom. There, he leaned the sledgehammer against the wall, stripped bare, had a brief look in the mirror, and took a thorough shower. After toweling off, he dressed in the spare set of surgical greens he'd tucked away in a plastic container inside his physician's bag and then reused the container for his bloody clothes. He took the damp towel and wiped down the shower and the floor, then stuffed the towel in the same plastic container. On the way out of the neat and tidy bathroom, he grabbed the sledgehammer and proceeded back down the hallway, retracing his steps toward the front door.

When he stepped outside, Amos paused to gaze at the moon and was overcome with a sense of calm and peace. His thoughts returned to Vicky and Dorothy in recovery, and he began the walk back through the woods, as if he'd been up to nothing more harmless than a moonlight stroll in the woods to clear his head. The peace lingered during the return trip. Amos felt relaxed, as the strong urge had been satisfied.

It had all started eleven months prior, when Lois Winston began having an affair with the hospital chief of staff. Lois was married to Kevin Winston, a male nurse at the hospital who was one of Amos's good friends. In fact, the friendship extended further, for Amos and Cynthia often went on outings with the Winstons. About three months into the sordid affair, Kevin found out about it, and the Winston family began to unravel. The anger and hurt from the betrayal was intense—so intense that one evening, it led to an argument that escalated into a physical altercation. As a result, Lois called the police and had Kevin arrested for domestic abuse. He spent two nights in jail before Amos was able to post bail for his release. A week later, the Winstons were separated, and Lois filed for divorce. Two weeks after that, Kevin Winston committed suicide. His death was a blow to Amos, who felt enraged by way the entire situation had unfolded. Adding further insult, although Lois appeared remorseful about what she had done, she had no problem reuniting with her lover, Dave Garth, the hospital chief of staff.

But now it was over, and all was well. Even the New York State Thruway was an ally, providing a relatively traffic-free path back to the hospital, where he entered through the same side door. At 2:13 a.m., it was on to another set of rounds, starting in the I.C.U. His two patients were stable, and he penned their status into the I.C.U logbook, along with the time.

By early afternoon, Old Wilderness was buzzing with activity. There were numerous police cars and an ambulance. The air was filled with sounds from police radios and walkie-talkies, and a small group of campground visitors had gathered around a nearby restroom facility, where they whispered and hoped they were close enough to eavesdrop to find out what had happened. Among them was a middle-aged female, who emerged from the ladies' restroom wearing only a bathrobe; her hair was still wet from the shower. She boldly approached another curious camper. "Anything new?"

"Well, I've only been here about ten minutes, but a cop just drove up in an unmarked car. He's probably important."

That cop was one Lieutenant Tom Wallace, a detective with several years of experience working in homicide.

"Really? Which one?"

"That tall guy over there by the ambulance. Looks like he's asking that lady some questions."

Wallace was easy to single out from a distance. He stood six-eight, and he'd tacked more than a few pounds on to his once-athletic high school basketball physique over the years. He was a big man.

"The big guy? Yeah, I see him. He does look important."

"Who is he talking to, I wonder?"

"I don't know, but she's wearing an Old Wilderness shirt. I'll bet she works here."

"She must know something."

The woman talking to Tom Wallace was Maria, a housekeeper, a member of the campground staff. When Wallace arrived on the scene, he was briefed by Detective Jerry Donaldson, who directed him to the already dazed and visibly shaken campground employee.

"Hi, Maria. I'm Tom Wallace. Can we go over this one more time?" Wallace asked, attempting to get his own up-close-and-personal version of the story from her. "What time did you arrive at the cabin?"

"It was about 11:00 a.m."

"Then what happened?"

"I knocked twice, but nobody answered, so I used the master key," Maria said, getting a little excited.

"Okay, good. Now, calm down, relax, and breathe deeply. So, are you saying that when you arrived, the door was locked?"

"Yes."

"What happened when you went inside?"

"I went to the bedroom and saw them there," Maria answered, her voice trembling. "I was so shocked. I screamed and ran back into the kitchen to use the phone to call the office."

"The office here at the campground?"

"Yes."

"Did you see or hear anything else this morning that looked suspicious?"

"No. I saw nothing. I-I can't believe this. I'm so sad for them," Maria said, nearly hyperventilating.

Wallace didn't get much more than what Donaldson had already told him, so he gestured for the emergency medical technician to intervene. "Thanks again, Maria, for your cooperation. I'll need you to come down to the police station later to give an official statement. I'll be in touch."

At the cabin, Wallace saw Detective Jerry Donaldson examining the front door and went over for the scoop. Donaldson was an experienced officer and was always thorough. In his twenty-some years on the force, he had never managed to move up beyond detective rank, but that was his choice. Office management and politics didn't interest him in the least.

"Find anything, Donaldson?"

"There's no sign of forced entry, Lieutenant. All the windows are locked, and the back door is bolted from the inside."

"What about this door?"

"It has one of those locking mechanisms that allows the door to be opened from the inside while remaining locked from the outside."

"Okay, keep going. Sounds like you're on to something."

"Well, sir, I think it's unlikely that the perpetrator would so carelessly leave a clue behind by deliberately locking the door on the way out after committing the crimes. Maybe the murderer used a key to enter and then locked the door behind him once he was inside. After the murders, he could have opened the locked door from the inside, and when he closed it, the door would have been locked from the outside."

"Hmm. Sounds like a logical theory to me, Donaldson. Now the question to be answered is, how many people had access to a key?"

CHAPTER 2

THE AFTERMATH

News of the murders spread quickly. The Thursday evening television news permeated the hospital walls, and the buzz intensified as Wallace interviewed the hospital staff. When Amos arrived for work the following morning, on Friday, it was the pervasive topic of conversation.

When Amos entered through the familiar side door from the parking garage, he was accosted by Nurse Wilma Hadley. "Dr. Konklin, good morning," she said, walking toward him in the hall.

"Good morning," Amos said.

Nurse Hadley, now in her late fifties, had been working at the hospital for over thirty years. She was a stout woman, flat-chested and strong. Amos didn't recall who had said it, but someone had once told him that if he hugged Nurse Hadley with his eyes closed he would mistake her for a man. Amos could relate, considering his sense of smell offered no additional clues of femininity; there was never even a hint that she was fond of perfume. Everyone knew her because she loved to talk—preferably to share or glean juicy tidbits of gossip—and Amos generally dreaded having to engage with her in lengthy conversations.

"Oh, Dr. Konklin, I suppose you've already heard the news by now." She peered out over the bifocals that rested midway on her less-than-feminine snout.

"What news is that?"

"You know...about Dr. Garth and Lois Winston."

"What about them?"

"They're dead! Both of them! It happened Wednesday night or Thursday morning, to be more exact. They apparently found the bodies at the Old Wilderness Campground."

"Really?" Amos responded in an incredulous tone. "No, I had not heard. Well, that's just awful."

"Awful indeed, Dr. Konklin. I just can't believe it. First Kevin and now this."

"What happened to them?" Amos asked, hoping he hadn't opened the door for an extended chitchat.

"Well, according the news, they were murdered," she said, whispering the last word as if it was the world's biggest secret and only she knew it.

"Murdered? Are you sure?"

"Yes, Dr. Konklin...murdered!"

"Wow. That's just...shocking. I don't know what to say. Is there anything else?" *Great. Now I've gone and done it, asking Nurse Hadley an open-ended question.*

"Well, I heard there wasn't no sign of forced entry, which means they might have been murdered by someone they knew," she said, whispering the final three words again. "It's just shocking, I tell you. These are evil times,

Dr. Konklin—evil times! Why, just the other day I was reading about this couple who was stabbed to death during a camping trip in Georgia, and that turned out to be a twisted love triangle. You know, Doctor, if you ask me, I can tell you plenty. Oh, if these hospital walls could talk! Now, heaven forbid I should say something out of line, but I see things around here. You know what I mean? Why, just the other day—"

The conversation was headed right down her alley, and Amos wanted it brought to a quick conclusion, before she gained momentum. He shook his head and took Nurse Hadley by the hand, interrupting her babble. "Wilma, thanks for telling me. I hate to run, but I need some time alone to process all of this before my rounds this morning."

Amos took the familiar walk toward his office to drop off his briefcase. From there, it was a quick set of rounds so he could finish in time for his 10:00 a.m. appointment. This morning, it was with a relatively new patient, Jane Smythe, a sixty-eight-year-old widow whose recent tests had revealed an abnormal mass of tissue in the brain. These situations often led to Amos having to disclose to people the thing they most definitely did not want to hear: A disease was killing them, and cutting an invader out of their head, perhaps along with part of their brain, was the only viable option available. It was news Amos had been forced to deliver on numerous occasions, yet the conversation never became easier.

At 10:03 a.m., Amos found Ms. Smythe waiting for him in the small lobby outside his hospital office space. "Hi, Ms. Smythe. You can come on back with me," Amos invited as he kept walking. "Sorry I'm late," he apologized, holding the door open for his patient. "Please have a seat.

I appreciate you meeting me here at the hospital today instead of my normal office."

"That's okay, Dr. Konklin. I don't mind."

"Well, Ms. Smythe, as you know from our follow-up phone conversation, the tests revealed an abnormal tissue mass in your right temple area. Now, we've come a long way with diagnostics in the past few years, but the next step will be to obtain a sample of the tissue so we can analyze it and be certain what it is."

"I was told on the phone not to draw any early conclusions. I know it's possible I simply have an abscess or something, but tell me the truth, Doctor. How likely is that?"

Amos heaved a heavy sigh. "Not very." He was always honest and direct, and he knew the statistics were not in her favor. Furthermore, he was facing additional uncertainty in her case. At least for the time being, Amos had to yield to conventional medical wisdom, for Ms. Smythe had not appeared in any of his dreams.

"I appreciate your candor, Dr. Konklin."

"The good news is that the first step only requires a less-invasive procedure. It will take less than an hour; we will use local anesthesia and minimal sedation."

"I don't suppose I have many options."

"Well, Ms. Smythe, I tell all my patients that there is always one other choice. You can choose to do nothing at all. There is risk with all surgeries, even those that are routine."

"Do you believe in God, Dr. Konklin?"

The question seemed to come from nowhere, and it took Amos by surprise, although it was a pleasant one. "Yes. As a matter of fact, I do."

"How refreshing. You know I'm sixty-eight, and while I suppose I could live another fifteen years or so, I've had a good life. I just might decide to leave this matter in God's hands instead of yours, though I'm sure you are most capable."

God's hands? It's not often I hear that anymore. "I can understand that," Amos briefly replied as the room fell silent. He noticed a tear had formed in her right eye, and he watched as it dropped to her cheek.

"I lost my husband to cancer, you know. He was a good man. We went through all of it together—the surgeries, the chemotherapy—and in the end, he was dead in less than two years. I didn't anticipate sitting here in this chair myself someday, but now here I am." Again, the room was quiet as she looked deeply into Amos's eyes, managed a partial smile, and then unexpectedly rose to her feet. "I need to leave now, Dr. Konklin. I'm sorry I'm such a mess today."

"Sure. That's not a problem." Amos rose from his chair and escorted Ms. Smythe out of the office and back to the hallway.

There wasn't anything left to say, so Amos stood in the hallway for a moment reflecting on their brief interaction, watching until Ms. Smythe made her way into the elevator. Inside, she turned around for a final wave. Amos sincerely wished the best for her, but now it was time to get on with the business of the day, so it was off to the nearest nurses' station.

As Amos approached, he noticed Nurse Erica Emerson watching him closely. He was able to read her lips as she whispered to her good friend, Nurse Patty, "Mm-hmm... here comes that fine Dr. G.—the doctor with golden hands."

Amos entered a small room next to the nurses' station to grab a chart. The door was cracked, and he could hear the whispering. Nurse Patty was a black woman, proud of her roots, and a straight talker. "Girl, I'd like to remind you that Dr. Konklin is old enough to be your father," she said to Erica. "Besides, he's wearing a gold band on that golden hand of his already."

"I wonder if those hands are golden in the bedroom," Erica said.

Although Amos wasn't interested, he did recognize that Erica Emerson was a looker and received plenty of male attention. She had curly, auburn hair that dangled on narrow shoulders, which rested on a slim, long column that led to a nice, round, petite bottom. Her long and slender legs, hidden beneath the medical garb, had made an indelible impression on more than one alpha male during social occasions away from the hospital; she typically flaunted short skirts and high heels,—and rumor had it that she had willingly wrapped those long legs around more than one lucky guy on more than one occasion in the janitorial closet down on the O.R. wing.

"You'll never find out," Nurse Patty answered. "That man is a fortress. I've been here over ten years and never heard anything juicy about Dr. Konklin. He's a keeper, for sure. His wife is a lucky woman."

"Yeah, I know—perfect man, perfect doctor, perfect husband. But you can't blame a girl for trying, especially with a sweet ass like that," Erica answered.

When Amos emerged from the room, Erica broke off the conversation to engage him. "Good morning, Dr. Konklin. I must say you look nice today." Erica scanned him from head to toe. Rumor had it that Erica was overheard to say, "Amos

Konklin is a man in full, intelligent and confident, with soft brown eyes that make me weak in the knees and wet in the middle."

"Thanks, Nurse Emerson," Amos simply replied, as he always did.

"About Mr. Weider in Room 478, I took him for a walk down the hall earlier. He seemed to have more energy today."

"That's great news. Anything else?"

"Do you have any lunch plans?" Erica asked.

"Uh, as a matter of fact I do. I'm meeting Dr. Stearns."

Erica smiled, but Amos knew her mind must have been racing, especially considering the countless times Brian Stearns had told him about his futile attempts to date her.

"Maybe some other time then?"

"Perhaps. Since you mentioned it, I think I'll visit Mr. Weider right now," Amos said, directing the conversation back to hospital business.

"Okay, see ya," Erica said.

Amos walked a few steps and then caught the rear hallway view in a large, round mirror on the wall. Erica was lingering, no doubt long enough to stare at his backside until Room 478 obstructed her view.

Around noon, Amos went to the cafeteria and met up with Brian Stearns, his excuse for avoiding Erica Emerson's lunch invitation on that particular day. Stearns was a likeable man, at least seventy-five pounds overweight, and had recently reached his fortieth birthday. He generally appeared unkempt and was not the kind of person one would guess to be a cardiologist at first sight. He hated the politics of the medical profession and was not afraid to share his opinions. When Amos spotted him, Stearns waved and motioned for Amos to join him at a table. Amos returned a nod before heading to the cooler to obtain an egg salad sandwich and an orange-mango juice drink.

At the table, Stearns was already taking the final bite of a greasy cheeseburger. His hair was as disheveled as always, and a stethoscope hung around his neck with its end piece tucked away in his front pocket. "Sit down," he said to Amos out of the corner of his mouth, still chewing on his cheeseburger.

"Good afternoon, Brian."

After swallowing the bite and not bothering to wipe away the grease that had gathered in the corners of his mouth, Stearns took a drink of his soda pop and then looked up at Amos. "Hey, man. By now I'm sure you know about what happened to Garth."

"I know he's dead, but that's about it," Amos said.

"Well, did you know I'm a suspect?"

"A suspect? What do you mean?"

"I mean I'm a suspect…and so are you." Stearns paused, sliding what looked like a third of a pie slice into his mouth. "This big dude from the police, Tom Wallace, has been snooping around since last night and then again early this morning. Let me tell you, the guy is huge. He looks more like a linebacker than a cop. Anyway, he has been interviewing people, asking questions. It seems Garth was most likely knocked off by someone he knew, or so this hulk Wallace thinks."

"Why is that?" Amos asked.

"Well, the way I understand it, everyone who has used the cabin is a suspect. According to Wallace, the killer had a key. We all know there is an official keychain, but hell, everyone who went to the cabin regularly made his own key. Shit, even I have one. I never liked that bastard Garth, but I didn't have a reason to kill him."

"Has Wallace spoken to you yet?"

Stearns paused again for another large spoonful of pie. "Nope, not yet."

"Well, you had better keep the not liking Garth comment to yourself."

"I know. I'm just talking to you, Amos, my old buddy."

"What else do you know?"

"I heard the murder scene was some old-school, hard-ass stuff. It seems the murderer bashed in their heads with some kind of blunt instrument, bludgeoned them to death while they were all cuddled up in bed."

"That seems a bit dramatic."

"Yeah. Man, I'm really sorry about Lois. I know you didn't speak to her a lot after that whole disaster with Kevin, but you two used to be good friends."

"Thanks, Brian."

"If you ask me," Stearns began, pausing to guzzle down the final third of the pie, "the murderer was probably after Garth. Poor Lois was probably just in the wrong place at the wrong time."

"Perhaps," Amos said.

"Well, I've gotta run," Stearns said, having polished off two cheeseburgers and a slice of chocolate pie.

"What? So much for our lunch date I guess."

"Sorry, buddy. Another time."

"If you keep eating like that, you're going to be making an appointment with yourself someday."

"Yeah, I know, but what the hell? You only live once!"

Amos smiled and watched as Stearns dropped off his tray and headed out the south exit. After washing down the last bite of his sandwich, Amos was debating on dessert when he noticed someone approaching the table, someone who looked just like what Brain Stearns had earlier described.

"Dr. Amos Konklin?" the big man asked.

"Yes, I'm Amos Konklin."

"Detective Tom Wallace. I'm investigating the Garth and Winston murders. I apologize for interrupting your lunch, Doctor, but could I have a few minutes of your time?"

"I suppose I have a few minutes," Amos said. "Have a seat."

"Dr. Konklin, let me get right to the point. I believe Dave Garth and Lois Winston might have been murdered by someone they knew, someone who had a key to the cabin. I understand that all of the senior physicians, you included, have access to the cabin."

"Yes, that's correct."

"Dr. Konklin, we're both busy men, so let me get right to the point."

"Go ahead."

"Where were you on the night of the murders?"

"What night was that again?"

"According to our coroner's report, the murders occurred early Thursday morning, most likely between midnight and 3:00 a.m."

"I'm impressed. You guys work fast."

"We try to. The bodies were found late yesterday morning. By evening, we already had positive identification and autopsies."

"I see."

"So, do you have a key to the cabin, Dr. Konklin?"

"Yes. I made my own copy, but that's pretty common around here."

"Okay," he said, jotting something down in his notepad. Without looking up he asked, "Can you tell me where you were Thursday between the hours of midnight and 3:00 a.m.?"

"Well, I was here at the hospital. Wednesday is one of my planned surgery days, and I have a custom of spending those nights here, to remain close to my patients."

"Did you see or speak with anyone between those hours?"

"Hmm...let me think. I finished a round in the I.C.U. before midnight, then crashed on my couch to catch a few hours of sleep. I believe I made another round at about 2:30 a.m. You can check the I.C.U. logbook if you would like."

"Did you know of anyone who might have wanted to hurt Dr. Garth or Ms. Winston?"

"No."

"I understand you and Ms. Winston were friends."

"Yes. We were close at one time, but not so much as of late. She was once married to a good friend of mine, and we were closer friends back then."

"You are referring to Kevin Winston."

"Yes. Boy, you guys are on top of things."

"Did you blame Lois Winston for what happened to your friend Kevin?"

"No. I really didn't blame anyone. I knew Kevin was upset, but divorces happen. Kevin was responsible for his own actions."

As Wallace attempted a response, he was interrupted by the hospital P.A. system. "Code Blue! Dr. Konklin, E.R. STAT! Code Blue. Dr. Konklin, E.R., STAT!"

"Excuse me, Mr. Wallace, but duty calls."

"I'll be in touch," Wallace replied as Amos hurried away.

Tom Wallace remained seated in the cafeteria, scribbling in his notebook, until he got a phone call from Detective Jerry Donaldson.

"Lieutenant, it's possible that the perpetrator drove here in a car last night, on the dirt road that leads down to the lake. We have a fresh set of tire tracks."

"Tire tracks are good, but a suspect and a car would be a whole lot better," Wallace replied. "Make sure you get good photos and casts."

"Already done, sir. I sent the digitals off this morning. The tread indicates a set of Michelin UltraWears, the kind used on high-end automobiles."

"You mean like the kind of car a *doctor* might drive?"

"Yes, Lieutenant—Mercedes, BMW, Caddies…, cars like that."

"All right. I'm going to be here at the hospital for the rest of the day. Call if you have anything else."

"Will do."

Downstairs in the E.R., Amos was greeted by the attending physician. "Sorry, Dr. Konklin, but we are understaffed. This is our third head case today, and the other two are presently in surgery."

"That's what I'm here for," Amos said.

It was tradition for Amos to be on E.R. call, and although no one was the wiser, Amos had already anticipated what was coming. When he pulled back the curtain that concealed a transport cart, there lay a thirty-something gentleman, a stranger to all but Amos. It was the man from his dream—or perhaps more appropriately his nightmare—from the night before.

The attending physician held up the results from the magnetic resonance angiography (MRA) while Amos pretended to notice the whitish coating around the cerebellum for the first time. "Looks like ruptures of multiple posterior aneurysms. Do you concur?"

"Yes, Dr. Konklin."

"Prep Bach," Amos ordered. It was the Konklin code, and everyone had been waiting for it with anticipation. It was an unconventional request in preparing an operating room, on-demand classical music, even for emergency surgeries. The code was terse yet diverse, for the musician of choice was up to Amos Konklin's whim. Hence, the simple utterance from Amos was akin to the drawing of a lottery ball. This time it was Bach, and Amos knew from the reaction that David Cox, the resident-in-training had won. "How much?" Amos asked.

"Forty dollars."

"The losers?"

"Beethoven, Verdi, Wagner, and Liszt," Cox replied.

"Spend it well, Mr. Cox."

Immediately, the journey to the operating room was underway. Amos followed close behind the moving convoy, and although he gave the appearance of listening to the medical briefing from the attending physician during transit, he was thinking only of his dream the night before. The dream had been vivid: The patient had four large aneurysms on the right *vert*, a neurosurgeon's vernacular for the right carotid artery. For Amos, it was easy, for he knew the precise coordinates of the aneurysms, and even the operating microscope was unnecessary. The dream had begun as all others, with Amos successfully completing the surgery. Yet, true to form, it had escalated into a nightmare. The situation always repeated, but this time everything went wrong. First, the O.R. lost power, and that was quickly followed by the patient experiencing cardiac arrest. Then Amos was grabbed from behind; he struggled to break free as he helplessly watched his surgical tools fall to the O.R. floor. It seemed like an endless struggle as Amos slowly lost the battle, gasping for each breath as the intruder's grip tightened around his chest. It was then that he sat upright in bed, startled, pausing only to wipe away the sweat, and then taking time to look over at Cynthia, who had clutched his hand—an automatic reaction, he assumed, because she otherwise remained still, with her eyes closed, in apparent tranquil sleep.

Upon reaching the set of double doors that led to Operating Room 8, Amos broke off from the group and made his way to the scrub sink. He had always enjoyed the ritual, the water, the cleanser, and the elegance of the heavy gage #3 brushed finish stainless steel. Undeniably, though, in recent years, his call of duty had lost its excitement. The dreams were wearing on him, and they seemed excessive, especially considering the types of cases that had been wandering into his office as of late. With the advancement of the less-invasive endovascular techniques, most of the surgeries could be easily handled, even by the young residents on staff. At least this time, the size and locations of the aneurysms somewhat backed his decision to opt for invasive surgery, a dying art form. Moreover, Amos missed the old days, those times in the past when only he had seemed able to discover and correct what the more primitive brain scans had missed.

By the time Amos entered the O.R., Bach was at his best, and the team ready for the next order. Assisting was O.R. Nurse Myrna Tobin, who had worked with Amos for many years. She was accustomed to his approach to surgery, which was a bit unconventional. When Myrna was assisting, Amos's medical directives were reduced to visual cues. He preferred pointing and hand gestures to speaking, which he reserved for debating with the residents. Observing was David Cox, resident and recent lottery winner. Amos enjoyed a healthy banter with these almost-ready-for-primetime surgeons, reminding them that they still had plenty to learn in spite of their book smarts. He quickly focused on Cox, who was forty dollars richer.

Amos walked to the front of the table, looking down at the exposed, bald head of the patient. He began the operation with the precision for which he was known, interjecting comments directed to Cox as he created a window in the skull. "Mr. Cox, did they tell you in school that this procedure is one of the most dangerous?" Amos asked, purposely refraining from addressing the young resident as "Doctor."

"Yes."

"And why is that?"

"Well, you have to lift the brain and move it away from the base of the skull," Cox replied, an easy and obvious answer to an elementary question.

"And why is that such a big deal?"

"Swollen brains are especially difficult to move, Doctor. They are delicate."

"Why on Earth would the brain be swollen?"

"Generally due to hemorrhaging."

"I'd say that's what we have here," Amos said, as the exposed brain lay before him. "Now it's time to take care of those aneurysms."

Cox looked on as Amos navigated through a jungle of blood vessels, using his unorthodox methods, especially the hand gestures to Nurse Tobin. "Why did you choose to open his skull?" Cox asked.

If only he really knew how unorthodox, Amos thought as he isolated the aneurysms one by one, attaching the tiny clips to the neck of each lesion. "A gut call," Amos said, pretending to use the operating microscope.

It wasn't a very scientific answer. "You know, Dr. Konklin, the results from the ISAT trials were pretty conclusive," Cox answered, referring to the multiple trials comparing less-invasive endovascular versus invasive open surgery.

"I'm aware of the trial results, Mr. Cox. However, I must tell you that if you specifically compare the results of my patients with ISAT endovascular data, you'll find that the survival rate of my patients at one year was significantly better than those who had endovascular surgery, not limited to just coiling as in the first trial. It's simple math really, since all my patients were alive after one year!"

The young resident was silenced for the moment.

Amos continued, "Mr. Cox, in a nutshell, I can only say from firsthand experience that I'm less impressed with ISAT data and endovascular advances and more impressed with the brain itself. It's a marvel of God, wouldn't you say?" Amos said, purposely engaging the young resident on a separate controversial topic.

"A marvel? Perhaps. Not so sure it has anything to do with God, but rather a refinement over millions of years of natural selection," Cox replied.

"I see. So when you encounter something impressive like the human brain, you're the type who doesn't assume the existence of an intelligent designer?"

"I didn't say that. It's by design, all right, but I believe that designer is nature, which has done its best. If I had to drag God into the argument, I'd have to say the brain is a bit of a disappointment."

"How so?"

"Well, it's not exactly a flawless design. The brain is located at the top of the body. If I were the one making the blueprints, engineering the body, I think I would put the brain in the middle of the body, where it would be more protected and less vulnerable."

"I think you are confusing topics, Mr. Cox. The design of the brain itself versus its placement in the body is a different subject altogether. But even when it comes to that subject, I think you have to appreciate that design has much to do with art. In other words, an aesthetic quality must be considered, because in the end, all parts of the body are ultimately vulnerable."

"Dr. Konklin, if there is a God, He or She manages to hide very well. It will take more than the human brain to convince me otherwise."

"Isaac Newton once wrote that the thumb was enough for him," Amos said. He looked up at the cocky resident, who seemed silenced for the moment. "You think you're smarter than Newton?"

"No, but I have a little more information to consider. A lot has been learned in the past couple of centuries."

Amos appreciated the candor and outspokenness of the young doctor and continued to test him as the surgery progressed. Toward the end, though, Amos was ready to return to an earlier point Cox had made. "I think it's time to close," Amos said, having successfully dealt with the critical medical situation at hand. "Now, back to this need you spoke of earlier—you know, of being convinced of God's existence. Let's just say that for me, it took an on-the-road-to-Damascus experience."

"A what?"

Amos paused, wondering if a further explanation was worth the effort, and then took a different approach to the response. "I was not raised in a religious family, Mr. Cox. I was not a brainwashed child."

Finally, it registered with Cox. "Oh, okay. So you are a convert? Fair enough, but I haven't had any such experience.

In fact, I have no reason to believe God would be interested in my life in any way."

"That's probably true, Mr. Cox, assuming you keep your nose clean."

"Meaning?"

"Perhaps God doesn't like germs to spread. Maybe He cleans things up every now and then."

David Cox frowned. He was intrigued by the riddle for only a brief moment before Amos spoke again.

"That's it. We're done here."

☆ ☆ ☆

Amos woke up at 3:11 a.m., but it was not a dream that had his eyes fluttering open; rather, it was the doorbell. When he wandered downstairs, he was greeted by Tom Wallace, search warrant in hand. At once, Amos looked out at the end of his driveway and noticed that the garbage can was out at the road, still awaiting the Saturday morning pickup. Inside the garbage can was a plastic container holding the bloody clothes. Then, he looked at Wallace, as he delivered the legal spiel. "A warrant at this time of night?" Amos asked.

"The hospital security tapes showed what appeared to be your car, leaving the parking garage at 11:20 p.m. and returning at 2:08 a.m. on the morning of the murders. It was enough to awaken Judge Matthews from sleep."

"I see," Amos said. "Please come in."

The evidence was soon uncovered, and, within fifty-one hours from the time of the crimes, Amos Konklin was arrested for murder—an abrupt ending to a series of executions that had spanned nearly forty years. Nevertheless, the arrest came as no surprise to Amos. Two months prior, following an incident one night in the hospital garage, he had personally spearheaded the request for installation of security cameras. As sitting chair of the Hospital Staff Committee, Amos had taken the lead by casting the first vote in the affirmative for the cameras, spawning a unanimous decision of agreement from the rest of the committee. Truth be told, Amos had grown weary of his work. He had become comfortably numb. He had tested God, and God had answered.

CHAPTER 3

THE NIGHT AT THE JEFFERSON COUNTY FAIRGROUNDS

Hugh Konklin was a convert, an intelligent mechanical engineer who'd abandoned a respectable job in favor of "joining the circus," so to speak. Actually, he was a carny, a gypsy, of sorts, who moved with a traveling road show known as "The Amazing Wilkes Clan Carnival," taking its name from owner Clarence Wilkes.

Of course, leaving behind a respectable mechanical engineering job in the midst of the Roaring Twenties had some people thinking Konklin was crazed out of his mind; however, that kind of rare insanity seemed practical to Hugh, considering that the close of the decade sent the country falling into the Great Depression. At least Hugh was doing a job he loved, and it honestly gave him many opportunities to use his mechanical skills. After all, he ran the High Striker, one of the carnival's most popular side-show games.

Hugh had studied the mechanics of the High Striker in college, and he was absorbed by the subject, an intense interest that primarily grew out of his fascination with the striker during a carnival encounter of his own, back when he was a teenager.

Hugh remembered that day well. The wind was calm that summer night in 1915, even still, at the Jefferson County Fairgrounds. The teenage Hugh Konklin, like everyone else, was meandering around, enjoying the sights and sounds, when he heard the invitation: "Hey, boy! Wanna come see how much of a man you are?"

Hugh turned to the source of the voice, and his eyes fell upon an old, wiry man of small stature, almost as greasy as the deep-fried goodies in the kiosk across the midway. In a more polite voice than necessary, Hugh asked, "Uh...what was that, sir?"

"I'm askin' you to come prove whether yer a man or a boy!" the old man replied.

Hugh had been warned in advance about the sideshow antics and the clever carnies who would use any means necessary to separate people from their hard-earned money. However, that advice did little to curb his curiosity, so he responded without hesitation. "Well, I'm not a weakling, if that's what you're saying."

"Really? Hmm. Then why don't ya come prove it, boy!"

"I don't have to prove anything to you," Hugh responded, beginning to get agitated.

He was waiting for the next taunt when the old man directed his attention to a new passerby, just as quickly as he had engaged Hugh. "You look like a strappin' lad. Wanna show that girlfriend of yers what you got?"

Hugh looked over his right shoulder and saw the couple walking behind him. A cute girl was holding hands with a young, broad-shouldered man, dressed in a Navy uniform. Already forgotten by the carny, Hugh stepped back, ready to watch the show that was surely about to unfold. It was a sideshow aimed at challenging the male ego.

"Yeah, why not?" the young naval officer responded, confidence dripping from his every word.

As he stepped forward, the sales pitch began.

"So, what's yer name?" the old carny asked.

"Stan," came the response as a small crowd began to form.

"Well, Stan, this here's a High Striker. That pole there is twenty feet high, and there's a bell up at the top. In order to ring that bell, you gotta strike the platform and send that block of metal attached to that cable all the way to the top of that pole. You got that so far?"

"Yes," replied Stan, still confident and smiling as he handed his money over to the old man.

"Okay, son, I'm gonna give you some help," the man said as he snatched Stan's cash, as if to imply he was actually doing Stan a favor.

"And what might that be?" Stan asked.

"Well, I'm gonna let you use this maul—this here sledgehammer—to strike that platform. If you strike it hard enough to ring the bell, I'm gonna let you pick any one of them there prizes from that wall to give to that pretty little girl of yers." In what seemed to be almost one continuous motion, for the sake of example, the old carny manhandled the maul, as he put it, with one arm, hurled it way above his head, and then struck it with full force back down on the High Striker platform.

Although the entire experience encapsulated only a few seconds in time, it filled every one of Hugh's organs of sensory perception. The salty, buttery smell from a nearby popcorn cart filled the hot, humid air as Hugh slid a grease-slimy but tasty French fry into his mouth. Before he could bite down, the visually stunning presentation was over, the sound of the bell echoing out into the night.

Turning around to face Stan, the old man blurted out, "See how easy it is?"

A grinning Stan stepped forward, took the maul, and approached the platform. As he stood there, tall, broad, and proud, in his crisp Navy whites contrasting visibly with the darkness of the night, he grasped the maul with both arms and swung. Unlike the old man, Stan's approach was more traditional, more representative of someone who'd grown up swinging an axe. Nevertheless, and former experience and skill aside, Stan's results were quite different. As the maul made contact with the platform, Stan released a loud grunt and watched as the metal block traversed about three-fourths of the distance up the pole and then plummeted back down, as if mocking his pathetic attempt. Stan paused for a moment and tried again. This time, the grunt was louder, but the results were similar. Finally, on the last swing, when the metal block only made it about halfway, Stan shook his head in dejection.

Immediately, the disappointment spread to all the spectators, and the small crowd dissipated as quickly as it had formed, heading off to find something more entertaining.

When the old man reached out to take possession of the maul, Stan willingly relinquished his grip, but Hugh lingered.

With no one else to yell at, the old man once again turned his attention to Hugh. "Well, boy, I see you decided to stick around."

"How did you...where did you learn to do that?" Hugh asked.

"Do what?"

"You know, ring the bell. Is it some kind of trick?"

"No trick here, boy—just strength and technique."

"Okay, but who taught you this so-called technique?"

"You gotta lot of questions, don'tcha, boy? You think somebody can tell you something like that and then you just do it?"

"Well, no...I guess not." Hugh inched closer to the old man. "I suppose you must have practiced a lot, but I'm sure somebody gave you some tips along the way. That's all I'm saying."

"I like you, boy. You seem pretty smart, but the thing is, smart only cuts it about halfway. Got any brawn to go along with those brains a yers?"

"Well, I'd like to find out," Hugh said, now thinking that perhaps he had established a relationship of sorts.

"I'll tell you what, kid. I'll give you five chances at the price of three," the carny said, posing an irresistible offer to someone who was already mostly committed.

"Deal," Hugh said as he dug in his pocket for money.

After the monetary exchange, Hugh grabbed the maul and walked up to the platform. Hugh, unlike Stan, didn't have an audience. Passersby did just that; there was no crowd forming, and nobody seemed to be watching. At that moment, Hugh contemplated all possible strategies. He thought about trying to replicate the old man's technique but quickly dismissed the idea. He stood there with purposeful hesitation, like an apt pupil awaiting advice from a teacher.

"Well, go ahead, boy. No sense in waiting. Thinking about it too long ain't gonna make it any easier."

With that, Hugh took a big swing. At the point of contact with the platform, Hugh felt an enormous resistance, almost as if the platform was pushing back against the hammer. He at once thought of his idol, Sir Isaac Newton. As he'd learned from Newton's ideas, stationary, inanimate objects tend to stay that way until they are acted upon by some outside force. In this case, Hugh knew he was that outside force, but overcoming the inertia of the striker proved even more challenging than he'd have thought possible. In the next instant, he saw the metal block rise about one-third of the necessary distance.

"Good try," said the carny as it began its descent.

Hugh was a bit irritated by the mocking encouragement and reacted immediately with another swing. This time, it appeared the metal block went close to half the distance; it was progress, yes, but still nowhere near the intended goal. "Dang it," Hugh lamented in a quiet whisper. The next three swings followed in slow, deliberate succession. "Damn it!" Hugh shouted loudly and then quickly surveyed the surroundings for spectators who might have been listening. He initially thought about his mother; regardless of the situation, he knew she would not be at all sympathetic to his use of profanity. After noticing the coast was clear, he spent the next ten minutes swinging, depleting his cash reserves, much to his own chagrin and the carny's delight. When Hugh finally departed from the High Striker sideshow stage that night and walked away, he briefly turned to look at the old man, who was already focused on his next victim in the crowd. Then, Hugh looked at the High Striker, the inanimate mechanical monstrosity that had managed to taunt him even more than its gatekeeper. There was simply nothing more to say. He had failed, and the High Striker had defeated him. All that remained was a mental acknowledgement of the impressive, cold, merciless machine. "I'll see you again someday," Hugh mumbled before he disappeared into the night.

CHAPTER 4

HUGH KONKLIN AT COLLEGE

On a wet, rainy day in 1920, Hugh Konklin peered out the window of the mechanical engineering lab of the Carnegie Institute of Technology. Going to engineering school was the fulfillment of a lifetime goal, one that had begun in his pre-teen years, though it had been delayed due to his mother's illness and death. Hugh's mother was a devout Christian, and his exposure to religion as a youth had made an undeniable impact. One of his fondest memories growing up was the time he'd asked his mother for proof of God's existence. Rather than express her opinion, his mother had simply handed him a copy of the Bible, opened to Hebrews 3:4. Hugh read the words, *"For every house is built by someone, but God is the builder of everything."* It was on that day, in that instant, that Hugh became a true believer, and he kept the Bible she'd given him as a personal gift. Hugh believed God to be the greatest engineer of all, and as a man *"made in God's image,"* as the holy book proclaimed, he was certain he'd found his calling.

Earlier that day, Hugh had overheard a lot of talk among the students about an interesting project they were going to be studying in Mechanical Engineering 1102. The professor, he'd heard, was somehow connected to the original inventors of a "striking machine," an obscure reference that Hugh did not fully grasp. It was on that day, as the rained poured outside, that Hugh, sitting comfortably dry at his desk inside the lab, would connect the dots.

Hugh was a very bright young man, and even the tough curriculum at engineering school was not capable of keeping him fully engaged. Till that time, his studies had centered mostly on a large volume of reading and solving mathematical problems. Although those assigned tasks did, in some ways, pique Hugh's interests, he considered himself more of a hands-on type. Eager to find out what the buzz was all about, Hugh felt immediately disappointed when Professor Johnson—a short, bearded man whose attire generally matched the stereotype of his profession—walked up to the chalk board and wrote:

$$W = \Delta E_k = E_{k2} - E_{k1} = \tfrac{1}{2}m\Delta(v^2)$$

Oh God! Not the work-energy theorem again. It had been the focus of discussions all week, and Hugh's theory was that he was growing weary of it. However, just as Hugh rolled his eyes back into his head, the professor walked over and pulled down the covering that was hiding an object in the corner of the classroom. As the very large drawing came into focus, it was a surreal experience for Hugh, jolting his mind back to that still, humid, summer night in 1915 at the Jefferson County Fairgrounds. Although his eyes were fixated on the drawing, his ears were tuned to Professor Johnson.

"This, class, is known as a striking machine. Perhaps some of you have seen one."

At once, Hugh raised his hand, as if he could anticipate the next question.

"Yes, Mr. Konklin? Do you have a question?" the professor asked.

"Uh…no sir," Hugh said in reply. "I just wanted to say I have seen one of those before."

"Thanks for sharing," came the response. "Has anyone else ever seen one of these up close?"

The class sat quietly.

Then the professor asked, "Has anyone been to a carnival or fair recently?"

At that, the mental connection had been made, and a few hands went up.

One student, who always sat in the front row and was exceptionally vocal during class, asked, "Isn't that the game where you take that big hammer and hit the platform hard to try and ring a bell or something?"

"Why, yes. I would say that pretty much sums up the essentials," Professor Johnson responded.

Actually, the drawing itself made the guesswork easier. The front page was an artistic finished drawing or rendition that hid the other pages of technical specifications behind it.

"You see," said the professor, "the hammer used in the striking machine game is basically a force amplifier. It works by converting mechanical work into kinetic energy.

In physics, mechanical work is the amount of energy transferred by a force acting from a distance. According to the work-energy theorem, if an external force acts upon an object, causing its kinetic energy to change from E_{k1} to E_{k2}, then the mechanical work (W) can be described by this equation." He pointed to the familiar formula he'd scrolled on the chalkboard. "In the case of the striking machine, though, there are more variables in the mix, including the hammer."

For the next couple of minutes, Professor Johnson had Hugh's full attention. However, the lecture eventually began to digress into pure physics again. At that point, try as he did, Hugh could no longer focus solely on the professor's words. His mind was racing with thoughts, pondering how he might construct a striking machine of his own. For the duration of class, Hugh's attention to the professor's lecture faded in and out as he reminisced about that night at the fair five years prior.

After class was dismissed, Hugh went up to take a closer look at the poster-sized drawings of the striking machine. As he flipped the pages, he found it fascinating to look at the mechanical breakdown, at all of the various parts and dimensions. As he stood there, he thought about each and every one of those components and how putting all of those pieces together could result in such a machine, a thing that existed for the express purpose of entertaining people—and ripping them off—at a carnival sideshow game.

"Hello, Hugh," came a voice, interrupting his focus.

Hugh turned to see who it was. "Oh…hi."

Ronald Lynn, a classmate, seemed insistent on making friends with Hugh. "So you've really seen one of these?" Ronald asked.

"Yeah. Haven't you?"

"Maybe. I've been to carnivals and fairs and stuff plenty of times. I guess I just never really noticed."

Hugh acknowledged him with a nod but remained silent.

"Did you actually *play* the game?" Ronald asked, determined to keep the conversation alive.

"Yes, yes I did."

"Well, how did you do? Isn't it supposed to show how strong you are or something like that?"

"Yeah, I guess it's sort of like that, but not exactly. I think it might be a combination of strength and technique. I also wonder if it's rigged somehow at carnivals, since a lot of those sideshows are a rip-off."

"Yeah, maybe, but you didn't answer my question. How did you do?"

"Sorry," said Hugh. "I think you asked two questions actually. I suppose I did okay, but I didn't win, if that's what you're asking. Like I said, a lot of those sideshows are rip-offs, and carnies are pros at talking people out of their money."

"Right. Hey, where are you headed next?"

"I think I might actually hang out here for a while and have a closer look at these drawings. Then I'll probably head over to the library."

"Okay. Well, I guess I'll talk to you later."

"All right," Hugh said as he turned back to face the drawings.

As Ronald walked away, Professor Johnson approached. "So, Mr. Konklin, you seem very interested in the striker drawings."

"Yes, sir. I would really like to build one. Can I ask where you got these?"

"Of course," the professor said as he made eye contact with Hugh. "The front page was drawn by an artist, but the rest of the drawings are enlarged copies from the patent specification by Nokes and Gordon, granted back in 1908."

"Really? Can I possibly get a copy of the patent?"

"Fortunately, Mr. Konklin, I have a few extra sets on my desk. All the drawings are in there as well, just much smaller versions than these, of course." He pointed to the classroom prop that had so mesmerized Hugh.

"Fantastic! Can I get a copy right now?" Hugh inquired.

"Sure. Follow me."

The High Striker was actually invented in 1907 but patented in 1908 as a "Striking Machine." R.A. Nokes and W.W. Gordon filed original U.S. Patent 898,129 on July 20, 1907, and that patent was issued on September 8, 1908.

When the professor handed Hugh the document, the following words jumped out of the page:

"To all whom it may concern:

Be it known that we, Royce A. Nokes and William W. Gordon, citizens of the United States, residing at Washington, in the District of Columbia, have invented certain new and useful improvements in Striking Machines, of which the following is a specification. This invention relates to striking machines and particularly that class thereof wherein a person strikes upon a pivoted lever with a hammer or maul, which lever causes a block to ascend along a suitable support provided therefore, and over and opposite indicating numerals located at different heights whereby to indicate to the person the force of the blow struck by the hammer or maul."

✲ ✲ ✲

The next day, Hugh thought more about the maul, the sledgehammer, and techniques for using it. He recalled that night at the fair when the old man had whipped that hammer over his head and onto the striker platform with just one arm. As he recalled from his own sorry attempts of winning the game, the sledgehammer didn't seem to weigh all that much. He thought about one of his previous lectures and then flipped through his notebook until he found the energy formula scribbled in his notes:

E = 1/2 mv^2, where m = mass, v = velocity

Based on this formula, the amount of energy delivered to the striker platform by the sledgehammer would be equivalent to one-half the mass of the head multiplied by the square of the head velocity at the time of contact with the platform. That was interesting to Hugh because it meant that, while the energy delivered increases linearly with mass, it increases geometrically with the velocity of the sledgehammer. As he had told Ronald Lynn after lab that day, he wondered if success had more to do with technique than raw strength, perhaps even more than the size and weight of the hammer. Moreover, considering the somewhat less-than-ethical carnival reputation, he could only assume there was a good chance that something else was going on as well—something that would give the carny the advantage.

Thoughts about building a striker began to dominate Hugh's mind, and as the next few months in college passed, he became more of a loner. He mostly spent his evenings in the mechanical engineering lab building things, never taking his mind off the striker. Hugh fancied himself a fan of the great engineer and inventor Nikola Tesla, and true to form, he preferred reality to theory. Due to his relentless lobbying for a grant to make the building of the striking machine a real lab project, Hugh's otherwise good relationship with Professor Johnson became strained.

At Carnegie, the wheels turned slowly. When it came to money for projects, there was only so much to go around. Cash allocation was typically aimed at lab projects and replications or improvements on things that had already been built before. It irritated Hugh that learning about the physics of the High Striker was only a paper exercise, because it had become far more important to him than that. He was resolved to build a striking machine of his own, one way or another, with or without the college helping to finance his efforts.

By the start of his senior year, Hugh was discouraged by college politics, and he decided to stop wasting his energy requesting to build a striking machine while at the university. In the meantime, he recovered the social life he had sacrificed. In the summer months following his junior year, he reignited his relationship with a girl named Susan Winters, a student at Margaret Morrison Carnegie College, the nearby girls' school. Susan possessed the All-American girl look: shoulder-length blonde hair, a great smile, and blue eyes. He seemed to be the perfect match for her: tall, smart, and handsome, according to Susan, with light brown hair that he parted on the right side and combed over. As their senior year progressed, Susan talked often to Hugh about life after college. On more than one occasion, she made known her interest in pursuing marriage and starting a family, if she met the right person.

As Christmas approached, Hugh received an invitation from Susan to spend the festive season at her parents' house. Not only did he accept the invitation quickly and wholeheartedly, but he also volunteered to drive in his car, a 160-mile road trip west from Pittsburgh to near Columbus. Hugh suspected she wanted to use the alone time to discuss their future together, and he was okay with that.

On the day of the trip, Hugh stopped by the lobby of Susan's dormitory and picked her up. Knowing her the way he did, he expected an enormous amount of luggage, so he dropped his items off at the car first. Susan didn't let him down: She stood in the lobby holding one sizeable suitcase, and there were two others sitting on the floor next to her.

"Is that it?" He pointed to the suitcases on the floor.

"Yep…and this one of course." Susan laughed as she spoke.

"All right then," Hugh said. "I'll just grab them, and we can get going."

"Wow. My own personal bellhop? Sounds good to me!"

Once the car trip was underway, Hugh made a conscious effort not to discuss the High Striker, so he was very surprised when Susan broached the subject herself.

"Hugh, I've never really asked you this before, but why was building the High Striker so important to you? It's just a game, isn't it? Does it still matter to you? You don't talk about it much anymore."

"Yes, it's still important to me, but I've come to realize that college isn't the time or place. I was trying to force the matter instead of letting things play out naturally." Hugh paused for a moment and then spoke again. "I don't think I ever told you this before, but…well, see, my mother was a very spiritual woman. She converted to a belief in God soon after my father died, before I was born. She was a great woman and taught me to appreciate that things happen for a reason."

"Aw. I know you must miss her. It doesn't seem fair that she died right before you started college. She'll never get to see what a great engineer you're going to be."

"I try not to think in terms of fairness. I don't think the world works that way, to be honest. While most people think life is just filled with random events, I look for signs."

"Signs? What do you mean?" Susan asked. "And what does any of this have to do with the High Striker, some carnival game?"

"Well, I think most people are disconnected from the Divine. They simply live and don't look for God in their lives. I know it sounds strange, but when I first played the Higher Striker game at a county fair back in 1915, it happened for a reason. I can't really explain it or expect you to understand. I just…know. Growing up, I read the Bible a lot, and I believe faith is a very personal thing. I know mine is, anyway. I also know God is always there, opening doors and presenting opportunities, but people don't recognize it."

"Wow, Hugh. That's some deep stuff."

"One thing I know is that you have to be willing to take a leap sometimes. I don't think the door God opens is always the one we'd expect. It's not always the most obvious or even the most practical choice."

"Hmm. Interesting."

"Have you ever heard of Abraham? You know, from the Bible?" Seeing Susan's nod, he said, "Well, he did *exactly* what God said, no questions asked. God commanded that he leave his home for a land that God would reveal to him in time. God promised to bless him and create a great nation from his seed. It wasn't the obvious, practical choice, and it wasn't easy for Abraham, but he did it anyway. I'm sure he didn't fully understand the higher purpose at the time, so what he did was a massive leap of faith. That allowed him to become a friend of God. I'm not pretending I'm anything close to the caliber of Abraham when it comes to my faith and obedience and trust, but I know God has a plan for me, and somehow, the High Striker is part of it."

"You are a wonderful man, Hugh Konklin—the smartest bellhop I know." Susan reached over and grabbed his hand for a reassuring pat.

When they arrived at Susan's parents' place late in the afternoon on Christmas Eve, the yard was already filled with cars.

As they pulled up, Susan's dad walked out of the front door to greet them. By the time the car stopped, he was right there by the passenger door. The window was open, so he peeked inside and said, "Hey, nice car. I love the Rambler 83. These old five-seaters are great, especially when Susan's along for the trip, what with all her baggage and whatnot!"

"Yeah, it's definitely, uh…convenient," Hugh chuckled, attempting to get the initial meeting off to a good start.

"Daddy," Susan said happily, "it's so nice to see you." She opened car door, pushing back against him so she could get out and give him a hug.

"You too, honey," her dad said, but before he could get out the next sentence, her arms were already wrapped around him in a tight embrace.

Hugh watched the happy father/daughter reunion for a brief moment before he opened his door and walked around the front of the car. "Hello. I'm Hugh." He held out his hand.

"Nice to meet you," Susan's father said, gripping Hugh's hand in a firm shake. "Carl. Welcome to our home." To Hugh, it seemed like a very sincere moment, and he instantly felt at ease.

"Okay, Hugh. Let's get these suitcases, and we can go inside and meet everyone else."

Hugh took the cue and walked to the other side of the car, where he had left the door open. He grabbed the remaining suitcases, and they headed into the house.

The first to greet them was Susan's mother, Gloria. After hugging Susan, she looked into Hugh's eyes. "You must be Hugh." She extended her arms, inviting a hug.

Hugh put down the suitcases so he could be a willing participant in the embrace of the friendly woman. "Yes, that's me."

Later, when the meet-and-greet was over and Hugh had settled in, he went outside for a breath of fresh air. In the backyard, he saw a young man, perhaps in his early twenties, standing by the fence, smoking a cigarette. "How are you doing?" Hugh asked the young smoker politely.

"I'm good," came the nonchalant, disinterested response.

"I don't think I've met you yet," Hugh said.

"Nope. Been out here for a while. I'm Donny," he said as he took a shallow drag.

"Hugh."

"Oh yeah, Hugh. Well, I'm Susan's cousin. She told me a little about you."

"Good, I hope."

"Well, mostly that you're interested in striking machines."

"Yep, that would be me," Hugh responded, arching a curious brow at Donny. "I find the whole idea quite fascinating. Striking machines don't generally mean much to people, and most folks don't even know what you are talking about."

"Yeah, I suppose that's true. Kind of an oddball thing to know about, I guess."

"So, I take it you are an exception?" Hugh inquired.

At that, Donny laughed. "I guess Susan didn't mention me."

"I don't recall her every saying anything about a cousin with obscure interests, no."

"Well, my mom is Katherine Grant. You probably met her inside. She's Aunt Gloria's sister. We actually used to live outside Pittsburgh before we moved back to Columbus."

"Okay." Hugh wondered where the conversation was headed.

"Well, we lived just a few miles from Kennywood Park."

"Oh yeah! Kennywood." Hugh recalled having learned about the amusement park that was built in 1898, just five years after the great Chicago World's Fair. The park was iconic, a catalyst for all the other parks, fairs, and carnivals that followed. "So did you visit Kennywood often?"

"I wouldn't call it visiting, exactly, but I was there a lot. Fact, I started working there right out of high school. They put me on a bunch of odd jobs—tightening bolts here and there, picking up wrappers and trash, painting things in gaudy colors, and even working some of the games and rides. I was assigned to the High Striker game. Now, I don't know all that much about the mechanical engineering part that interests you college types, but I did have fun running the game. Anyway, when Susan mentioned your unique interest in striking machines, I thought…well, what a small world, I guess."

"Yeah, I suppose it is," Hugh said, now fully engaged and eager to discuss the topic further.

About that time, Susan opened the back door and walked out into the yard. "There you are! I was wondering where you went." Susan then caught sight of her cousin. "Donny!" she exclaimed, running over to give him a hug. "I see you've met Hugh."

"Yeah. Just tellin' him about my job at Kennywood back in the day."

"Oh. Well, sorry I interrupted, but I wanted to let you know that we will be eating in about fifteen minutes." At that, Susan gave Hugh a kiss on the cheek. "I'll see you guys back inside. I need to go help Mom." Then she briskly walked back into the house.

For the next few minutes, Donny shared his experiences with the High Striker game at Kennywood Park. A couple of the anecdotes were quite hilarious, but Hugh couldn't help thinking Donny's insights were mostly superficial. It was obvious the former makeshift handyman-turned-carny had no real connection to the sideshow; he was just an employee at Kennywood Park. Hugh was ready to take the initiative. Looking at his watch, he declared, "Well, Donny, we had better get inside, or else they'll be out here looking for us."

"Let them. They know where to find us."

"Well, actually, I, uh…I need to use the bathroom." Hugh pointed toward the house.

"Well, in that case, man, let's go," Donny said, giving way to the suggestion.

The two men entered through the back door. The holiday spirit was in full swing, and all enjoyed their time together.

✲ ✲ ✲

On the morning of December 31, Hugh and Susan left Columbus for the return trip to Pittsburgh. They wanted to get out early so they would be back in time to celebrate New Year's Eve with some friends back at school.

It didn't take Susan long to bring up the topic of life after college, just as Hugh had been expecting she would. "Hugh, you know how much I care about you, don't you?"

"Yes, I know," Hugh said, knowing what was coming next and half-expecting that little four-letter word.

"Well, actually, I…well, Hugh, I love you. I really do. You are a great guy in so many ways, and my family really likes you, and…" She gulped and trailed off, as if the words were difficult to speak.

"And…?" Hugh said, coaxing her to go on.

"Well, I guess I'm trying to say we should have a serious talk about our future," Susan announced, to no surprise.

"Our future? Like, how far into the future are you talking about?"

"I'm talking about *our* future—you know…life after college, our relationship, our commitment to each other, that kind of stuff."

"Can't we just take one day at a time? I mean, I love you, but I don't want to make plans and commitments right now. I just…well, Susan, I just can't, to be honest."

"I can appreciate that, Hugh, but I need to know what you want out of life."

"I'm sorry, Susan, but I don't have all the answers right now."

"I'd just like to know if you see me in your future, that's all," she said, burgeoning impatience beginning to seep through her voice.

"I don't have a crystal ball, Susan, and I don't believe in them anyway. I can't see my future. As I told you on the trip up, I really believe God has a plan for me, so my future consists of being open to living and seeing how things unfold. I hope you are part of that plan, but I cannot see the plan from here. I have to live and learn, at least for now."

Susan sat quietly and gazed out the window, saying not another word.

After a short break, Hugh continued, "Let's just talk about something else, like the party tonight."

"Hugh, we have to talk about this eventually. I understand that you don't want to feel pressured, and I know you are a thinker who likes to really look at things from all angles before making your move, but please try to understand things from my perspective. I'm just trying to be practical.

You can't always just live one day at a time without planning ahead...or at least I can't."

"I don't understand why it has to be so complicated. We love each other. Isn't that all that matters? Let's just keep it simple."

"Not everything is that easy, Hugh."

"Okay, maybe you're right, but I just don't want to talk about it right now. We had a good time at your family's place. Let's not ruin the happy spirit before we're even back at school. Besides, it's almost New Year's, and I want to ring it in with a kiss. That's part of my immediate plan, anyway," he said, trying to flatter her and lighten the mood a bit.

Susan looked disappointed, but she didn't push the issue. Instead, she took a shot at a compromise. "Well, will you promise to think about it so we can discuss it soon?"

"Okay, I promise," Hugh responded, hoping she'd let go and change the subject to something more pleasant.

As the time passed, the mood remained light as the ongoing sparse conversation often yielded to the quiet hum of the open road. They had just about reached the halfway point back to the university when it started to rain. It was as if someone had opened the floodgates, and, as Hugh leaned forward to strain to see through the torrential rain beating down on the windshield, the accident just...happened.

✦ ✦ ✦

College commencement in 1923 was bittersweet for Hugh Konklin. After all, he had achieved so much in his life, even though graduation had occurred a year later than he had planned. It had taken months to recover from the car accident. And, in the midst of the aches of his broken bones, Hugh had other healing to do. He never got the chance for that New Year's kiss or to discuss a future with Susan because that car accident ended any future they might have had together. It had taken Susan's life.

As he listened to the speeches that night, his thoughts returned to those days following the accident, as he lay helpless and broken in the hospital bed. At that time, graduation seemed a distant goal. Now the time had arrived, and he found himself reflecting on his final one-way conversation with Susan.

Weeks after the accident, he visited Memorial Gardens Cemetery. With crutches nudged uncomfortably up under his armpits, Hugh managed to make his way through the maze of graves until he arrived at Susan's final resting place. She lay beneath a beautiful headstone, etched with *"Beloved Daughter."* The time for closure had arrived; Hugh had lain unconscious in the hospital during her funeral, but now it was time to honor his final promise, to answer the questions that had lingered in Susan's mind, perhaps her last thoughts before her final breath. "Susan, it's me," Hugh said softly, leaning over the grave. "I am so sorry it's taken so long. I was pretty banged up and just recently got out of the hospital. I didn't forget, you know, about what I said in the car. You are a great person, and I do love you. I know I told you I believe in a grand plan for my life, orchestrated by God, but I have to say, times like these make me question it all. It's hard to imagine such an ending for us. But anyway, to answer you, yes, I could have imagined being with you, had things been different." The pause was long before Hugh uttered his final words to her. "Maybe it's less about me and more about you. Maybe this was part of God's plan for you."

His mind returned to the graduation as his name was called. He arose and made his way to the stage as thunderous applause permeated the auditorium. Hugh had overcome adversity, persevering in a demanding college engineering curriculum. Now, the grand moment had arrived. There he was, receiving that valued piece of paper, a college degree. There he stood, the young man who'd lost his girlfriend, who'd willed himself back to health, and who'd graduated with honors from one of the most difficult engineering programs in the country. It was a special moment, but like far too many special moments, it was also a fleeting one.

At first, events in Hugh's life unfolded as expected. He got a good job with an engineering firm and made a decent living. He was even content at times. However, as time passed, Hugh realized that no one was watching any longer. College was in the past. His story would continue to be told, but in reality, it had ended the night of his graduation. The young man who'd been captured in the minds of those who told his story was a snapshot in time. The real Hugh Konklin, the evolving one, had to live with what had happened and what he had become. While his life was speckled with happy moments here and there, it was not a life of complete fulfillment and satisfaction. It was a life devoid of the High Striker.

CHAPTER 5

HUGH KONKLIN JOINS THE CARNIVAL

The aftershave was a giveaway: Gary Russell was near, and Hugh felt nauseated.

"Good morning, Hugh," Russell said as he entered Hugh's office.

"Good morning, Mr. Russell," Hugh replied.

"Look, Hugh, I need to get right to the point. You've been working on this project for three months, and we are now over two weeks late. I need those drawings finished this afternoon."

"Mr. Russell, I understand. However, as you know, things have continued to shift and change, yet I've been busting my butt here every night to get it done. I just think—"

Russell interrupted, "Hugh, I don't want to hear another of your damn excuses. You work late. I get it. But so do I, and so does everyone else around here. In fact, I've been working late for a long time, so you might as well get used to it and stop complaining. If you want to keep your job, I suggest you finish your work today." At that, he turned around and walked out.

It was a painfully familiar scene, and Hugh hated the predictability with every fiber of his being, but it came with the job as a mechanical engineer for Perkins and Graf.

Almost two years had passed since the newly graduated Hugh Konklin had sat in Russell's office, interviewing for the job, and standing there, his blood boiling at the man's impatience, his mind drifted back to that day.

"Well, Hugh, we take great pride in our work here at Perkins and Graf," Gary Russell had said. "I've been with the company for seventeen years. This company represents what living in Pittsburgh is all about, hard work. I see that you're a smart guy. Here at Perkins and Graf, we're looking for smart people, but most importantly, we need people who know how to follow the rules and get their work done."

I should have known better, Hugh thought, still reflecting on the day he'd willingly become the servant of a schedule-driven taskmaster who left no room for creativity.

"Knock-knock," a voice interrupted his daydream.

"Oh, hi. Good morning, Grace," Hugh said to Ms. Evers, the office busybody.

"Good morning, Hugh. I don't mean to interrupt. I know you're busy. Just wanted to say hello. How are you doing?"

"I'm good," Hugh said, tolerating the needless chitchat to the best of his ability.

"Did Mr. Russell visit you this morning?" Grace asked, feigning naïveté.

"Yes. He just left a few minutes ago."

"How was his mood?"

"Same as always."

"Great. Well, do you need help with anything?" she asked, as if she really had a service to offer.

"No thanks. I'm just trying to get this drawing done."

"Okay. Well, have a good day."

"I will. Thanks, Grace."

Hugh sat back in his chair and noticed the flyer on his desk, an advertisement for a carnival at Scott Township. He couldn't help but let his mind wander again. He thought about the night at the Jefferson County Fairgrounds and about carnival life. There was something appealing about the idea: freedom, adventure, and living life without the boundaries of office walls. However, those were just dreams, and Hugh's reality was much different. He was, in fact, sitting in an office with a pencil in his hand and there was... the drawing. *Yes, the drawing,* he thought, sighing as his mind came back into focus on the dull task ahead.

When lunch hour arrived, Hugh put the pencil to rest, proud of his accomplishment. The drawing was done, and it was the perfect time to refuel. Although the streets of Pittsburgh were crowded and noisy, there was something about the openness. It was apparent to Hugh that the confines of office walls did not suit him well. Getting outside for a walk seemed to be the perfect remedy for him most of the time, and this day was no different, so he ventured out. "Afternoon, Charlie," he said to the familiar street vendor.

"What'll it be today?"

"I'll have a bratwurst, fully loaded."

"You got it."

"You're a godsend, Charlie."

"How so?"

"If I had to leave work and go somewhere else, into some other grim, dull building, to eat lunch, I think I'd go crazy."

"I take it you like the outdoors, Mr. Konklin?"

"I sure do, Charlie. Look at you. You've really made it. Here you are, working outside, being on your own. And it's Hugh for you, Charlie. Just call me Hugh."

"Nothing like a bratwurst and a park bench, huh, Mr. Hugh?"

"You nailed it," Hugh said with a smile.

As he walked away, bratwurst in hand, Hugh suddenly realized it had to be the day. *So it's finally here.* He was single and had no commitments to anyone except Perkins and Graf and Gary Russell, of course. *So why do I endure the torture of a job I hate? Why not just quit and live in the moment—like good ol' Charlie? Heck, I could run off and join a carnival. After all, that one's right nearby, and I could...* His imaginings and delusions of carnival freedom were cut short when he'd barely walked through the door of his office and saw Gary Russell. He turned in order to avoid making eye contact and then bumped into Grace Evers, who dropped an armload of papers. "Sorry, Grace." Hugh bent to help her pick up the papers from the floor.

"It's okay," Grace said. "Accidents happen."

When Hugh stood up, Russell was in his face. "I hope that project is priority one," Russell said. "Some of us have been working through our lunch breaks, you know," he scowled, glancing down at Hugh's bratwurst wrapper, seemingly perturbed at Hugh's audacity for eating and taking a much-deserved break.

A sarcastic smile came over Hugh's face, and he shook his head at the irony. It was both a serious and a comedic moment. He considered blurting an obscenity, but Hugh was more diplomatic than that. Instead, he responded with an invitation. "Mr. Russell, could I have a few minutes of your time? It's about, uh…the project."

"Give me five minutes, and I'll meet you in your office. I hope you have good news for me." In the end, he didn't take the news of Hugh's resignation very well.

Through the office window, Hugh saw Grace again, and she appeared interested in the heated, loud voice of Gary Russell emanating out of the doorway.

"Of course I'm upset, Hugh! I can't believe how unprofessional this is. You know I was counting on you to finish that drawing!"

"Mr. Russell, the drawing is done."

"Done?"

"Yes. Done."

"Why didn't you tell me that to begin with?" Russell pointed to the paper on Hugh's desk. "Is that it?"

"That's it, and I'm sure you will be pleased," Hugh said.

"You must have been very close this morning."

"Yes. Just needed a few refinements."

"Well, thanks for honoring your commitment," Russell said, a rare gesture of gratitude that Hugh wholeheartedly welcomed. "But as far as your job is concerned," Russell continued, "I won't beg you to stay. That's not my style."

"I didn't expect you would."

"Well, nevertheless, I suppose good luck is in order." It was another compliment, at least relative to Russell's usual demeanor, and it took Hugh by surprise.

"Thank you," was all Hugh could think to say.

And just like that, it was over. He was a free man, escaped from Alcatraz. Hugh dismissed himself from Russell and then said his goodbyes to everyone. By mid-afternoon, he was on the street again, this time as a former employee of Perkins and Graf. It was a surreal experience, and Hugh was glad for it. The pressure had immediately lifted, and he was finally free.

☆ ☆ ☆

The next morning, Hugh awoke early, eager to begin the next chapter in his life. After stopping at a local bakery, he headed out of the city toward Scott Township, prepared to apply for a new job—a *new* job in every sense of the word. As he drove, he thought about the conversation he'd had with Susan about Abraham, the man of God who willingly and faithfully left everything behind in pursuit of a nomadic life. *A friend of God,* he recalled, and the thought made him smile.

Hugh arrived before the official opening time, hoping to talk to someone before the crowds arrived. When he walked up to the front gate, no one was there. The carnival looked lifeless, but he spotted a few carnies out, prepping for the opening. Hugh was fond of his ability to whistle loudly, but for the sake of good manners, he constrained his actions to a loud shout and a wave. "Hey! Over here," Hugh shouted, waving his right arm.

The initial attention-getter went ignored.

Hugh found himself feeling a bit uncomfortable and self-conscious for a moment. He did not dwell on the emotion for long, though, and followed up with an even louder shout, this time with both arms waving about in the air. "Hey! Over here! Over here!"

This time he caught the attention of a teenage girl. As she made her way closer, Hugh was immediately taken by her good looks, which were accentuated by a charming, beautiful smile and her dainty wave. "Well, hello there, mister!"

Hugh was captivated for a moment by the precocious teen, but he finally managed to speak up. "Well, hello there yourself. I'm Hugh, Hugh Konklin."

"Samantha Cohen. It's nice to meet you, sir," she said, showing off her gorgeous set of teeth.

"I suppose I'm a bit early," Hugh said, glancing at his watch.

"Well, yeah, if you're waiting to get into the carnival. I'm 'fraid we don't open for another two hours, Mr. Konklin."

"Well, actually, I'm here on business."

"You sellin' something? People are always comin' by here trying to sell stuff."

Hugh smiled. "No, I'm not selling anything. Are you the carnival spokesperson or something?"

"No. I just happened to see you. Not many good-looking men just show up outside before business hours," she said in a flirtatious manner, toying with a strand of her long, black hair.

"I see," Hugh said. "Well, perhaps you might know who I could talk to about some work."

"You mean, like, working here?"

"Yes, work…and maybe here."

"Well, that would be nice." She gave him a good, hard look from top to bottom. "I think I might know who you can talk to then. His name is Mr. Wilkes."

"You mean Wilkes, as in—"

"Yep. Mr. Wilkes. He's the owner."

"Well, Samantha, I must say that sounds very good."

"I can't let you inside because that's against the rules, but if you wait right there, I can go get Mr. Wilkes. He's a really nice man."

"That would be great," Hugh replied. "Thanks."

"Okay then." Samantha turned to leave, but after she'd taken a couple steps, she stopped for another quick look at Hugh. She smiled again, giggled, and trotted off.

Hugh kept his eyes on her until she finally disappeared into a trailer some distance away. It was one of those warm August mornings, Mother Nature's version of hot flashes, and the sun was already beginning to unleash its wrath. Hugh was anxious, and it began to stretch every moment to an eternity. He glanced at his pocket watch again and realized that forever had really only been a couple of minutes. Hugh released a nervous, heavy sigh and began to walk in large circles, kicking pebbles as he went. He let his mind wander to ease the nervous tension. When he found himself near his car, he decided to sit on the hood.

Just as he sat, he noticed some activity off in the distance. The trailer door Samantha had entered opened again. Out came Samantha, followed by a short, rotund fellow. They walked together a while before Samantha broke off and headed toward the interior of the carnival while the man continued toward Hugh.

Hugh stood at once and approached the gate again, this time even more anxious than before. When Hugh reached the gate, he stopped and waved as soon as he made eye contact, or so he thought.

The man did not acknowledge him and kept his slow, steady pace.

When he was within speaking distance, Hugh waved and then spoke. "Hello."

The man acknowledged his presence with a mere nod of the head.

Hugh felt it best to maintain eye contact and would have been prepared for a handshake had it not been for the locked gate that separated them.

He was finally put at ease when the man smiled and spoke. "Good morning to you, sir. Samantha said you want to talk to someone in charge, and I s'pose that'd be me. I'm Clarence Wilkes." Up close, Wilkes appeared pleasant enough. He had a round, jolly face that went along well with his pudgy body. The top of his head was bald, with a patch of gray hair on each side, just above the ears.

"Nice to meet you, Mr. Wilkes. My name is Hugh Konklin. Actually, I'm interested in finding out what I would need to do to work here, to be part of the carnival."

"Do you have a job now?"

"No, sir. Well, I did, but I just quit my job yesterday."

"What were you doing, if I may ask?"

"Actually, I'm a mechanical engineer. I was working with a firm in town and just...well, I guess I just got sick of it all, if that makes any sense. Sick of the everyday routine, the grind."

"Hmm. I don't think I've ever heard this particular story before. Quitting your job as an engineer to join the carnival? That's a new one, mister. If anything, it usually goes in reverse."

"I suppose it does sound unusual," Hugh replied.

"Well, I might have something, but this is no place to talk." Wilkes pulled a chain of keys from his pocket, and, after briefly fumbling around, found the right one to open the gate.

They shook hands and walked down the path, back to Clarence Wilkes's trailer.

The next hour in the trailer was spent forging a deal. During the final negotiations, Hugh made clear his terms. "I really appreciate your offer, Mr. Wilkes, and I would very much like the job as foreman. However, I really would like the opportunity to run a sideshow game of my own, if that's at all possible."

"After what you've told me today, I can only guess you're wantin' to run a High Striker. Unfortunately, like I said earlier, we don't have one," Wilkes replied.

"You may not have one right now, but I can build one."

"Like I told you, the foreman's job is pretty demanding. It involves keeping all the other shows and rides up and running. Some of our contraptions have really been around the block a time or two, so it's going to be a lot of work. You think you can handle being a foreman and building a High Striker at the same time, then runnin' the game once it's built?"

"Absolutely," Hugh replied enthusiastically.

"I like you, Konklin. You're a confident young man. As long as you can do the job I'm hiring you for, I'm willing to let you figure out the High Striker thing in your spare time. If you do manage to build one, I'll let you run it. Do we have a deal?"

"Yes. Yes, we absolutely do!"

Within the span of two days in August of 1925, Hugh's transition into the family of The Amazing Wilkes Clan Carnival was complete. He had gone from being a formal mechanical engineer to a carnival foreman. He believed God had opened a door—a door he'd willingly stepped through, even if it did come with a lesser paycheck. Finally, he would have the opportunity to run a carnival sideshow game, and not just any game! Hugh Konklin was going to be the sideshow master of the High Striker, the game that had been his nemesis, his obsession for so long.

CHAPTER 6

HUGH KONKLIN BUILDS HIS OWN HIGH STRIKER

During part of his first week on the job, Hugh pitched a tent until Clarence Wilkes finally arranged for a small trailer to be delivered for his new foreman. The weekend following its arrival, with the help of Daniel Key, his new carny buddy, Hugh moved all his personal items out of his apartment in Pittsburgh and made the transition to his trailer.

Daniel Key, the man in charge of the ever-popular Ferris wheel, was one of the first to establish a friendship with Hugh. Daniel was a high school dropout, and he'd taken over the Ferris wheel at the ripe old age of nineteen, quite by chance, following a brief stint as an assistant. Daniel's old boss, who had operated the wheel, had left the carnival abruptly, right before Hugh's arrival. Daniel was a slender, wiry young man who was particularly good with his hands. He had learned about Ferris wheels by tearing them down and putting them back together. That part came easy, but he had an appetite for learning as well, something that became apparent to Hugh following an early encounter during his second day on the job.

"Good Morning, Mr. Konklin," Daniel had said as Hugh approached the Ferris wheel.

"Good morning. It's Daniel, right?"

"Yes."

"Remember, you can call me Hugh. How's the Ferris wheel running?"

"She's runnin' well."

"That's good to hear. Do you have any questions for me today?"

"Actually, I do. I've been meaning to ask someone something, and you seem like the one who might know."

"Sure," Hugh had responded, curious as to what Daniel was going to say next.

"Well, I heard you were an engineer before becoming foreman, so I hope this doesn't sound dumb."

"I don't believe there are any dumb questions, Daniel. Go ahead and ask."

"Well, I'm pretty good at building things, like this Ferris wheel here, but I don't really understand *why* it works the way it does—you know…why you get the queasy feeling, like you're gonna fall out or something."

Hugh had paused for a moment. "That's a good question. Actually, I'm going to have to think about it for minute." Hugh had scratched his chin, looked up at the wheel for a few seconds, and then spoke up. "Did you graduate from high school, Daniel?"

"Nope," he'd said, sounding somewhat ashamed.

"Well, that's all right. Before you left school, did you ever learn about Isaac Newton?"

"Can't recall. Maybe. The name sounds familiar."

"Did you ever learn about gravity?"

"Sorta. That's the stuff that keeps us glued to the planet, right?"

"Yes. When people ride a Ferris wheel, they feel the effects of gravity. On a Ferris wheel, the force at work is called centripetal force, because it's curved as a result of moving around a circle. Now, this force is basically a combination of the mass—or just think of it as the weight of the passenger and the acceleration of the passenger due to gravity—which is roughly thirty-two feet per second per second. You can think of it as being how fast and far you are falling, thanks to gravity pulling you down."

"Um...okay."

"Now, here's the interesting part. When you're riding around the wheel, your acceleration is always pointing toward the center of the Ferris wheel. When you are down at the bottom, it's pointing up, and when you are up at the top it's pointing down."

"I'm sorry, but you kinda lost me already." Daniel had looked puzzled.

"I don't think there's an easy way to explain it. Anyway, you asked about the queasy feeling, the butterflies you get when you're at the top of the wheel, right?"

"Yes," Daniel had responded right away.

"Well, those butterflies are the result of a feeling of weightlessness. This is because the centripetal force and your weight are essentially the same thing when you are at the top. Actually, your weight is that force that's pointing down toward the center of the wheel. Now, what happens when you reach the bottom of the loop?"

"I'm not as queasy, that's for sure."

"That's because at the bottom, you feel heavier than normal because the centripetal force is coming from the seat on the wheel. It's now pointed up toward the center of the wheel, and the seat is actually supporting your weight."

"It makes sense when you describe it like that, but I'm not sure how much will sink in."

"That's okay. All learning takes time. We can talk about it again someday if you'd like," Hugh had replied.

"I'd like that."

"Okay then. I'm just going to continue making my rounds."

From then on, Daniel and Hugh had enjoyed a true connection, and when Hugh had to make his move from his apartment, Daniel was happy to volunteer a little manpower.

Hugh's first night in his trailer was spent amongst boxes of his stuff. It was not until the second night that things began to succumb to some form of organization. By the third night, Hugh had set up a small table in the kitchen area and was about to do some Bible reading when Daniel arrived at the door. "Come in," Hugh said.

"I hope I'm not interrupting. You told me to drop by sometime, so here I am."

"That's fine. I'm still trying to get things organized. Here…take a seat." Hugh dragged another chair up to the small kitchen table. "I really appreciate all your help getting me moved in, Daniel."

"Happy to help you. So, uh, are you reading the Bible?" Daniel gestured to the Good Book opened up on the table.

"Yes."

"May I?"

"Sure, go ahead. It was a gift from my mother."

"That's nice," Daniel said. "I didn't go to church when I was growing up."

"My mother was a devout woman. It was always a big part of my life."

"Hey, I recognize this name! Isaac Newton," Daniel said, referring to their conversation about the Ferris wheel. "Did you write his name in here?" Daniel pointed to the inside cover of the Bible.

"Yep, back when I was twelve. I loved math and physics, even back then, so I was a big fan of Newton...and still am."

"What about this other name? I'm not sure I can even pronounce it."

"Oh, that's Nikola Tesla, another hero of mine. He's a great engineer and inventor. Have you ever heard of Thomas Edison?"

"Yes, of course. We even knew about him back in third grade."

"Well, Edison and Tesla worked together and later became foes. I actually think Tesla was the more gifted one in the partnership. Anyway, my father was an electrical engineer, and he met Tesla in Colorado Springs in 1899. They even worked together briefly. My father died soon after that in an accident, while my mother was pregnant with me."

"Man, I'm sorry. That's rough," Daniel said. "Did you ever get to meet Tesla?"

"No, but he was nice to my mother following the accident. After I was born, my mother wanted to move to New York to be near some relatives, and Tesla gave her the money she needed. I've always followed Tesla and tried to keep up with his work."

"That's quite a story."

"You see that clipping folded up in the cover? Go ahead and open it up."

"What is it?" Daniel asked as he took it.

"It's a passage from Tesla's 1919 autobiography."

"I'm not a very good reader," Daniel said.

"That's okay." Hugh grabbed the paper. "Let me read it to you. '*At this time, as at many other times in the past, my thoughts turned toward my mother's teaching. The gift of mental power comes from God, Divine Being, and if we concentrate our minds on that truth, we become in tune with this great power. My mother had taught me to seek all truth in the Bible; therefore, I devoted the next few months to the study of this work.*'"

"So this Tesla was a Bible reader, too, huh?" Daniel said.

"Yes. After I read his autobiography, I felt an even stronger connection to the man, so I added his name to the inside cover next to Newton's. Each night before I read, I look at those names. They mean a lot to me."

Daniel smiled. "Thanks for sharing that with me, man." He placed the Bible back on the table.

Hugh nodded, folded the clipping, and returned it to its place.

"So, have you found those drawings you were telling me about? Those ones of the High Striker?" Daniel asked.

"Ah, the High Striker." Hugh slid a box across the floor. "This would be it. I tell you, Daniel, the striker will be fun to build." Hugh took the original striking machine patent and specifications from the box, handling them with care. "I got this in college and will never forget the first time I read those words."

"Which words?"

"These." Hugh gestured to the patent he'd received from Professor Johnson in college. "This is a copy of the High Striker patent. *'Among the objects in view is to provide a machine of the character described which will be simple in construction, inexpensive, and efficient in operation.'*" Then, as he flipped through the pages, the breakdown of the intriguing machine lay before his eyes. There they were—four separate drawings that captured the composition and essence of striking machines, a mechanical engineering marvel so simple, yet so complex. It was man's intellect, his concept of a making a machine that would, in turn, provide a mechanism that would challenge its maker's brawn, become a pawn in carnival capitalism, and ultimately provide amusement. However, for Hugh Konklin, it was much more than that. "Take a look at these drawings." Hugh handed the patent to Daniel.

No. 898,129.

PATENTED SEPT. 8, 1908.

R. A. NOKES & W. W. GORDON.
STRIKING MACHINE.
APPLICATION FILED JULY 20, 1907.

4 SHEETS—SHEET 1.

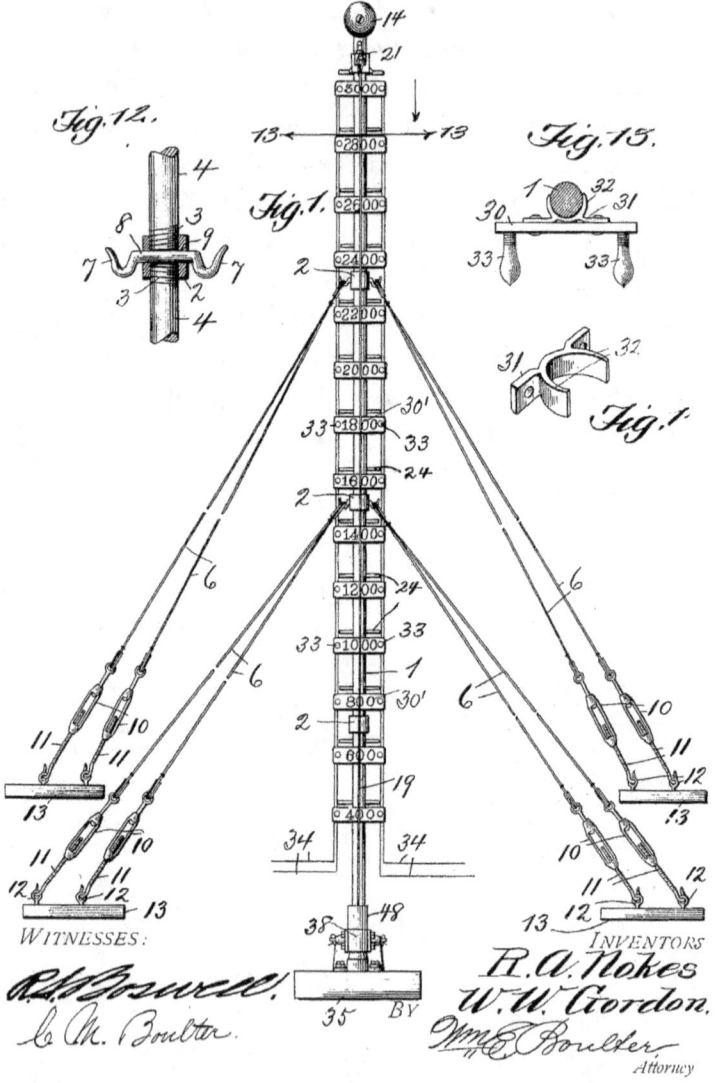

Fig. 12.

Fig. 1.

Fig. 13.

Fig. 1

WITNESSES:

R. W. Boswell.

C. M. Boulter.

INVENTORS

R. A. Nokes
W. W. Gordon.

BY

Wm. E. Boulter,

Attorney

No. 898,129.

PATENTED SEPT. 8, 1908.

R. A. NOKES & W. W. GORDON.

STRIKING MACHINE.

APPLICATION FILED JULY 20, 1907.

4 SHEETS—SHEET 2.

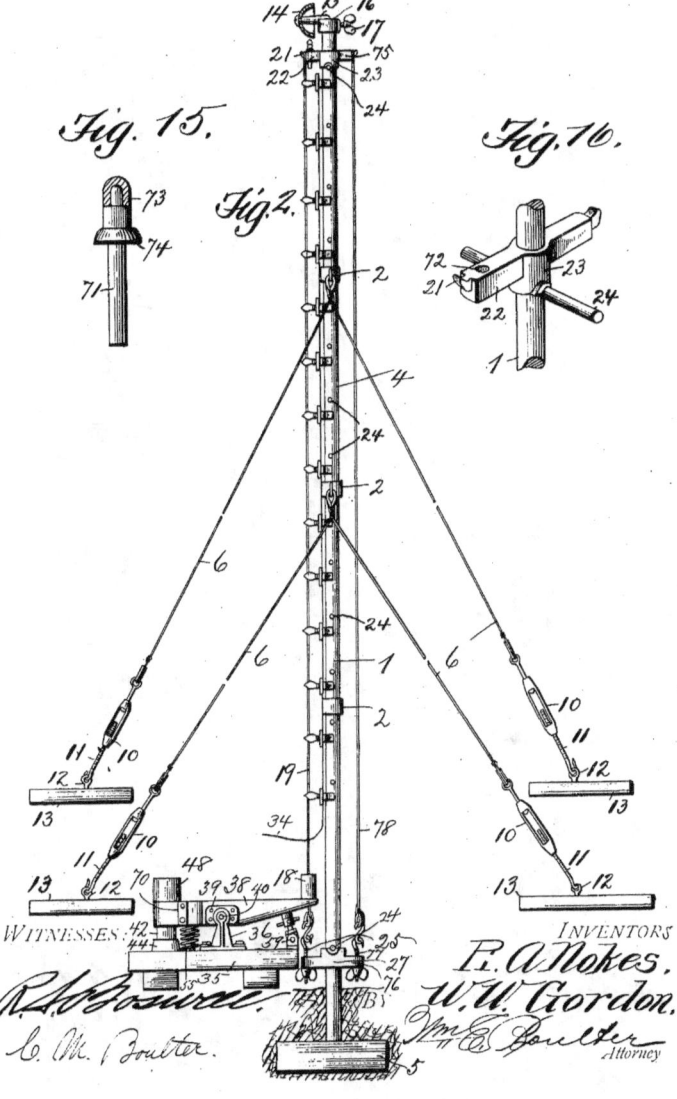

Fig. 15.

Fig. 16.

Fig. 2.

WITNESSES:

R. A. Boswell.

C. M. Boulter.

INVENTORS

R. A. Nokes.

W. W. Gordon.

Wm. E. Boulter.

Attorney

81

No. 898,129.

PATENTED SEPT. 8, 1908.

R. A. NOKES & W. W. GORDON.
STRIKING MACHINE.
APPLICATION FILED JULY 20, 1907.

4 SHEETS—SHEET 3.

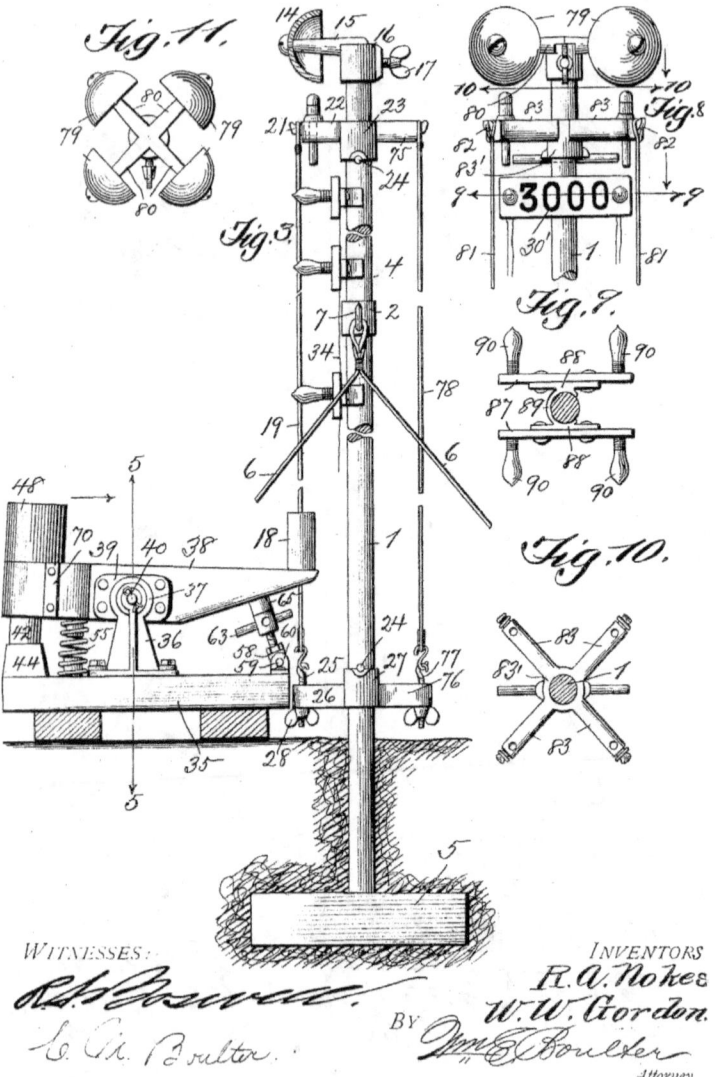

WITNESSES:

R. L. Boswell.

E. A. Boulter.

INVENTORS
R. A. Nokes
W. W. Gordon.

BY *Wm. E. Boulter*

Attorney

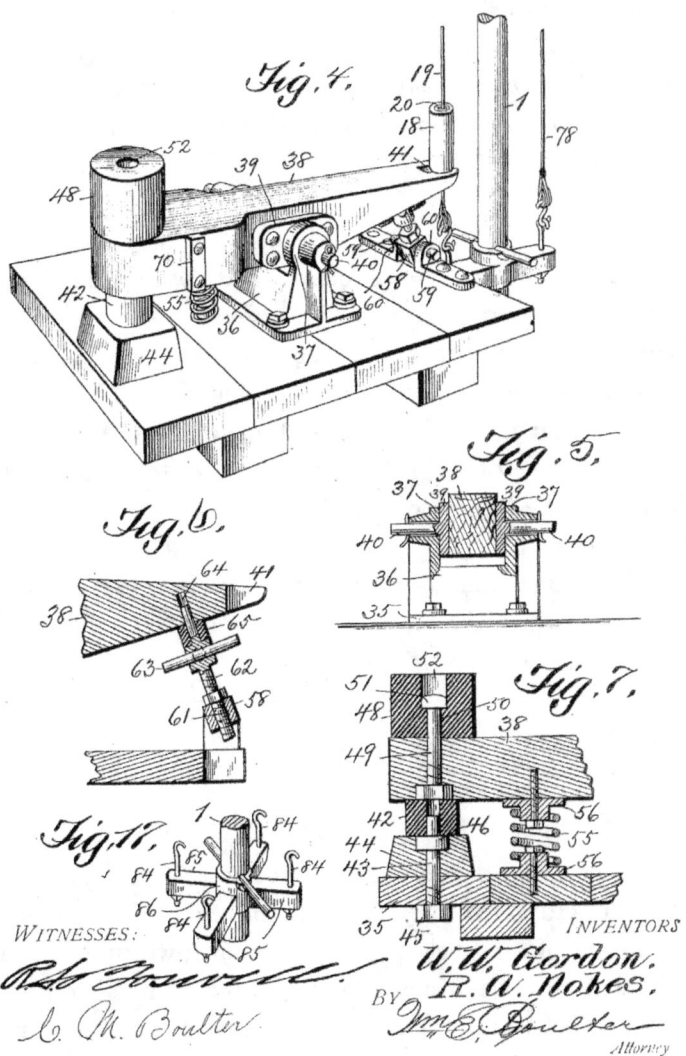

No. 898,129.

PATENTED SEPT. 8, 1908.

R. A. NOKES & W. W. GORDON.
STRIKING MACHINE.
APPLICATION FILED JULY 20, 1907.

4 SHEETS—SHEET 4.

Fig. 4.

Fig. 5,

Fig. 6.

Fig. 7.

Fig. 1?,

WITNESSES:

INVENTORS
W. W. Gordon.
R. A. Nokes.
BY
Attorney

"Wow," Daniel said.

"Yeah, when I look at these, it makes me think about a Bible lesson my mother taught me long ago. It's simple logic that design implies a designer. It was something Newton believed as well. He once said, *'Gravity explains the motions of the planets, but it cannot explain who set the planets in motion. God governs all things and knows all that is or can be done. The Supreme God is a Being Eternal, infinite and absolutely perfect.'*"

"I suppose that makes good sense," Daniel said.

"Daniel, take a close look at the drawings. They represent but a tiny subset of the physical universe. The High Striker is an elegant machine, physics in its most basic form, a game that is a metaphor of life. The physical laws that govern success and failure in the game are representative of the same laws that govern success and failure in the larger context of life. They are, in essence, God's laws."

Daniel sat quiet for a few seconds, pondering, and then spoke. "So when are you going to start building it?"

"Soon, Daniel. Very soon."

Exactly 283 days after he started his job as the carnival foreman, Hugh Konklin finished building his High Striker, at the end of a 3-week stay near a small town in Arkansas. The next stop was Kansas, where Hugh planned to put it all together as a fully functional machine that could be used in an operational sideshow.

The night The Amazing Wilkes Clan Carnival settled near a small town in Kansas, Deborah Cohen was the squeaky-wheel. It was clear that her daughter Samantha had an adolescent crush on Hugh, and Deborah was protective. Therefore, when it came to matters concerning Hugh Konklin, Deborah Cohen cranked up her difficult-to-please personality an extra notch.

"You're sort of giving me a hard time tonight," Hugh said as Deborah followed him toward a tent.

"I know you're busy organizing all the trailers, Hugh, but I want to make it clear that I don't want to be too close to rides or noisy sideshows, especially those with big-mouth men like Bob Connor. I swear, you'd better not put me anywhere near him."

In the world of the carnival, Connor represented what many people considered to be a main attraction. He was the master of "Freaky," a catchy one-word title that exemplified Connor and his cast of strange characters. They were a group of loners, a tight-knit clique who minded their own business. Connor, on the other hand, was an extrovert, a salesman, an exploiter of the world's oddness for his own gain. What Deborah Cohen hated most (and she was not alone in this despise) was that obnoxious megaphone that never left his side.

"You tell me that every time, Deborah. I've been doing this a while. Don't you trust me by now?"

"I'm just making sure."

"You know, I've heard rumors, but I've never asked. Can you fill me in on Bob Connor's story?"

"Oh God! Well, it was a long time ago, somewhere in West Virginia. That night, I was battling a migraine, a rambunctious crowd, and Bob Connor's loud, irritating voice amplified by his ridiculous megaphone. Although my show is inside a tent, it doesn't offer much privacy whenever Connor's parked close by. You know the audiences I get sometimes. Snake charmers and belly dancers draw a particular male crowd. Anyway, a half-lit, cantankerous customer stood in the front row during my show, and he started an argument with Connor."

"How so?"

"Connor was loud—louder than usual. The man walked back through the crowd, disrupting the show. He went to the back of the tent, stuck out his head, and started yelling at Connor to shut up."

"Did you stop the show?"

"No. I continued dancing. Connor ignored him, of course, and kept spewing his sales pitch. He knows the rules regarding customer engagement."

"There are *rules*?"

"How long you been here now?" Deborah replied sarcastically. "Yes, there are rules, written and otherwise, and one forbids provocation, except in cases where carnies need to protect themselves from harm. I later found out, unofficially of course, that Connor felt like breaking the rules and served up the middle finger. 'Cause of that, a shouting match began, and pretty soon the other men at my show found the argument more exciting than me. It was the first time during my career when I was unable to finish a show."

"I see," Hugh said. "I'll tell you what. I'll make sure Bob Connor is not anywhere near you."

"You need to tell him at once."

"Now, Deborah, I've been with the carnival nine months. Have I ever let you down?"

"Not yet...and I don't want there to be a first time under your watch."

"I'll go speak to him now," Hugh said, attempting to be the peacekeeper.

It had been a long day, and Hugh was tired. *I need to get out of here and put up some High Striker road signs along the way. What's a grand opening without a little gratuitous self-promotion?*

Two days later, the carnival opened, and the High Striker was ready for business. That day was one to be remembered in the annals of Hugh's history, for it marked the end of a longtime quest and the beginning of a new adventure. From that day forward, Hugh Konklin never looked back. He had a dream to fulfill, and he wasn't going to let go of it.

✫ ✫ ✫

Time passed, and Hugh was happy. Months turned into years, and as the decade closed, there was a new interest in Hugh's life. In 1929, Samantha Cohen turned twenty years old. Hugh Konklin, on the other hand, was a decade ahead of her, approaching thirty. Samantha's crush had not been a phase after all, and her actions made that blatantly clear to everyone. From the time she was sixteen, she'd boldly proclaimed her love and told everyone she met, "Someday I'm gonna marry Hugh Konklin." Her mother dismissed the whole idea for years, hoping Samantha would grow out of the ridiculous fantasy, but in 1929, Hugh Konklin had no problem returning the girl's admiration.

Their first official date was in early August, and within a month, their relationship had crossed the lines into a sexual one. By the end of October, the stock market crash was the big news, but Samantha had news of her own one evening.

"Why aren't you eating tonight?" Hugh asked, while Samantha sat quietly.

"I'm not hungry."

"It's quite a spread," Hugh responded, alluding to the customary evening cuisine. Supper in the carny world was a collective experience during carnival setup week; they all convened under a large tent. It was a Clarence Wilkes tradition, a way to reconnect with fellow carnies before the next show cycle began.

"Yuck," Samantha responded. "I'm getting sick just looking at that chicken leg."

One of the things Hugh loved most was Samantha's feistiness, and he had a way of pushing her buttons. "Boc-boc-boc!" Hugh flapped his arms, waiting for Samantha's next reaction, but when none came, he could tell something was wrong. When she just laid her head down on the table, pushing her dinner away and refusing to acknowledge his silly barnyard bird impression, he asked, "Hey, are you okay?"

"I've just been nauseous a lot lately."

"A lot? For how long?"

"A few days."

"Why haven't you said anything?"

"I'm telling you now, aren't I? I assumed it would go away."

"Have you told your mother?"

"I haven't said anything to her, but Mother just...well, she knows things."

"Do you have a fever?" Hugh placed the back of his hand on her forehead. "Hmm. You don't feel hot. Did you eat anything that might have made you sick?"

"Hugh, it's not that. That wouldn't last this long. Do I have to spell it out?"

"Spell what out?"

Samantha raised her head and gave Hugh the stare. "Why else do women who are having sex get sick to their stomachs?"

Hugh paused, and then a panicked look came over his face as he was bathed in an understanding of what she was saying. "Uh...you mean...?"

"Yeah, that's what I mean. I also missed my menses."

"Uh, s-so..." Hugh stammered. "I-I don't know what to say."

"You don't have to say anything. Besides, I think I'm about to throw up."

Hugh sat speechless, but Deborah Cohen suddenly appeared. She had arrived for supper, and Hugh was rescued from the awkward silence wafting between him and Samantha, hovering over her uneaten chicken leg.

"Samantha, honey, come with me." Deborah extended her hand. "You just stay here," Deborah said to Hugh. "I need to take care of my daughter."

Samantha shrugged and went with her mother, giving Hugh a glance that said, *"See? She knows things."*

✡ ✡ ✡

By mid-November, the news of Samantha's pregnancy was official, so during Thanksgiving, Hugh added to the festivities by asking Samantha to marry him. She agreed, of course, and the date was set for Christmas Day. They agreed on a simple wedding ceremony, and Clarence Wilkes did the honors. In the carny world, it didn't include any official paperwork. It was simply symbolic, a day for Samantha to let the other carnies know Hugh was her man and that she was his woman. In other words, *"Hands off."*

By January of 1930, Hugh and Samantha were husband and wife; technically, that only meant Samantha had moved into Hugh's new trailer, a Christmas gift from Clarence. In addition to being thoughtful and generous, Wilkes was a wealthy man. He'd made a fortune in the carnival business and had been shielded from the recent economic collapse, for he kept all his money in a safe that moved with the carnival. Clarence Wilkes had his own personal bank, and during the next five months of Samantha's pregnancy, the carnival continued to survive the harsh economic woes, thanks in good part to Clarence Wilkes's good graces.

On June 1, 1930, the carny clan was back in Kansas again, the place where Hugh Konklin had opened the High Striker for the first time. It was the first day of carnival setup.

"Good morning, beautiful," Hugh said as he walked up from behind and wrapped his arms around the very pregnant Samantha, who stood in the doorway of their trailer, enjoying the fresh air. "This is where it all started, you know."

"Where what started?"

"We're back in Kansas, where I had the grand opening of the High Striker—you know, back when you were a skinny little girl."

"Ha-ha." Samantha gave him a soft elbow to the ribs.

"I remember that day well. I was trying to get some work done and didn't think I'd ever get rid of you."

"Git ridda me? Right. You were begging me to stay so you could impress me with your big hammer."

"And did I?"

Samantha turned around to face Hugh and smiled, slightly blushing as she looked down at her ample belly and back up at him. "What do you think?"

"I think I swing the hammer pretty well."

Hugh was expecting a classic Samantha comeback, but suddenly her expression changed. "Oh God!" She leaned into Hugh. "I need to...to sit." She attempted to take a step and then collapsed in his arms.

As Hugh picked her up, he noticed blood streaming down her legs, and he quickly carried her to the couch. "Wait right here, honey. I'll get help!"

It was a quick sprint to Deborah's trailer and then to Martha Penley, the midwife. Martha had helped bring several babies into the world, and on this morning, Hugh found her outside at the clothesline.

"Martha! Come quick! It's Samantha. Something is wrong!"

Martha immediately dropped the damp pants she was holding to the ground, along with the two wooden clothes-pins, and quickly followed a frantic Hugh to his trailer. Inside, Deborah had managed to get Samantha back to the bedroom.

Hugh rushed to the bedside to hold her hand, and when he glanced down, he saw that there seemed to be even more blood. The otherwise cool Hugh Konklin was out of his comfort zone, feeling panicked. "We need to do something before she bleeds to death!"

"Calm down, Hugh." Martha approached the bed to better assess the situation. "We need someone to drive to the nearest town to find a doctor. In the meantime, we need to stay calm…for Samantha's sake."

"I love you," Hugh said to Samantha as he released his firm grip. "I'll be right back. I need to find Daniel." A few minutes later, when Hugh returned, Samantha was unconscious. "Daniel is on his way to town," Hugh stated as he entered the room. "How is she?"

"She's sleeping right now," Deborah replied.

"Good," was all Hugh could say, as he stood looking down at Samantha, feeling helpless.

The day dragged on at a painfully slow and uneasy pace, and by the time Daniel returned, three hours had passed. Samantha was now fully awake, and her violent contractions had begun.

Fortunately, Daniel was not alone; an elderly Kansas doctor was with him. "Where's the father?" the old medic asked as he entered the cramped bedroom.

"Here. I'm Hugh Konklin."

"Solomon Price," the doctor said as he met Hugh in the middle of the room. As they shook hands, Price asked, "Is this your first child?"

"Yes."

"Okay, sir, now listen. There's not much room to move about in here. I think it would be better if you could kindly wait outside. We'll come get you if we need anything or need to fill you in on progress."

"But Samantha's lost a lot of blood, Doctor. She's—"

"I can see that, sir, but please let me be the doctor here. To do that, I'm gonna need room to work."

Hugh left, albeit reluctantly, and eventually settled on the front porch steps, where he remained as the afternoon hours ticked by. Praying was helpful, yet every half-hour or so, he ventured to the bedroom, only for a moment, as a way to ease his mind before returning to the steps.

Finally, as sunset approached, a distinct new sound came from the bedroom: the cry of a newborn.

Just as Hugh leapt to his feet, Martha came out of the bedroom. "You have a son."

"A son? I have a son! And Samantha? How is she?"

"She's lost a lot of blood, but Dr. Price can tell you more. He'll be out in a few minutes."

Hugh forsook the front porch and made his way to the couch. He leaned forward and buried his head in his hands.

After a few minutes, as promised, Dr. Price appeared, looking grim. "Mr. Konklin, uh, your wife would like to see you."

As Hugh entered her room, Deborah passed him in the doorway, sobbing. The room was suddenly and ominously quiet. The newborn was nestled next to his mother, atop the crimson-stained sheets. Samantha's eyes were dull and lifeless, but her farewell smile invited him in.

Hugh knelt down and took her hand. "I love you, Samantha."

There were no other words exchanged between them. It was yet another tragedy, another loss for Hugh Konklin, but at least this time, he was able to say goodbye.

CHAPTER 7

FAREWELLS

Bill Konklin was born on June 1, 1930, the child of Hugh Konklin and Samantha Cohen, a second-generation carny who had died giving birth on that warm summer day. As for Bill, growing up without a mother was hard at times, but his grandmother, Deborah, was a steady female influence in his early life. His early years were full of experiences and exploration. As a child growing up in the carnival, his life was filled with spontaneity and change. There was the routine of moving from town to town every month or so, and every part of the country was a little different, as were the people who came to see the shows when the carnival showed up in their towns, luring them in with posters and loud music and the smell of wonderful foods. Although it was the same show, every event was very different, so little Bill never found himself bored. For a little boy who was naturally curious and demanded constant new experiences and loved to learn (much like his father), life was good.

It was late in May of 1936 when The Amazing Wilkes Clan completed a show in Oklahoma and settled in Texas. On a Tuesday morning, after Bill finished eating breakfast, he ventured out of his grandma's trailer and ran toward Hugh with his arms open wide.

"Hey, little man!" Hugh exclaimed as he knelt for his little boy to leap into his welcoming embrace.

"Daddy!"

Hugh stood with his arms wrapped around Bill. His eyes met Deborah's, peering out of the window. He offered a smile of acknowledgement and appreciation; it was all he could manage as of late. There was no longer brightness in Deborah's eyes, and that made Hugh sad. The week after Bill's fifth birthday, the not yet fifty-year-old Deborah had taken ill and was later diagnosed with cancer. Hugh had helplessly observed her decline. A once strong, dancer's physique slowly wasted away. In Iowa, a doctor had given her only a few months to live. Now, almost a year later she was still alive, albeit thin and frail. Hugh tried not to dwell on the thought of losing her, for she meant a lot to him and even more to Bill.

After a tight hug, Hugh relinquished his tight grip, and Bill slipped through his arms, landing back on his feet. "Did you have a good breakfast?"

Bill nodded his head in the affirmative.

"Well, buddy, I'm all packed and ready to go," Hugh said. "I need to do a few more errands though. You can come with me." Hugh had to make a final round to make sure all was well before he departed. It was the time of the year for an extended break, a two-week lag before the next setup and opening day. For Hugh, it was off to Dallas with Clarence Wilkes's blessing, where he planned to pick up some extra cash working as an engineer on a new roller coaster construction. Considering the decline in Deborah's health, Hugh thought having more money might leave them more options, just in case. "Let's go over here, little man. I need to talk to Daniel about the Ferris wheel." Hugh watched as Bill ran ahead of him, skipping along in the grass and leading the way to Daniel. "Daniel, how are you doing today?"

"I'm good."

"How's the bracket situation?" Hugh asked.

"Hopeless, I'm 'fraid. I'm gonna need to make a trip into town to get some parts."

"Do you need my help?"

"Nope. I can handle it. I wouldn't wanna delay your trip."

"All right, Daniel. I know you can handle it. Is there anything else before I take off?"

"Actually, yeah, if you have a minute. How about a quick physics lesson on roller coasters, since you're gonna be building one?" Daniel asked, having become accustomed to learning interesting things from Hugh.

"Just a second," Hugh said to Daniel in order to address the youngster yanking on his shirt. When Hugh looked down at Bill, he saw that the boy's mood had changed. It was written all over his face; Bill wanted his attention. "Bill, I need to talk to Daniel for a while. It's kind of important. Why don't you go back to Grandma's, and I'll be over soon to say goodbye." Hugh then gave Bill another warm hug, which seemed to satisfy him for the moment, and he trotted off.

"That boy is sure gonna miss you," Daniel said.

"I know. I'll miss him too, something awful."

"Well, don't you worry about anything. We'll be fine till you get back."

"I know," Hugh said. "Anyway, back to your question. You remember all those physics concepts I told you about regarding how the Ferris wheel works, like acceleration, force, and gravity?"

"Yep."

"Well, those are fundamental concepts, and they can help explain roller coasters just like they do for Ferris wheels. However, I'll throw a new concept out there. When you climb the first hill on a coaster, gravity is what brings you down and causes the coaster to accelerate. Now, during the ride down the first hill, there is a conversion to kinetic energy. In fact, there is enough kinetic energy, which is energy generated by motion, needed to take the coaster around the remainder of the track, assuming, of course, that the track is designed properly. There are other factors like friction that are involved, but the most important part to remember is that the only external energy comes from something helping the coaster climb to the top of the first hill. After that, all the energy comes from the motion of the coaster itself."

"Really? Hmm. Okay, I guess that makes perfect sense," Daniel said.

"Good, because now you have a new wrinkle. That's about all I have right now. I'm sure I'll learn more about it on this gig, and I'll be happy to fill you in on my findings when I get back."

"I'd like that, Hugh. I always enjoy learning from you. Take care and have a good trip."

"I will, and I'll see you soon."

After Hugh finished his rounds, he headed back to Deborah's trailer, where he found Bill sitting on the couch, noticeably upset; he had never been apart from his father for any long period of time, and it had him worried.

"Bill, I'm not going to be here tonight to tuck you in, so I want to tell you a Bible story now, before I leave."

Although Bill enjoyed the nightly stories, Hugh at once noticed that his son seemed less than enthused. It was time to adapt, and there was no sugarcoating about it. The time for a heart-to-heart, man-to-man moment beckoned.

"Actually, I'm not going to tell you a Bible story after all." Hugh took a seat beside him.

Bill looked at him strangely and curiously.

"Instead, I'm going to tell you something my mother once told me. God loves you, Bill. Always listen to Him and pay attention to what He does in your life. Always remember that without God, a man's life will be dark. See, son, life is full of opportunities. God puts those in front of us, and this is one of them. Going away for a few days is an opportunity for me to make some extra money so I can take better care of you and your grandma. It's also an opportunity for you to be the man around here until I get back. I want you to take good care of your grandma while I'm gone...and make sure you listen to her."

"I will, and I love you, Daddy," Bill said, as the tears welled up in his eyes.

"Everything is going to be fine, Bill. I want you to be a big boy for Daddy, okay?"

"Okay," Bill said.

There was nothing left to say, only final hugs for Bill and then Deborah. "Thanks so much for your help," Hugh said to her sincerely. "I'll be back soon."

✫ ✫ ✫

Just over two weeks after Hugh departed, Deborah Cohen was outside enjoying a tranquil day when a car stopped alongside the road. A middle-aged man dressed in a suit exited the vehicle.

Deborah wasn't the only one who'd taken notice, for Clarence Wilkes emerged from his trailer and walked out to greet the gentleman. After they spoke for a few minutes, Clarence Wilkes turned to point to something inside the carnival. When he saw Deborah, he waved and motioned for the gentleman to follow him.

At that moment, Deborah was overwhelmed with a feeling that something was wrong. It was intuition, something she could never explain rationally. She did, in fact, just know things. Instead of waiting to find out, she began walking in their direction and met them halfway. It was then that her worst fear was realized: The solemn-looking traveler explained that Hugh Konklin had been killed in an accident while working on the new roller coaster. Deborah was unable to respond to such devastating, seemingly impossible news. At once she thought about the tremendous impact it would have on Bill, now tragically orphaned by both of his parents, and she began to weep.

The man reached into his pocket and retrieved a letter. "Ma'am, I'm sorry for your loss. I have a personal letter here from Mr. Kensington."

"Who?" she asked, tears streaming down her face.

"Mr. Kensington. He's in charge of the project Mr. Konklin was working on. Hopefully the letter will answer your questions." At that, the man said goodbye and returned to his car.

Stunned, Deborah watched until he drove away, unable to move.

"Deborah, I'm so, so sorry." A teary-eyed Clarence Wilkes reached out to embrace her.

She buried her head in his shoulder until the tears no longer flowed and then said, "Thank you. I...well, I guess I just need a moment, if you don't mind." She stepped back from Wilkes and opened the letter:

"Dear Ms. Cohen:

Allow me to introduce myself. My name is Marland Kensington, and I'm the man who hired Mr. Hugh Konklin. In the spring of this year, I ran an advertisement in multiple newspapers calling for mechanical engineers to help me finish the Triple Racing Coaster at the state fair here in Dallas. Mr. Konklin contacted me by phone, and I instantly took a liking to him. When Mr. Konklin arrived here in Dallas, we were facing many challenges with completing the coaster on time, and his contributions were immediately felt. During his first week here, I got to know him better, and he told me about you and his son Bill. I know he cared for you both very much, which was one of the reasons he took the job. Mr. Konklin was a brilliant engineer and an excellent worker. He was the victim of an unfortunate accident—killed when the cable on a crane broke. He was simply at the wrong place, at the wrong time, in the path of the falling object. I'm very sorry for your loss, Ms. Cohen, and I can only hope my letter brings some peace and closure. We will make all of the necessary arrangements to ensure that Hugh's body is returned to you for proper burial. I wish you and young Bill the best through this difficult time.

Sincerely,

Marland J. Kensington"

Bill took the news hard. Deborah was at a loss for words and could do little to comfort him. At least she was not burdened with making any arrangements. The body was returned just as Kensington promised, and Clarence Wilkes was kind enough to take care of all the funeral details.

Hugh's death had come as a tremendous blow to the already weakened Deborah, and two months later, her health took a turn for the worst. Burying Samantha and then Hugh had been an emotional drain no mother would ever want to endure, and the strain ignited the spread of her unrelenting cancer. By the middle of August, she was bedridden, and she had little time left to tie up loose ends. A month earlier, in July, she had written a desperate letter to her brother, John Canter, informing him of the events and requesting that he take care of Bill. Deborah had not spoken with John in years, and they were not very close. Although he was family, she didn't know what sort of man he was, but her options to place Bill in someone's care after her imminent demise were limited. Deborah passed away on August 26, 1936.

CHAPTER 8

YOUNG BILL KONKLIN

Bill was only six years old when, following the death of his father and grandmother, he went to live with his uncle, John Canter, a lifelong carny. John worked in The Carnival of the Ages, which was owned by Clarence Wilkes's brother Abraham, who had opened it after a disagreement occurred in the family business many years earlier.

Bill thought John to be an ugly man, and his distaste for John's appearance began on the day they met. In contrast to Bill's father's thin frame, John had a large stomach that hung over his pants. His face was red and oily, with little bumps everywhere. His nose looked hard and scaly, and most of his upper teeth were missing. But worst of all was the man's breath; it smelled of alcohol, cigarettes, and rot—an odor that incited Bill to vomit outside of John's trailer on that first day.

Fortunately, the ever-thoughtful Clarence Wilkes was there, ready and willing to intervene on Bill's behalf. "Sorry, John. It's just his nerves. He's been through some tough times recently, as you know," Wilkes said as Bill continued to gag. "Can ya give us a few minutes?"

"All right," John said.

Bill lifted his head and watched John walk away, mumbling something under his breath.

"Are you okay, Bill?" Wilkes asked, concerned.

"I want to sit down," Bill replied.

Wilkes motioned him toward the front door steps of John's trailer. "I hope you're not coming down with something."

"I feel sick. That man has bad, stinky breath."

Wilkes smiled. "Yes, I understand. It doesn't look like he's taken a bath in a while."

Bill returned the smile.

"Bill, I have something for you." Wilkes bent over to open a briefcase. "Here, son. This belonged to your father, and I just know he would have wanted you to have it."

"Daddy's Bible!"

"Yes, and it's yours now. Take it."

"Will John tell me Bible stories?"

"I don't know. John is not your father, and I don't think he's much of a Bible reader. I'm sorry, little fella, but that's about all I can tell you. There is one more thing I have for you though. I gave John your dad's High Striker, the one he built. I made it legal that when you turn twenty-one, the High Striker will be yours. I hope you are happy here, Bill. I've done all I can for you, and now I have to follow your grandmother's wishes."

Bill nodded, and Wilkes soon departed.

✵ ✵ ✵

As the years passed, life with his father and grand-mother in The Amazing Wilkes Clan Carnival faded, along with many of his memories. The day-to-day life with John Canter in The Carnival of the Ages now dominated Bill's time and his thoughts.

The morning after his tenth birthday, Bill was outside his trailer home near the High Striker.

John was leaning over behind the machine, making some adjustments. When he saw Bill, he stood upright. "There he is, the birthday boy. It's about time you and me had a good talk. I got this idea, see. I want you to master the High Striker. It's all about making money, and I think yer old enough to start earnin' yer keep 'round here. When all those proud men out there see a young boy ringing the bell, I think it'll bruise a few egos, and a few bruised egos means a few bucks for me when they try to prove us wrong. Men will give up plenty to prove how manly they are, Bill, my boy—especially when they don't wanna be outdone by a young'n."

Bill walked closer, with his hands in his pocket, wrin-kling his brow in confusion as he looked at the big metal contraption and its heavy hammer.

"What you need to know, boy, is that this game ain't got nothin' to do with strength. This here's all about technique. Just watch!" At that, John grabbed one of the sledgehammers lying on the ground by the High Striker platform. "It's just like chopping wood, see? When yer tryin' ta chop wood, you can swing that axe mighty hard, but you ain't gonna split any logs right unless you hit the target."

It was a saying Bill had heard from John more than once, and he stood there wondering what the next line would be.

John raised the sledgehammer with both arms over his head, just like a wood splitter. With a strong, clean, definite stroke, he hit the platform cleanly. The block shot up the guide wire to the stop, the bell. "Ding!" John shouted, in concert with the actual sound. Then, in order to make a point, he raised the sledgehammer again and repeated the feat. "It's that simple, boy. Now then…get yerself over here and give it a try."

Bill hurried over like he was told. He felt like an obedient dog, ready to please his cruel master, but he had come to discover that being too late to respond to John's commands had its unpleasant consequences. The most recent incident had occurred three weeks prior, when John had slapped him on the back of the neck with a yardstick, hard enough to break the stick in two against his flesh, all because Bill forgot to do one of his chores.

John walked behind the High Striker, adjusted the wires, and then repeated the ritual, this time without success. He swung again, and the results were the same: no bell. John walked over and grabbed one of the heavy wires attached to the High Striker. "Come over here and pull on this wire."

When John swung again, Bill felt the wire pull away, and he let go of it.

John failed again, and the bell didn't ring. "Do you know what just happened?"

"Not really," Bill answered.

"Well, dummy, you let go! Now grab that wire again and pull hard…and for the love of God, hang on tight this time, would ya?"

Again, Bill complied.

This time, as John swung the sledgehammer, the block traveled up, and the bell screamed out to announce his victory. "Now do you know what happened?"

"I reckon I helped you win," Bill said.

"Right. You see that wire that runs up the striker with that block attached?"

"Yes, sir."

"Well, after I rang the bell the first two times, I went back there and adjusted the guide wire so it would loop back behind the bell and connect to that wire you were just pulling on."

"Um...okay," Bill acknowledged.

"Now there ain't no way I can win, because that wire is loose. When you pull on it, that only makes it tight again, so the odds are even."

"Isn't that cheating?" Bill asked.

"Well, boy, I reckon it's my game, ain't it? I think that gives me the right to make up the rules however I damn well want, and if them fools are stupid enough to give me their hard-earned cash for a try, so be it."

"So when it's loose like this, no one can win unless you pull on the wire?" Bill asked, mostly sure of the forthcoming answer.

"Pretty clever, if I do say so myself, but I wouldn't just start grabbing on the wire and pulling it! That would be a bit obvious, don'tcha think? You see, boy, if I don't do nothin', everybody's gonna lose every time. That'll be too suspicious and have them askin' questions. So, every once in a while, if I feel sorry for some poor slob, I might walk over and lean up against the wire...you know, just to give him a fair chance to win."

"Okay," was all Bill could muster, unsure of what else he could possibly say.

"Anyhow, now that you're a big ten years old, you should be able to win when I'm a-leaning on that wire fer ya, so get yer bony ass over here and practice."

Bill walked over and grabbed the sledgehammer. His legs trembled, and perspiration dripped down on his face. He had taken a lot of practice swings when John wasn't around, and he already knew he couldn't win playing fair. Terrified of failing or upsetting John and inciting his wrath, he just stood there holding the sledgehammer for what seemed an eternity.

"Just what the hell are you waiting for anyway? Jesus fucking Christ, boy. Just get on with it, would ya? I ain't been out here bustin' my ass on this thing for you to stand there gawkin' at it like an idiot. Get to hammerin'!"

Bill's heart was pounding, and his hands were shaking something terrible. The handle of the sledgehammer was wet from his sweaty palms. With a mixture of anger and fear, he held his breath, raised the sledgehammer, and brought it down toward the platform with all his might. Overhead, the block barely moved, just like all the times when he'd sneaked in a little practice in fear of that very day.

In that instant, John laughed, a real belly-buster that made Bill clench his fists tightly around the handle of the hammer. John was standing by the wire, but his hands were off it. Bill was on his own; the fix wasn't in. John simply wanted to see him fail, just for fun. Cackling loudly, John shouted, "I'm sorry, boy. I just wanted to see how weak you are. Goddamn, you definitely need some help with those spindly arms of yers. Are you even a boy at all? I guess you's one of dem poor slobs I was talkin' about. I guess I'm gonna hafta cheat and help you out some," the sarcasm rang out, punctuating the moment. With that, John leaned against the wire and nodded at Bill for another try.

Now that he had the go-ahead, Bill repeated the action. This time, the block traveled about one-third of the way up before it plummeted back down to its resting place.

"Try again," came the response.

Again, Bill swung and failed.

"Try again, damn it!!"

Again, Bill swung and failed.

"Again!" John shouted.

And so it went for several attempts. After a while, the weight of the hammer began taking a toll on Bill's young arms, and he grew weary.

"Goddamn it! Goddamn it! You son of a bitch. What are you, some little girl? Why, yer dead grandmother could do better than that shit!"

With that, Bill threw down the sledgehammer and ran back toward the trailer home, tears streaming down his cheeks. He took a seat on the front steps. He felt powerless to do anything, and most of all, he wished more than anything that he could be successful at bringing that sledgehammer down on John's head.

"That's it, run away, you little sissy. Girly boy!"

The fellow carnies at The Carnival of the Ages generally minded their own business, but Bill looked on as John received what appeared to be quite a disapproving stare from Harold Collins, who was standing outside his trailer.

John didn't say anything; he just turned and walked back behind the High Striker, muttering under his breath, "What the fuck you lookin' at, old man? Don't make me come over there and kick yer ancient, nosy ass."

When Harold locked eyes with Bill and waved, Bill at once felt better; it was the same feeling he'd had when he'd first met the elderly gentleman and the old lady who lived with him, Miss Hannah. On that day, Bill had been seven years old, and it was right after John had just hit him for the first time. He'd been wandering around outside, visibly upset in the aftermath of his disagreement with his abusive custodial parent, when Harold Collins had spotted him.

"Hi, there. I'm Harold. I don't think we have officially met. Are you okay?"

"Yeah."

"Your name is Bill, right?"

"Yes, I'm Bill Konklin."

"Well, Bill Konklin, you seem upset."

Bill had shrugged his shoulders.

"I'll tell you what. I have something that's guaranteed to make a boy feel better. You like sno-cones?"

"Yeah, sure," Bill had said, trying to muster a half-smile.

"Come over here, and I'll make you one."

The concession stand was a small white trailer on wheels, with the words *"Harold's Famous Delights"* painted on the outside. Also painted on the trailer were the words, *"Popcorn, Candy Apples, Sodas, Hot Dogs, Hamburgers, and Sno-Cones."*

"What's your favorite flavor?"

"Grape, I guess," Bill had answered.

"Okay. Then grape it is."

Seconds later, Harold had handed Bill a grape sno-cone, with plenty of extra purple syrup, and a friendship had begun.

"So who's that lady who lives with you?" Bill had asked unexpectedly.

"Well, that would be Miss Hannah. Her stage name is Madam Millford, but she goes by Hannah to everyone who knows her offstage. She's a psychic, and we've been friends for a long time. She's older now, and we decided to live together so I can take care of her."

"What's a psychic?"

"Well, some people call her a fortune teller. She can see the future."

"Really? But…well, how can she do that?"

"It's a gift, Bill. I happen to think it's a divine one myself. Most people don't believe it's possible, but Miss Hannah is the real deal. She's a genuine fortune teller."

"Wow."

"Would you like to meet her?"

"Um…sure," Bill had said, not knowing what to expect.

"All righty then. Follow me. I gotta feelin' you two'll like each other a whole lot. Why, Hannah's even sweeter than that there sno-cone!" Harold had walked over to his trailer and opened the door. "Hannah, I have someone out here who'd like to meet you. Is now a good time?"

"Come on in," Hannah had responded.

Bill had followed Harold inside. The elderly woman sitting at the table in the small kitchen area was thin and gray with a prominent nose, and her wrinkled complexion combined with blindness in one patch-covered eye was less than inviting for the then seven-year-old Bill Konklin, so he'd kept his distance and stayed alongside Harold.

"Come on in, young Bill. Don't be afraid."

"You know my name?"

"Of course! You're Bill Konklin, the young master of the High Striker."

Bill had nodded.

"What are you eating?" she'd asked.

"A sno-cone."

"I like those too. My favorite's cherry."

"I like grape."

"Grape is good too. You know, someday, you and I are going to be good friends."

"We are?"

"Yes, absolutely, young Bill. I know many things, and that is one thing I know for sure."

Bill had nervously looked down at the goose bumps on his arms and then taken another bite of his sno-cone.

"I bet you like to play cards. Am I right?"

Once again, Bill had simply nodded in the affirmative.

"Well, we should start playing cards together, maybe after you do your chores in the mornings before the carnival opens. Would you like that?"

"Yes ma'am," Bill had responded, this time verbally.

Following that first meeting, Bill was a constant visitor. A day rarely passed without him playing a game of cards with Miss Hannah. John sometimes complained, but he tolerated the relationship nonetheless. So, on that day, as Bill sat on the front steps with tears in his eyes for his High Striker failure and John's cruel insults, he knew it was time to pay Hannah an unexpected visit. After gaining his composure, Bill got up and walked over toward the psychic's trailer.

Harold was still outside working and motioned for Bill to go on inside.

Bill knocked as usual, and Hannah replied in her predictable manner, "Come on in, young Bill."

At first, Bill had been amazed that Miss Hannah always seemed to know when he was at the door, but over time, he'd come to accept her uncanny abilities. When he entered that day, she was seated at the table; Bill suddenly realized he'd rarely seen her sitting in any other place inside her home.

"You seem upset, my young friend."

"I'm okay. I just hate John. He's such a...well, he's an asshole."

As usual, Hannah did not even attempt to scold him for his foul language or diminish his feelings about John Canter. However, when he sat at the table across from her, Hannah asked him to place his hands on the table, palms up. Bill felt the grasp of her cold hands, as she closed her only eye. After opening it, she laid out some cards on the table and said, "Young Bill, today is not a day for games. Instead, I'm going to tell you about your future."

Bill was too taken by surprise to respond. He just stared at her, awaiting his fortune. Bill had faith in Hannah, and he was more than willing to listen.

"Young Bill, I see a crossroads in your life. Your future is clouded, and I'm concerned for you. John Canter is a despicable man, but you must continue to tolerate him for now. One day, things will change, and you will have an opportunity to be free of him."

"How long till then, 'cause I sure wanted to hit him with that hammer today?"

"Maybe years, but you must choose wisely when the time comes."

"How will I know when the time comes?"

"You will just know."

Bill had grown accustomed to Hannah's vague and intriguing manner of response. She spoke with confidence, and Bill believed her. "He made me play the High Striker today, and I lost," he said. "Will I ever be able to ring the bell?"

"Yes, young Bill. Do not concern yourself, for I see the High Striker in your future. You must not abandon the machine. It is a legacy from your father, one he built with his own hands and his own mind, and that piece of him has passed on to you."

"I can't even remember what he looked like. It seems like a dream."

"Perhaps, but it was real. He was real. You carry his name, Bill Konklin, and you mustn't ever forget that. You and the High Striker are parts of him that live on."

Miss Hannah always had a way of making Bill feel better; however, when he returned to his home and life with John, his days were generally filled with sadness, and the time that followed with John Canter was more of the same, Bill failing at the High Striker and John taunting him. Bill couldn't wait for that crossroads to come, for he was ready to take a different route in his life—one that would lead him away from the cruel man he wanted to bludgeon with a sledgehammer.

CHAPTER 9

BILL KONKLIN, THE TEEN

By the time Bill was twelve, he had mastered ringing the High Striker bell with John's assistance. By the time he was fourteen, Bill no longer needed the services of John Canter, as he had developed enough muscles, skills, and know-how to ring the High Striker bell without any tricks. And through it all, Miss Hannah was a guiding force in his life. To Bill, Hannah was family. In the absence of Deborah Cohen, Hannah was a makeshift grandmother—a grandmother who shared his love of sno-cones and card games and knew more about his future than he did.

John Canter continued in his ways, drinking and always searching for an easy way out, for new ways to lie, cheat, and steal. In fact, by the time Bill turned fourteen, John had perfected his High Striker cheating mechanism. His old act of leaning on the wire wasn't exactly subtle, so he'd devised a method to control the wire tension with a trick lever hidden under a loose board in the striker platform. This way, John could manipulate the outcome by standing on the board, which forced a metal pin against the bracket, holding the guide wire in place. This caused the bracket to bend just enough to reduce some of the tension of the wire.

When Bill first learned about this clever use of cheating tactics, he sought Miss Hannah's advice. He brought up the subject after playing cards one afternoon.

"You seem distracted today," Hannah said as Bill yielded another bad hand of rummy. "Anything you want to talk about?"

"Do you believe honesty is important?" Bill asked.

"We live in a dishonest world, Bill, and that's an odd word to be using around here, for sure. But not all carnies are liars or cheaters. I know my gifts to be real, so I've never had any reason to lie."

"What if you knew something bad about someone's future? Would you tell them the truth? Do you ever fib to them to spare their feelings so they won't worry?"

"Well, Bill, I suppose I do. The truth isn't always easy to hear. But then again, I don't always know everything. Some things are clouded. No one's future is set in stone."

"Well, John has always cheated in the High Striker, and he keeps inventing new ways to do it."

"Does that bother you?"

"Not really. That's why I'm asking you. *Should* it bother me?"

"We can't control everything. Cheating at High Striker is John's choice, and he will have his own consequences to deal with. You should not feel guilty because you are not the one doing the cheating."

"Maybe, but it's not just the cheating. It's John. I hate him."

"Be patient, young Bill. Things will change. You will not always have to live with John. Someday you will be free, as I've told you all along."

"But when? You've been telling me that for such a long time, and I'm still stuck with the brute."

"Someday soon, Bill. I promise. You must only wait and watch."

"I could run away."

"And where would you go?"

"I don't know. Maybe I could join another carnival somewhere."

"You are much too young to think about such things. Life is hard sometimes, and we must endure. Running away is not the answer, Bill. Often, the pain will follow you, no matter where you go. The only cure is time. We must be patient."

"Okay. I suppose you're right."

"Promise me that you will be patient, Bill?"

"Yes, I'll try to—at least for now."

"Good. Very Good," Miss Hannah said. "Now, let's play another hand of rummy."

✫ ✫ ✫

In 1946, Bill turned sixteen. Business was booming, though John Canter was rarely sober enough to enjoy the fruits of his cheating. The relationship was cold and indifferent on the surface, but underneath Bill detested John. Moreover, a day rarely passed without Bill daydreaming about some elaborate scheme to end John's miserable life. He had shared his cruel intentions and desperate homicidal fantasies with Miss Hannah, but she always advised him to be patient and not to do anything rash.

It was summer, and The Carnival of the Ages had just finished a run in a small Texas town, so it was time to pack up and move on. Generally, it was the time when the carnies took a short break, a short period of rest and relaxation. The first day of the break happened to be a rainy Monday. Bill rose early, as was his routine. Entering the kitchen in his small trailer home, he saw John lying on the couch in the tiny living room, snoring loudly and sleeping off his drunken stupor. Bill raised his eyebrows in disgust and wiped the man's alcoholic stench away from his nostrils, then peeked out the tiny window over the sink in the even tinier kitchen. He had hoped to take a trip into town to do some shopping.

As the rain poured, he noticed Harold Collins walking out of the front door of his trailer. Harold ran over to his car, and Bill realized he was likely headed to town. Without thinking, Bill ran out toward the car. He arrived just as the car was backing out.

Harold rolled down the car window. "What are you doing, Bill?"

"Mr. Collins, if you are going into town, could I go with you?"

"Where is John?"

"Asleep on the couch. He got really drunk last night… again."

"Well, I've gotta leave now. You're still wearing your pajamas, and you're getting soaked."

"Can you give me five minutes to throw on some real clothes?" Bill asked.

"Okay, okay. Just go…and hurry! I wanna get driving before this weather gets any worse."

Bill ran back to the trailer and emerged within five minutes, fully dressed in dry clothes, just as he promised. When Harold backed the car up near Bill's trailer, Bill quickly closed the trailer door and entered through the passenger door. "Thank you, Mr. Collins."

"You're plenty welcome, Bill."

Going into town and getting way from John was a relief, but Bill never really felt entirely at ease anywhere. By the middle of the afternoon, the rain had ceased, and Bill imagined John would soon awake from another familiar hangover. It was predictable and annoying. John's first order of business was urinating, which he did sitting down. He never bothered to close the bathroom door, and on more than occasion, Bill had witnessed part of the event. The bathroom visits were often painful; John moaned and groaned about his prostate problems. Bill imagined the scene as he perused a storefront display in town and wished for John's pain to be severe.

Later, during the return trip, the rain drizzled. As Bill and Harold pulled into carny land, Bill caught sight of John standing on the front steps of their trailer. He was staring at the car. He had no doubt been awake for a while and had most likely been drinking from the bottle of amber-colored, smelly liquid in his hand.

"Oh no," Bill said in a low voice, just loud enough for Harold to hear. "He doesn't look…happy."

"You stay there and let me handle this, okay?" Harold parked the car and turned off the lights. Bill didn't say a word as Harold got out and walked toward John.

"Hey, old man, where in the hell have you and that boy been?" John slurred, pointing at the car, in which Bill was still sitting.

"John, everything is all right. We just went into town for a while."

"You little prick! Get the hell outta there, all leavin' without permission! I'm the one that looks after you, damn it—not this old fool," John said as he pointed at Bill while ignoring Harold.

"Now, John, you just calm down," Harold stated as he stopped near the porch steps.

"Don't tell me what to do, you old fucker." John pulled out a pistol and aimed it at Harold's head.

Bill leapt out of the car. "Put that away! Mr. Collins didn't do anything wrong!" he screamed as he ran toward the front porch of the trailer.

At that, John squeezed the trigger. The gunshot rang out into carnival land. Thankfully John had aimed it up into the air, away from Harold.

"You're an asshole! I hate your fucking guts!" Bill shouted.

John reacted by taking another swallow of whiskey from the bottle in his left hand. "Well boy, guess what. I hate yer fucking guts too," John said, hurling the pistol at his great nephew.

Bill ducked, and the weapon flew over him and sank into the mud near the front of the car. When he stood back up, he shook his head. Without hesitation, he ran over and picked up the gun and removed the bullets. By the time he turned around, John had already gone back inside the trailer. Up until that time, John had never fired a gun, and Bill was scared that he'd gone to that level of hatred.

"Bill, you can stay with me tonight if you want to," Harold said.

"Naw. I'd better get back inside. I don't want him to come lookin' for me later, after he drinks the rest of that whiskey and is even worse. I'll be okay. I'm really sorry about all of this, Mr. Collins."

"It's all right, Bill. You don't have to apologize to me. You take care, and I'll see you later. You need anything at all, you know where to find us."

The next morning, Bill made a visit to Miss Hannah's trailer while John was still asleep.

"Young Bill, I heard the gunshot yesterday, and Harold told me what happened. I see two futures for you now. You have been right all along. Bill Konklin, you must kill John before he kills you."

At sixteen, Bill was more than receptive to hear how he could be free of John Canter forever, so he listened carefully to the psychic's, his friend's, plan.

"Here, young Bill. Take this. It is poison, so be careful." She held out a small bottle with no label.

"Okay, but how do I use it?" Bill took it from her hand.

"Pour the contents in one of John's whiskey bottles. He won't taste it or see it, especially with all that liquor he guzzles. Then, rinse out the bottle, wash your hands, and throw the bottle away in the carnival trash bin."

"That's it?"

"Yes, young Bill, but you must do it soon...and tell no one! Don't even speak of this to Harold, for he would not understand. Only you and I can know of this, Bill."

"Okay," Bill said.

"Bill, you must know that it is not wrong to kill a bad man to preserve your own life. Remember that. Go now."

Back at his trailer, John was still passed out on the couch. Bill felt unusually calm and wasn't afraid of being caught. He was desperate and believed in Miss Hannah, so he followed her instructions to the number. He picked up the half-full whiskey bottle from the floor and poured the entire bottle of poison into it, careful not to spill a drop. Then he washed the empty poison bottle and his hands and disposed of it just as Miss Hannah had told him to do.

During the remainder of the morning, Bill remained outside. He took a long walk and then returned to take some practice swings on the High Striker. He tried to keep his mind off what was happening inside the trailer, but by noon, he was getting hungry and had to go inside for a bite to eat. At first there was no sign of John, but then Bill heard his gruff voice coming from the bedroom.

"Bill, get yer sorry ass in here."

From the entrance to the bedroom, Bill could see John sitting on the edge of the bed with that familiar hangover frown on his face. Bill was disappointed to see that the man was still alive.

"Where the hell have you been, boy?"

"Outside. I took a long walk and then did some practice swings on the striker."

"Are you done?"

"Yeah, but I'm going back out to do some maintenance work after I eat," Bill answered.

"You gonna do what the hell I told you to do or keep on fooling around like a lazy little shit?"

"I'm gonna sand and varnish the sledges, like you asked."

"About damn time you made use of yerself," John replied.

"Did you need something, or can I go?" Bill asked.

"Don't be a smart-ass. I just wanted to make sure you're working and not over there wasting time with Collins and that crazy old one-eyed hag. I'm gonna take a bath, and then I'll be outside to make sure you're not making a fucking mess outta everything like you usually do."

"Okay."

In the kitchen, Bill made himself a ham sandwich. John was rumbling around in the back of the trailer. He didn't see the whiskey bottle; John had taken it with him when he'd awoken. Bill took his sandwich outside with him and sat on the porch for his lunch break.

By 1:30 p.m., John had still not come out of the trailer to bother him, so Bill decided to go back inside again. He called out for John, but there was no answer. His hands began to tremble, and he felt nervous—or maybe happily excited. He stood there just inside the door for a while, breathing deeply and wiping the perspiration from his forehead. "John!" he called again, making his way toward the bedroom.

Finally, the spectacle lay before his eyes. John was on the floor, motionless, his eyes open, staring blankly at the ceiling. The bottle of whiskey had rolled over by the nightstand; some of the contents had spilled out onto the floor. John was dead as a doorknob, and Bill was finally rid of him. Bill had imagined such a moment for a long time, but now that his fantasy had become a reality, he realized he hadn't been prepared. He simply stood there, paralyzed, overwhelmed, relieved, yet scared. Feeling the need for further precaution, Bill took the bottle of whiskey in the bathroom, emptied the smelly contents into the sink, rinsed it out, and deposited it into the trashcan, clanging against all the other bottles John had consumed. He then walked over to Harold Collins's trailer to break the news: He had found John dead.

It was all too easy. Over the next few days, Abraham Wilkes took charge and had John buried. Just as Miss Hannah had foreseen, no questions were asked. After all, there was no cause for suspicion since everyone knew John was an old, angry drunk who was always treating himself and others with complete disregard.

By the time the carnival moved to the next town, Bill was running the High Striker by himself. After all, a sixteen-year-old boy reared in the carnival environment was generally equipped to handle big responsibilities, even running a sideshow like the High Striker.

Three weeks from the day John died, Bill received some shocking and sad news from Harold Collins. Miss Hannah had died in her sleep. Four days later, Bill found himself outside at a funeral in a small cemetery near where the carnival was stationed at the time. He was devastated as he stood there with a farewell bouquet of freshly picked flowers for his dead friend. Miss Hannah had been fond of wildflowers, and Bill had made it a habit of bringing her a fresh bunch whenever he could—only this time, Hannah was not there to take them and offer the kind words of gratitude that Bill had grown accustomed to hearing. She was forever silent, so Bill would have to be content to hold them for her.

Following a few words from Abraham Wilkes and Harold Collins, a local preacher gave a short sermon on the meaning of life. He was young and charismatic, and as his spirited and animated sermon drew to a close, Bill couldn't help but stare at the steady stream of sweat rolling down his face. He was obviously passionate, a feeling that eluded Bill. "I didn't know Miss Hannah Millford," the preacher said, "but she was a child of God, just as we all are. We are all children of God, and we are all sinners. Miss Hannah was a sinner. I'm a sinner! Today is an opportunity for you, my dear friends, to think about your lives. If your life ended tonight, would you be ready to stand before the judgment seat of God? If you haven't already done so, I urge each of you to turn your life over to God through faith in Jesus Christ. I'd like to close with a passage from John 3:16 which says, *'God so loved the world that He gave his only Son, so that whoever believeth in Him shall not perish, but have life eternal.'* Let us pray."

At that moment, Bill's mind was suddenly flooded by memories of his father, Hugh Konklin, the man who used to read the Bible to him and pray with him. It had been so long ago, but now it seemed like only yesterday. The final words of his father then echoed loudly, as if he were standing there in person: *"God loves you, Bill. Always listen to Him and pay attention to what He does in your life. Always remember that without God, a man's life will be dark."* Bill felt the darkness his father had spoken of; in fact, it had started when his father had died, and it had hovered over him like a cloud ever since, a cloud that never allowed the light to shine through. There had been rays of hope while Miss Hannah was alive, but now she was gone. Harold Collins was a good man, but his friendship was not enough to fill the emptiness inside of

Bill. Even the absence of John Canter had not brought Bill peace. So the tears came, flooding his eyes, and then rolling down his face in a steady stream, tears of sadness and tears of anger.

Shortly after the carnival had moved back to Oklahoma and settled near Tulsa, Bill spoke to Harold Collins about his unhappiness. Harold had suggested Bill pursue a spiritual path for a while to see if he might find some answers to his questions and concerns, so Bill convinced Abraham Wilkes to allow him to take a break from the carnival. In the fall of 1946, Wilkes arranged for Bill to stay for a while in a Catholic church in Oklahoma City. At one time, the church ran a sizeable orphanage that had dwindled down to only a few boys who worked for the church in return for food and shelter. The orphanage was actually attached to the church, and the plan was for it to serve as Bill's home for at least the remainder of the year.

CHAPTER 10

BILL'S SPIRITUAL PATH

On his first day at St. Mark's, Bill was greeted by Father Penderson, who was in charge of the orphanage. In his early sixties, Father Penderson had been a priest for the majority of his adult life. He was the scholarly type, known for his propensity to quote scripture, an admirable and rare characteristic among those in the priesthood. However, he had a troubled past, and in recent years, the Catholic church had moved him from parish to parish, the most recent being St. Mark's.

The first order of business included a tour of the church and the orphanage, followed by an invitation from Father Penderson as they arrived back at Bill's room. "You should get your life here off to a good start, Bill. I would suggest you come to confession later."

"Confession? What is that?"

"It is a place to confess your sins and ask God for forgiveness. Here. I will leave you this brochure to read. It will explain everything for you, and you can always ask me questions about anything you find confusing. I am here to help."

As Father Penderson exited down one hallway, a young boy approached up another. He had his head down, as if he was planning to ignore Bill, but Bill took the initiative. "Hi. I'm Bill Konklin. I'm new here."

"Hello there," the boy replied timidly, lifting his head. "I'm Joey."

Staring Bill in the face was a pale, freckle-faced boy with red hair that lay over in a straight line across his forehead. "Well, Joey, this is my first day here. What about you?'

"I've been here since I was eight years old."

"I'm sixteen," Bill said. "How old are you?"

"Twelve."

"Four years, huh? You've been here a long time."

"Yeah, I know. My parents died, and I don't got no other family, so the church took me in."

"Are you headed somewhere in particular?"

"Just to my room, right down there," he said, pointing, "at the end of the hall."

"Oh, I see," Bill said. "Father Penderson said supper will be served in about thirty minutes. Are you going?"

"Yeah, sure."

"Well, maybe I'll see you there."

"Okay," Joey answered.

Back in his room, Bill began to unpack his oversized suitcase and then took a break to read the brochure Father Penderson had given him. *"Confess your sins,"* it said, *"and let*

God fill your life with peace and contentment." Is it that simple?
Bill wondered.

Later in the dining room, Bill saw Joey sitting alone.
Bill had not anticipated the emptiness, the absence of any
adults. Supper was light, just lentil soup and bread, and
there was no indication of who had prepared it.

"Where is everybody?" Bill asked, as he sat by Joey,
soup in hand.

"There're only five boys here now, and you make six.
The others are away at St. Mary's. They volunteered to
do some work over there and will be gone for a couple of
weeks. It's just you and me."

"This just seems unusual, that's all. The soup is actually
quite good. Where did it come from?"

"Oh, that would be Sister Catherine. She just left," Joey
said.

"So what do you do around here every day?"

"I have a lot of chores to keep me busy."

"Do you like it here?"

Joey hesitated. "Well, it's better than no home at all."

"I'm thinking about going to confession. Have you
done that before?"

"Yeah."

"I'm not sure what to expect. What's it like?"

"Well, you go into this room. There's a wall in there,
and the priest is on the other side. There's a small opening.
First, you've gotta make the sign of the cross," Joey said as
he demonstrated it, "and then you gotta say, 'Forgive me,
Father, for I have sinned.'"

"Is that it?"

"Usually you've gotta tell the priest how long it's been
since your last confession, but since you've never done one

before, I guess that won't matter for you. Then, you just tell the priest all the wrong stuff you've done since the last time you asked for forgiveness."

"Does it work?"

Joey shrugged.

"Do you like Father Penderson?"

"Sometimes."

"Sometimes? What does that mean?"

"I don't know. I mean, he's nice most of the time, but..." Joey paused.

"But what?"

"Oh, nothing."

"Hey, I get it. I was raised by someone who wasn't always nice to me."

"Can we talk about something else?"

"Sure, but thanks for telling me about confession. I think I'm going to do it after I finish eating."

Joey remained silent for the rest of the meal, and when Bill got up for a second helping and returned to the table, the boy was gone.

After supper, Bill made a quick visit to his room and found the long hallway he had trekked earlier with Father Penderson. As he headed back toward the place Father Penderson had referred to as "the nave," Bill was quite taken by all the sights along the way: the stained glass, the statues, and the mesmerizing paintings. It was an impressive display, albeit a bit excessive, in Bill's opinion. Entering the nave, he found it was mostly empty, except for a couple of people down in front, kneeling before an altar.

Father Penderson walked toward him. "Good evening, Bill."

"Good evening, Father," Bill replied respectfully, thinking it an odd thing to say to someone who was virtually a stranger. It was very formal, and, having lived so long with John, uttering any sort of paternal greeting somehow seemed out of place.

"Did you eat supper?"

"Yes."

"I'm sorry not many were there to join you. Most of our boys are away with Father Richards, helping out with some church work."

"Yes, Joey told me."

"Oh, so you've met Joey? He's a good boy—quite an active imagination, that one, but a good boy."

Really? I didn't notice much of an imagination. "Well, I read the brochure you left me, and I think I'd like to go to confession, maybe even right now."

"Excellent. Come this way."

Bill followed as Father Penderson walked toward the back of the church and stopped in front of a small room. "Give me a minute, and then you enter through that door. You can talk about anything you like."

"Okay." Bill watched Father Penderson disappear behind a door. He counted out sixty silent Mississippis and stepped inside the room. It was cramped, and as he knelt to perform the sign of the cross, Bill took note of the tiny opening Joey had mentioned. Father Penderson was on the other side of the wall, but his face was hidden. "Forgive me, Father, for I have sinned. This is my first confession," he said, just as Joey had instructed.

"Speak, my child."

"Well, uh…" Bill hesitated. "I-I, um…for starters, I killed someone."

The room fell silent until Bill was no longer comfortable. "Father, did you hear me?"

"Yes. I am just thinking about what you've told me. This person that you say you killed, did you know him or her well?"

"Yes."

"Was your act deliberate?"

"What does that mean?"

"Was it an accident?"

"No. I knew what I was doing."

"Was anyone else involved, or does anyone else know about what you did?"

"Well, sort of. There was this lady, but she's dead now. She was a fortune teller, a psychic, and she gave me advice."

"A fortune teller, you say?"

"Yes."

"Well," Father Penderson said, "I think you were led astray, young one. Later tonight, I want you to read some verses of scripture found in Deuteronomy 18:10-12. I'll write it down for you and give it to you later."

"Can't you just tell me what it says?"

"The basic idea is that God does not approve of fortune tellers, but more importantly, are you truly sorry about what you did?"

"Well, not exactly."

"And why not?"

"Because the person I killed was a bad man."

"My son, vengeance belongs to God. To confess means to ask God for forgiveness, and to truly want to be forgiven, you must feel regret and sorrow for the wrong you have done."

"Well, I don't—at least not right now. I would like to be all right with God though. I'm not very happy. My dad died when I was very young, and I recently started having memories of him after forgetting about him for a long time. He used to talk to me about God, tell me Bible stories, and read the Bible to me. Maybe God is something I'm missing in my life. That is why I came here."

"It sounds like you are on the right path, my son. Is there anything else you would like to confess at this time?"

"No, but I wonder why God lets bad things happen to people. Why didn't God protect my dad? My life has been very hard with no parents, and other people have died too. I think I'm angry at God for taking people away from me."

"Well, my son, I cannot pardon you, but I can ask God to help you find peace. I offer this prayer in your behalf. God, the Father of mercies, through the death and resurrection of His Son, has reconciled the world to Himself, and sent the Holy Spirit among us for the forgiveness of sins. Through the ministry of the Church, may God grant you peace. In the name of the Father, and of the Son, and of the Holy Spirit. Amen."

After the confession, Bill didn't feel any different. As he retraced his way through the nave, back down the long hallway to his room, he wondered if the confession had meant anything at all. *Father Penderson did not promise a pardon or forgiveness, but he did offer up a prayer for my peace of mind. At least there was that.* There was no peace, though—at least not yet. There was only a partially unpacked suitcase. Bill lay on the bed, neglecting the suitcase for a few more moments of deep thought about his lackluster confession when he heard a knock at the door. "Who is it?"

"It's me, Joey."

"Hey there." Bill got up and opened the door.

"So did you go to confession?"

"Yeah. You can come in if you like."

"Thanks," Joey said, as Bill closed the door behind him. "Well? How do you feel?"

"I feel the same," Bill answered. "Father Penderson prayed for me, but I don't think it's working."

"Maybe you should give it some time."

"Time? Why? I mean, if it has anything to do with God, it seems to me like it should be immediate."

"Yeah. Anyway, it looks like you aren't unpacked yet," Joey said, changing the subject.

"I'll work on it."

"Okay. Well, I just wanted to let you know that breakfast is at 7:00 a.m. I'd better get going."

"But you just got here, and you already said none of the other boys are around to talk to. Sure you don't wanna hang out for a while?"

"Well, I've got some reading to do before bedtime," Joey said as he made his way back toward the door.

"Uh, okay. Goodnight, then, Joey."

"'Night."

After another look at the unpacked suitcase, Bill convinced himself he was drowsy. He grabbed the Bible on his desk before lying on the bed once again. Then he took the note Father Penderson had given him out of his pocket. He fumbled through the Bible and eventually found the passage in Deuteronomy 18 that the priest had scribbled on the piece of paper: *"Neither let there be found among you any one that shall expiate his son or daughter, making them to pass through the fire: or that consulteth soothsayers, or observeth dreams and omens, neither let there be any wizard...Nor charmer, nor any one that consulteth pythonic spirits, or fortune tellers, or that seeketh the truth from the dead...For the Lord abhorreth all these things, and for these abominations he will destroy them at thy coming."*

Not only had Father Penderson's prayer failed to bring peace, but now Bill was reading something that suggested Miss Hannah was not a good person. Bill felt confused, even angry, and closed his eyes to try to clear his head.

At about 1:20 a.m., Bill awoke with a strong urge to urinate. He had fallen asleep with the Bible still open, lying on his stomach. The bathroom was all the way down the hall, past Joey's room, and Bill was able to find his way using a dimly lit candle that was on the wall in the hallway. His visit was brief, and as he was leaving the bathroom, there was enough light from the candle for him to recognize the side profile of Father Penderson leaving Joey's room. The priest didn't see Bill as he quickly stepped back behind the wall. *This is strange*, he thought as he peeked around the wall again, watching Father Penderson until he melted into the darkness of the hallway. *Maybe this is the not-always-being-nice part Joey meant*, Bill thought as he made his way back to his room.

Bill didn't sleep very well that night, and the next morning, even before breakfast, he stopped by Joey's room and wasted no time getting to the reason for his visit. "Joey, I need to ask you something. Last night at supper, you didn't seem to want to talk about Father Penderson very much. Anything you want to tell me about him now?"

"No, not really."

"Joey, I need you to be honest. Listen, I went to the bathroom early this morning and saw Father Penderson leaving your room. Why was he in here?"

"Forget what you saw, Bill. Just forget about it."

"I can't, Joey. Listen, I came to live here because I want...well, never mind that. I just need you to tell me what's going on, if anything is."

"Father Penderson comes to my room a lot of times at night. It's been happening a long time. He likes to...uh, to do things with me."

"Things? What kinds of things?"

"He likes to take off his clothes and get into bed with me."

"Are you serious? What a sick bastard!"

"You shouldn't swear, Bill—especially here."

"Sorry if that offends you, but you've got bigger things to be concerned about. Don't you know what he is doing is wrong?"

Joey shrugged as if he was uncertain.

"Have you told anyone else? What about the other one, the other priest?"

"You mean Father Richards?"

"Yes, him."

"Father Richards knows about it because he does it too."

"You gotta be kidding me! Listen, Joey, you—no, we—need to get the hell out of here."

"And where would I go? I've got nobody, no place."

"Well, I don't know, but you can't stay here!" Bill paused for a moment. "Hey, I know. You can come with me. We can take the train and go back to the carnival."

"I can't, Bill."

"Sure you can. Let's just go right now."

"No! I'm not going anywhere!" Joey said.

"Listen, I'm leaving this place. It's full of liars, dirty old men. Confession was bullshit, and now this? I should have known. I don't know why I ever came here in the first place."

"Just go," Joey said. "You should get out of here."

"But I don't want to leave you here, with them. You should come with me, Joey. Really. You might like the carnival."

"Bill, just go."

"But—"

"Go. I'm staying here."

By late afternoon, Bill once again found himself at the Tulsa Union Depot; he had left Joey behind in Oklahoma City, which made him very sad, but Joey had no interest in leaving. Fortunately, Harold Collins had already exercised foresight and made arrangements so Bill could leave sooner than planned if he happened to change his mind. Actually, Bill never imagined such a short stay in Oklahoma City, and Harold's wisdom had proven itself convenient to facilitate the abrupt departure.

By evening, Bill was back home at The Carnival of the Ages. When he got there, Harold Collins's trailer was his first stop.

"My God, Bill! What are you doing here?" a surprised Harold Collins asked when he opened the door.

"I just got back. I need to talk to you."

"Sure. Come in."

Bill walked inside, suitcase in hand.

"You haven't even been to your trailer yet, I see."

"Nope." Bill dropped the heavy luggage to the floor.

"Tell me what happened, Bill. What's wrong?"

"I can't believe I was so stupid. After what happened to Miss Hannah…well, you know, it made me think of my dad and all those stories about God. But it's all a bunch of crap!"

"What happened to make you feel this way?"

"Well, I met this kid named Joey there, at the orphanage. He's twelve. I woke up in the middle of the night and went to use the bathroom, and I saw the priest, Father Penderson, leaving his room. Joey told me the priests do things with him."

"What kinds of things?"

"Well, things people do when they're naked. Things grownups do."

"Bill, are you sure? I mean, this sounds unbelievable."

"Yeah, but it's true. When I asked Joey, he said Father Penderson goes in his room a lot."

"Oh my! I'm not sure what to say."

"Well, that's not all. Joey told me the other priest there, Father Richards, does the same thing. Mr. Collins, you need to go there and get that kid. He wouldn't come with me."

"I'm afraid it may a bit more complicated than that, but I will try to find out more. I'm sorry you had such a bad experience, Bill."

"That's the story of my life. The church is fake. It's all bullshit! And if there is a God, He's a jerk for letting this crap happen to people and for taking good people away."

It had been a long day, and when Bill finally made it back to his trailer late that evening, he welcomed the comfort of his bed. He had dumped the heavy burden upon Harold Collins, so sleep came easily. He slept into late the next day, and by the time he awoke, Harold Collins had already departed for Oklahoma City. Bill spent the remainder of the day tucked away in his trailer, and except for a brief visit with Abraham Wilkes, he spoke to no one.

The following day, Bill arose early and sat outside most of the morning, on the lookout for Harold Collins. Around noon, he went back inside to find a snack. Before he had taken the first bite of his half-sandwich, he heard a car door slam. At once, he peeked out of the window and saw that Harold had returned and was walking toward him—alone. "Mr. Collins, you're back," Bill yelled through the window.

Harold waved. "I'll be right there."

By the time Bill opened the door, Harold was at the steps. "Come in," Bill said.

"Hi, Bill. Good to see you. Well, I went to St. Mark's yesterday and spoke to Father Penderson and Joey."

"And?"

"Bill, to be blunt, uh…well, I heard a different story."

"Different? How so?"

"Father Penderson is worried about you. He didn't know where you had gone because you left so suddenly, without telling any of the priests. I was frank with him about what you told me, and he seemed disturbed by the accusation."

"Yeah, I'll bet."

"Bill, he wasn't disturbed in the way you think. He didn't act guilty or admit anything. On the contrary, he told me that during confession, you told him about some things that had happened to you. He suggested they were sexual things, but he wouldn't say anything further because what is said in confession is confidential. He probably said more than he was comfortable saying, but he felt a responsibility to shed some light, given the circumstances."

"Sexual things? He's a liar! I never said any such thing."

"Well, that's not all. I actually spoke to Joey myself, and he told me it was you who came to his room in the middle of the night."

"What? That's crazy!"

Harold hesitated for a moment and then asked "Bill, did John do things to you?"

"Now you wait just a minute. John was a bastard, and he was mean to me. I hated his guts, and everyone knew that. But he never tried to fuck me, if that's what you're asking."

"Calm down, Bill. I'm just concerned about you."

"Then why don't you believe me?"

"I *want* to believe you. I'm just trying to get down to the truth. Joey told a different story to me than he told to you, and to be honest, it fits now that I think about it. I feel sort of responsible because I knew John was a bad man, and I didn't do anything about it. I didn't try to stop him from hurting you."

"Mr. Collins, listen to me. Yes, John used to beat the shit out of me, and he was an asshole, but I'm not making this up about Joey and that lying priest. I know what I saw. I don't know why Joey is changing his story, but I saw it with my own eyes, and I've got no reason to lie about it."

"Bill, I think you should talk to someone else, maybe get some help. I think you may have been reaching out for help, and that's why you wanted to go to St. Mark's to begin with."

"I did want to go, and I might be screwed up, but it has nothing to do with what I've told you."

"So why did you go to confession?"

"Because I wanted to talk to the priest."

"What did you have to confess? You have quite the, uh, worldly vocabulary, but that's not worth a confession."

"I can't say. Confessions are supposed to be private, between the person, the priest, and God."

"So you expect me to believe you, but you can't tell me?"

"I just can't."

"Well, Bill, I don't know what else I can do for you right now."

The trailer fell silent, and after a long, uncomfortable pause, Bill blurted out, "Okay. I killed John! I told the priest the truth, that I killed that bastard!"

"Oh my God!" Harold exclaimed. "So it's true?"

"No. That wasn't why I killed him."

"So why, then?"

"You really want to know?"

"Yes!"

"Because Miss Hannah told me to! Heck, she helped me do it!"

"Bill, are you really dragging Hannah into this? You do need help."

"It's the truth!"

"I'm sorry, but you need help I can't give you."

Anger swelled up inside him. The truth had been turned upside down, and once again, Bill thought, *Everything is against me.* "You know what, Mr. Collins—Harold—you don't know anything about me and Miss Hannah, even after all this time. You just assume things that are not true. Why don't you just get the hell out of here and stay out of my life?"

"Bill, please calm down. You don't mean that."

"Mr. Collins, I'm asking you to leave now!"

"All right, Bill, I'm leaving, but I'm not going to stand by and watch you destroy your life. I'm going to get you some help."

A week later, in the fall of 1946, Bill Konklin was admitted to a psychiatric hospital in lieu of prison, where he remained until his juvenile years had elapsed. For Bill, it was the culmination of a life filled with disappointment and betrayal. He was released in the summer of 1951, just after his twenty-first birthday.

Upon his release as a legal adult, he had nowhere to go, so Abraham Wilkes welcomed him back into the carny fold. For Bill, the decision to return was easier when he found out that Harold Collins, whom he thought had betrayed him, had passed away the previous winter. Abraham Wilkes had kept Bill's personal items packed away, and now at twenty-one, Bill was the rightful and legal heir to the High Striker that had been built by his father.

As the carnival continued to move, Bill made no friends and remained reclusive. By the time he reached his mid-twenties, he was a product of his own experiences in life. He was the victim of loss: loss of family, loss of good friends, loss of a normal childhood, and loss of God. He was emotionally damaged, and a bad temper began to boil to the surface as a symptom of his disturbed and scarred mind and heart. He had very little patience, and carnival work and the nomadic carny life began to bore him. He'd become physically repulsive and disgusting; rarely did he even bother to bathe. He'd also acquired a taste for alcohol, and he drank every day. He was a loner and a carny. He had become everything he hated. As the years passed, running the High Striker became a burden. Bill had grown to hate minding all the details to keep a High Striker game up and running.

By the time he was nearing his fortieth birthday, the decade of the 1970s had begun; he had lived another lifetime and a half since the dramatic events of 1946. Bill had become John Canter in every sense but one. Now he was prepared to take that final step. He would find a boy, someone like himself who would carry the burden and do just as he had done for John all those many years ago. He wondered if that boy would poison him in the end, but he really didn't care either way. The darkness no longer hovered as it had for so long; it had finally saturated his very soul.

CHAPTER 11

LARRY STEVENS, THE EARLY YEARS

The night Amos Konklin was born, July 21, 1963, the hospital nearest Centerville, Minnesota welcomed two babies into the world, but Amos Konklin was not one of them. His mother gave birth at home, just as she had before. Amos Konklin was actually born Larry Stevens, an unassuming name given to the child of the proud parents William and Wanda Stevens. William was the owner of a local shoe store, and Wanda was a stay-at-home mom. Larry was the youngest of four siblings: two girls, Janet and Frances; and two boys, Aaron and Larry.

By the time Larry came along, William had made it known that four kids were enough. Wanda would have preferred to bring more into the world, but she knew better than to make a fuss about it. She felt blessed to have four healthy children and was more thankful about her blessings in life rather than complaining about what she did not have. After Larry was born, the years passed quickly, and Wanda's desire for more children faded.

Life in Centerville was good. The Stevenses lived in Oak Estates, a nice section of town mostly comprised of middle-class families. The neighborhood was full of kids, and having four children was more common than not. Larry was well liked. He was a thoughtful boy, considerate of others. Academically, Larry stood out from his peers. By the time Larry started kindergarten, he was already an avid reader and had an IQ over 170; he was, in every way, an extremely gifted young man.

On the morning of May 23, 1970, the Stevens family left Centerville to visit Wanda's sister Betsy. It was about a three-hour road trip, down into farm country, and by the middle of the lunch hour, they had arrived at the Grimbal farm. When they pulled into the driveway, Larry was the first one out of the car. He really enjoyed visiting his cousins, especially Frank, who was a year older. As Larry ran toward the house, the door flew open, and Frank ran out to meet him halfway.

"Hey, Larry," Frank said.

"Hi there." Larry put his hands in his pants pockets.

About that time, Janet and Frances ran past the boys, heading toward the barn. Larry looked over his shoulder and saw Frank's two sisters, Katie and Gretchen, standing by the barn door. Aaron, the oldest and least excitable, remained back at the car with his parents.

"Want to go up to my room?" Frank invited.

Larry nodded, and they quickly entered the house.

At the top of the stairs, the boys turned left and proceeded all the way down the hall to Frank's room. As soon as they were inside, Frank closed the door and went to his desk and grabbed a piece of paper. He was noticeably excited. Larry waited in the middle of the room as Frank handed him the flyer and said, "Look at this."

"What is it?" Larry asked, reading the caption. As soon as the question came out, Larry knew the answer. "Oh! The Carnival of Ages? Neat!"

"Did you see it on the way here?" Frank asked.

"I don't think so," Larry said. "I'm sure I would have noticed."

"Pa says we can go later today. Have you ever been to a carnival before?"

"Maybe, but I can't remember."

"Me neither." Frank returned the flyer to his desk. "Pa says this is the best carnival in the whole country."

"How so?" asked Larry. "Do they have a lot of freaks or something?"

"Maybe," Frank answered with a smile, as if to hold back laughter.

"Frank! Larry!" Frank's mom called from downstairs.

Frank walked to the door and opened it. "Yes, Ma?"

"Is Larry up there with you?"

"Yes, ma'am."

"Okay. You boys come on down in about five minutes for lunch."

"Okay, Ma."

Downstairs, Wanda and Betsy were in the kitchen making the final preparations for lunch. Eating at the Grimbal farm was an event. Granted, some meals were more spectacular than others, but lunch on the weekends was generally special. The old family farmhouse was large and spacious, as was the formal dining room that was put to good use whenever the Grimbals had company.

"Remember our last Christmas dinner with Mom?" Wanda asked as she turned toward Betsy.

"Yes. Yes, I do," Betsy smiled. "Mom always did love to cook and entertain guests."

"That she did," Wanda replied, "and by the looks of this spread, I'm sure she would have been happy to be here."

"I know she would have. You know, Wanda, Mom could have done anything, yet she chose to marry a farmer and live in Iowa." After a brief silence, Betsy continued, "Anyway, I've been meaning to ask about Larry. We all know how smart he is, so I'm just wondering if—"

"If what?" Wanda interrupted.

"You know…if he has Mom's gifts?"

"Oh, well…" Wanda started to respond just as Frank and Larry entered the room.

"Five minutes, Ma, just like you said," Frank stated.

"Right on time," Betsy replied, "just like you always are for food, huh?"

The lunch was spectacular, but the boys were actually more interested in the topic of the carnival. Once they sat and began passing the food around the table, Frank initiated the discussion. The words tumbled out right after he had passed off the bowl of mashed potatoes to his sister. "So, Pa, I told Larry about the carnival."

"You did, huh?" Wayne replied. "Don't go gettin' anyone too excited. After all, I haven't said anything about this to Larry's mom and dad yet."

William responded. "A carnival? That sounds pretty fun."

"Can we go, Dad?" Larry inquired.

At that point, all the kids got excited, to the point where everyone starting talking at the same time, half-spewing mashed potatoes all over the place.

It seemed that the pressure was on William, and he bought into it by stoking the excitement and anticipation. "I wonder if it's that really good one I've been hearing about."

At that, the kids grew even more anxious and could hardly sit still in their chairs.

"Okay, I know you're all excited. Sounds like a great adventure for the Stevens family."

Larry had to ask just one more time for assurance. "Are you sure? We can really go?"

"Yes. That means we can go," William replied with a smile as the children all erupted, happy and pleased.

"I thought maybe we could go this afternoon, after lunch and after everyone gets a chance to settle in a bit," Wayne interjected.

"Sounds like a good plan to me," William said.

Betsy and Wanda managed to stay out of the conversation; they just looked at each other and smiled knowingly, as if they'd been in on it all along.

Around 2:00, both families headed out toward the carnival. Within the hour, they were standing inside the front gate near the High Striker. Bill Konklin watched and listened intently as Wanda laid out the strategy of what to do in case any of the kids were separated. The kids appeared distracted, and Wanda waved her hand in front of Larry's face.

"Larry, did you hear me?"

"Yes, Mom."

"Okay, then what did I say?"

"You said not to panic, and if we get separated or lost, we should walk back here to the front gate and stay put."

"Did everyone hear what Larry just said?" Wanda asked, surveying her entire juvenile audience.

"Yes, ma'am," came the reply from a choir of kids.

Although there was a group of kids, Bill Konklin focused on Larry. His search for a protégé was ongoing, and young Larry captured his attention right away.

"Hey, Dad, can I play this one?" Larry tugged on William's arm and pointed toward the High Striker.

"I don't know. Let's take a closer look," William added as they walked closer.

When they got within speaking distance, Bill initiated the sideshow sales pitch. "Hey there, young man, you look strong and healthy," Bill said, still focusing his attention on Larry. "What's your name?"

"I'm Larry Stevens."

"Well, Mr. Larry Stevens, how old are you?"

"I'm six years old, almost seven."

"Six? Hmm. Well, ya know what? I played this game for the first time back when I was six years old!"

"You did?" Larry responded, wide-eyed.

"Yep. It's pretty simple. See, ya take this here sledgehammer and strike that platform with it. If you hit it hard enough, a buzzer will sound, and you can pick out any one of the prizes you see."

"Okay," Larry said.

"You folks from around here?" Bill asked the adults.

"We live about three hours away, in Centerville, Minnesota," William said.

"Mr. Stevens, I presume?" Bill said, attempting to make the familial connection since Larry had already been forthcoming about his last name.

"Yes, that's right, William Stevens, of Stevens Shoe Store."

It was a stroke of luck; the salesman gave Bill all the information he needed.

"Well, Mr. Stevens, are you gonna give it a try?"

"I don't believe I'd be very good."

"Well, sir, it's just a game."

"How about you, Larry? You wanna give it a shot?" William asked, deferring to his son.

Larry did not speak; he only nodded his head in the affirmative as a big smile emerged.

Bill had conceived the plot one night following a rare week of sobriety, but in each of his three previous attempts, the master plan had failed. It was supposed to be simple: He would let a young boy win at the High Striker, give him a Hot Wheels car, steal it back, follow him home to return it, and then kidnap him. Bill initially thought a plan with so few basic steps was sure to succeed, yet as Larry Stevens came forward that night to play the game, Bill had not yet achieved success. Giving a boy a Hot Wheels and then stealing it back had proven to be the most challenging part thus far, and he had no intention of failing that task again.

"How much to play?" William asked.

"I'll tell ya what," Bill replied, "I'll let this young man have five chances for fifty cents."

"And you said I get a prize if I can ring the bell?" Larry asked.

"Of course! Winners always get prizes, don't they? See all those stuffed animals up there? Well, those are the prizes I *usually* give away, but since I like you, I'm gonna give you something extra if you win." Bill reached into his apron and pulled out a Hot Wheels car. "Ever seen one of these?"

"Cool!" Larry said excitedly, right on cue.

"This here's a Shelby Turbine. She's a brand new model."

"That's a nice-looking car." William stepped forward with the money in his hand.

As the money exchanged hands and Larry walked into the High Striker stage, little did the boy—or his parents—know that he had officially entered Bill's world.

Although Bill was still using the cheating tricks John Canter had taught him, when it came to kids, Bill had rigged up something extra. He had an electric wire powered by a battery that was connected to a buzzer behind the High Striker. In order to build the anticipation, Bill waited for Larry's fifth and final strike before he pushed the buzzer button. Then he shouted, "You won!" Larry dropped the kid-sized sledgehammer on the ground and walked back toward William. "You've got a mighty powerful swing there, young man." Bill held out a stuffed animal in one hand and the Shelby Turbine in the other. "They're all yours, just like I promised."

Larry smiled, took the prizes, and acknowledged Bill with a polite, "Thank you."

As the Stevens family walked away, Bill hurried into his trailer and emerged wearing a baseball cap, a black windbreaker, and a pair of sunglasses. The Stevens family remained in his focus, Larry in particular. Bill followed for a few minutes until the Stevenses settled inside a food tent. He watched from his vantage point nearby as Larry gobbled down sticky pink and blue cotton candy and accidently knocked the Hot Wheels off the table and onto the ground without noticing. Thankful for his bit of good fortune, Bill swooped in, confident in his disguise, and grabbed the toy without anyone realizing what had happened. He hurried back to his trailer, removed the hat, jacket, and glasses, and then opened the High Striker for business once again. There was no sign of the Stevens family for the remainder of that day, and he was sure his patience had finally paid off. Bill was now ready to execute the next step of his plan.

CHAPTER 12

THE BIRTH OF AMOS KONKLIN

The Stevens family returned from the Grimbal farm late Sunday afternoon on May 24, 1970. Later on that evening, The Carnival of the Ages closed up shop. The next day would be the beginning of a short three-day break, followed by a day of teardown, and then moving on to the next town.

After Bill Konklin closed the High Striker that night, he did the complete teardown and packed the hauling trailer. It was a late night, and by the time he got into his truck to head for Centerville, it was already Monday, May 25. He arrived in the wee hours of the morning and passed through the middle of town while the streets were empty—the perfect time to get a feel for the place since the town had not come to life yet. The small size of Centerville made it convenient for Bill, and around 4:00 a.m., he found the Stevens Shoe Store on the corner of Pinto and Main. By 5:00 a.m., a local phone book had revealed the address of the Stevens home and the elementary school that Larry no doubt attended.

Later that morning, Bill parked a block down from the Stevens home, keeping watch on the white, wood-framed, colonial house. At precisely 7:30 a.m., a boy walked down Trowell Avenue and stopped outside the house. One minute later, the door opened and Larry came out, dressed in a distinguishable yellow t-shirt. His mother stood in the doorway as Larry greeted the other boy at the sidewalk, and they began walking together. Larry's companion was noticeably bigger, no doubt older.

That afternoon, Bill was again on stakeout. This time, he waited across from the elementary school and watched from a distance as Larry, dressed in jeans and that familiar yellow t-shirt, left school along with two other boys, one of whom Bill recognized from the morning walk. After getting permission from the crossing guard, the boys traveled another block and took a right at the next corner. Bill cranked up his truck and followed at an unnoticeable distance. They headed down Lemon Street. One of the boys stopped, said goodbye, and entered a gate in front of a house. Larry and the bigger boy continued walking for two more blocks and then took a left on Rose Avenue. After another block, they crossed over and cut through a small park, home to a swing set and a lone seesaw. They exited the park onto Trowell Avenue, and after one final block, Larry headed up to his house. The bigger boy kept walking, but Bill was no longer interested in him or his place of origin.

Bill stayed in Centerville that night instead of making the long trip back to the carnival. His pickup had a small, attached camper on the bed, and Bill found an isolated place to park. He figured that in order to snatch Larry, he would have to deal with the other boy. Grabbing two kids would certainly be more of a challenge, but chloroform was powerful stuff. He didn't really have a perfect plan; he was content to follow them again to see if their pattern was consistent.

The next day, Bill repeated the routine in the morning, and in the afternoon, he again watched as the same three boys left school together. He followed at a distance, and when they crossed over to cut through the park, Bill thought it was the best possible opportunity for him to make his move, assuming no one else was there. He decided it best to wait patiently, something Hannah had taught him to do; he would be confident and ready to follow through the next day.

Wednesday, May 27, 1970, began as any other normal day in Centerville, Minnesota. Larry waved goodbye to his mother and was off to school again. That afternoon Bill Konklin sat in his truck, waiting for the boys to cross the street to the park, just as they had done the day before. On this day, however, fortune would be in the kidnapper's favor and pay him for his patience. Larry Stevens was alone this time, and Bill Konklin was waiting.

As Larry began to cross the street, Bill took a final look to make sure no one was around. Once the coast was clear, he stuck his head out the window. "Hey there, Larry."

Larry was startled for a moment and stopped in the middle of the street.

"It's Bill, from the carnival. Remember the High Striker game you won?"

"Oh, yeah! But…well, what are you doing here?" Larry asked.

"Well, that night after you won your prizes, I was helping clean up and found a Hot Wheels in the grass.

Immediately I thought about you, since you were the only winner of the car that day. Just so happens the carnival is moving on and passing near your town here. I remember your dad telling me his last name, so I found him at the shoe store today. I offered to give him the car, but he said you would appreciate it more if I hand delivered it. He told me you'd be walking home from school. I guess it's just luck I found you. I was actually headed to your house to meet your mom and give it to you there. I just stopped here for a moment because I don't know where Trowell Avenue is, and I don't have a map."

"Trowell is the next street over," Larry said.

"Imagine that! I was just about to turn the corner up there, and then I looked up and saw you. I suppose it's a waste of time to follow you home. I might as well just give it to you right now." Bill put his arm out the window and opened his hand, revealing the Shelby Turbine.

"Gee, sir, that's...well, it's very nice and super thoughtful of you to make a special trip and all." Larry reached out to take the car.

Bill grabbed his arm, pulled him to the window, and covered his face with a chloroform-soaked rag. The boy struggled for only a moment, then dropped to his knees. Bill got out of the truck and pulled Larry into the front seat, then reapplied the chloroform to his face. The struggle was brief, and Larry relented as the drug took full effect.

The final step was completed as Bill moved Larry from the front seat to inside the camper. Just like that, it was over.

Later that day, while the small town of Centerville was beginning to notice that young Larry was missing, Bill Konklin was already back in his carnival trailer home with his new protégé. Bill got drunk that night, as usual, but he was sober enough to realize that he was going to have to give the young boy a new name. As Larry lay in the corner of the room, frightened and lethargic from the aftereffects of the chloroform, Bill snatched up his father's Bible from a nearby desk drawer. Bill had kept it all these years, though he rarely bothered to open it anymore after that fiasco at the Catholic orphanage that had left a bitter taste in his mouth about God and his so-called Good Book. However, on this night, he set the book down on a table and, without any direction or purpose, opened it up to the book between Joel and Obadiah. After glancing down at the name of the Bible book that lay open before his eyes, Bill looked over at the trembling and drugged Larry Stevens and said, "Amos. Your name is Amos Konklin." Then Bill turned to the inside front cover of the Bible and added an entry. When he finished writing, he spoke aloud in a sarcastic tone, "Isaac Newton, Nikola Tesla, and Larry Stevens/Amos Konklin. I guess that makes you a fucking genius, boy."

For Bill Konklin, the plan was working perfectly. For a while at least, he knew there would be a lot of focused activity centered on finding Amos. He had already decided to separate from The Carnival of the Ages and had made plans to later join another carnival group on a Canadian circuit. However, his first order of business was to cross into Canada quickly and hide out for a few months. His destination was an isolated cabin he had located on one of his scouting trips, so early the next day, with his young captive in tow, he began the trip up Minnesota 35W North.

CHAPTER 13

THE CABIN

Larry awoke in an unfamiliar place, feeling groggy and terrified. There was that strange man again, hovering, forcing him to open his mouth and swallow. The taste was simply awful; it reminded him of the cough syrup his mother used to give him when he was sick. He couldn't hold back the tears, so he just let them flow as he drifted away, unable to keep his drugged eyelids open.

When he awoke again, it was daytime, and the sunlight gushed through the window, illuminating the room. Everywhere Larry looked, there was wood; even the ceiling above the bed looked like tree trunks. He was alone, but the spoon and nearly empty bottle of Vick's on the nightstand conjured memories of the night before. Instantly, his heart raced, and he sat up in bed, looking for the strange man.

Larry was sad, scared, lost, and alone, but there didn't seem to be any tears left to cry. He got up and walked out of the tiny bedroom. In the next room, he saw the carnival man, sitting on the couch in the small living area of what looked like a cabin. It was similar to a place Larry had stayed once with his family. *My family! They must be looking for me!* For a brief moment, that thought comforted him, but then his captor spoke.

"Okay, boy. Take a seat. I need to talk to you about something."

Larry walked to a nearby chair and sat down, just as he was told.

"Listen, kid. I know you're upset and miss your mommy and daddy, but you're gonna live with me now. I gave you a new name. It's Amos. Larry is no more."

"But...but my name's Larry. My mom and dad named me that first."

The man shook his finger at him. "Now you listen here! From now on, I'm in charge. I know where your mommy and daddy live, and if you try to run away or call anyone, I will go to that place and kill them. My name is Bill Konklin, and from now on, your name is Amos Konklin, and that's final. I don't ever wanna hear you call yourself Larry again. Do you understand?"

Larry sat quietly, so upset he was unable to cry.

"I said, do you understand?"

Larry was upset, but the tears would not come.

"Listen, kid, I know you're sad for losing your parents. Hell, my own mommy died when I was born, and my daddy died when I was about your age. Shit happens. At least your mommy and daddy are still alive. If you wanna keep it that way, you'd better do whatever the hell I tell you to, or your parents will be as dead as mine. Besides, life with me will be fun. Later, when you've calmed down, we're going to join up with a carnival."

Over the course of the first week, Larry tried to run away once. He didn't get very far, and it didn't take him long to realize what the consequences were for disobeying Bill's commands. By the end of the first month, Larry was mentally exhausted, worn down, and no longer felt like resisting. Bill's threats were intimidating, and he believed them. He also began to respond to his new name just to avoid Bill's wrath.

The time spent at the cabin seemed like it would never end, but one day, Bill packed their things up, and they left. They took a long drive on the open road, until they finally reached their destination—a carnival in Canada, just as Bill had said.

CHAPTER 14

LIFE WITH BILL

As each year in the carnival passed, Amos lost more of his true self. He allowed his former life as Larry Stevens to fade away; it was easier that way. Living with Bill was difficult. He was drunk most of the time, and his harsh treatment of Amos intensified as time wore on. Amos hated Bill more and more each day, but with the help of the friends he'd made during his captivity, life was tolerable. His life with Bill centered on running the carnival High Striker game, and in late July of 1972, Bill invited him outside one morning for what he had described as a "special lesson" involving the striker.

It was a Saturday, early, before the carnival crowds arrived. Bill was outside waiting for him. "Well, boy, did you know this game ain't got nothin' to do with strength?"

Amos didn't say anything.

"You see, boy, this game is all about technique. Just watch!" At that, Bill grabbed one of the sledgehammers lying on the ground by the High Striker platform. "It's just like chopping wood. You can swing that axe mighty hard, but you ain't gonna split no wood right unless you hit the target."

Amos watched as Bill raised the sledgehammer with both arms over his head just like a person with an axe, cutting wood. With a strong, clean, definite stroke, Bill struck the platform, and the block quickly traveled up the guide wire to the top, where it was stopped by the bell.

"Ding!" Bill shouted, emphasizing his feat. "It's that simple, boy. Now get over here." As Amos walked closer, Bill moved behind the High Striker and adjusted the wires. Then Amos heard him mumble to himself, "I'm a-doing it just like you, you old dead son of a bitch." When he finished the adjustments, Bill grabbed the sledgehammer.

Amos stood watching as he swung again, but the bell didn't ring.

Next, Bill grabbed one of the heavy wires attached to the High Striker. "Come over here and pull on this wire," he barked.

Amos did as he was told.

Bill grabbed the sledgehammer and swung again.

Amos felt the wire pull away and he let go of it.

Bill failed again, and the bell didn't ring. "Do you know what just happened?"

"Not really," Amos responded.

"Well, you let go, you little pussy. Now grab that wire again. Pull hard and hang on tight with those weak hands of yers."

Again, Amos complied, feeling he really had no other choice.

This time, as Bill swung the sledgehammer, the block traveled up quickly, and Amos heard the sound of the bell once again. "Now do you understand, boy?" Bill asked.

"I think I get it now," Amos replied.

"Oh yeah? Well, it's about time, you little dumb shit. But I don't think you do!" Bill ranted. "You see that wire that runs up the striker with that block attached?"

"Yes."

"Well, after I rang the bell, I went back there and made it so that it'll loop back behind the bell and connect to that wire you were just pulling on."

Amos remained silent but nodded in acknowledgement. Whether he fully understood or not, he was not going to give Bill any further reason to insult or punish him.

"Now, there ain't no way I can win if that wire is loose. When you pull on it, that tightens the shit, evening the odds and giving me a better chance to win. You got that?"

"I understand," Amos said.

"You understand now, genius? Jesus fucking Christ! It's about fucking time. But you can't just start yanking on the fucking wire," Bill continued. "That would be a bit obvious to those fools considering giving us their money, don't you think? You see, boy, if I just stand around and watch and don't do nothing, people will lose the game every time. Unless, of course, we just so happen to be dealing with an abnormally strong son of a bitch, and I ain't never met one of those. Anyway, every once in a while, if I feel sorry for some poor idiot, I might just walk over and lean up against the wire to give him a shot and keep everyone's suspicions down."

"I thought you only used the trick lever under the platform?"

"Don't be a smart-ass, Amos! Of course I do. I'm just showing you something I was taught a long time ago. Now that you're nine years old, you should be able to win when I'm a-leaning on that wire for you. Now get your ass over here so we can practice."

Amos walked over, grabbed the sledgehammer, and brought it down toward the platform with all his might. The block barely moved, and he heard laughter.

Bill was standing by the wire, but his hands were not on it; Amos was on his own, and the fix wasn't in. Bill wanted to watch Amos fail, just for the fun of it, sick as that was. "Goddamn, boy, you failed! Why? Because I let you fail, you little shit!" On the subsequent swing, Bill leaned on the wire, but it made little difference in the outcome. "Now try again!" he demanded.

Amos swung as Bill did his part. However, even with the tension applied, Amos failed to move the block up any farther than a few feet.

"Goddamn it! You are a little pussy, aren't you?" Bill shouted.

Amos kept going—swing after swing, failure after failure—while Bill stood by berating him.

"Ready to give up yet? Go ahead. I know you wanna run away and cry, like the little pussy you are."

"I don't run away from stuff," Amos said sternly.

"Okay, that's enough, smart-ass."

But Amos kept swinging; his entire being was fuelled by intense anger.

At that, Bill yelled, "I said that's enough! Stop it!"

After the last swing, Amos stood upright, stared at Bill long enough to convey his disapproval, and then dropped the sledgehammer on the ground. Amos went about his chores after that, and the carnival got underway that Saturday morning like other countless times.

Generally, during the day Amos would wander off and make his tour around the carnival, which was comprised of an interesting cast of characters. At the Ferris wheel was Paul, a short, bald man with a spider tattoo on his right shoulder. Paul kept a pack of Camel cigarettes folded up under his short-sleeved t-shirts, exposing the spider at all times. At the Tilt-A-Whirl was Jim, a tall, skinny fellow with a patch over his left eye, which he'd lost in the jungles of Vietnam. Jim was talkative, especially when it came to war stories. The Scrambler, Amos's favorite ride, was manned by Jeff, a quiet guy who loved listening to Bob Dylan tapes. He never made eye contact, but his lips never stopped moving in sync with the Dylan tunes that steadily flowed from the eight-track stereo he kept near The Scrambler at all times. The remaining rides were all run by men, except for The Himalaya. Nell Long was a second-generation carny, a good-looking woman who always seemed to draw a crowd to the ride. The Himalaya was popular anyway, and with a recently upgraded stereo system and siren, Nell managed to preside over her ride kingdom with a queen-like intensity and power that drew the crowds in again and again.

Unlike the ride operators, the sideshow game masters were a different breed. Instead of waiting for the people to come to them, the tricksters actively solicited participation. It didn't take Amos long to suspect that most of the games were rigged, much like Bill's High Striker. This was later confirmed by what he learned behind the scenes. His first hands-on realization occurred one day when Lucas Carlson handed him a milk jug that he used in his game; even though it was empty, it was significantly heavier than a typical jug filled with milk. Amos had watched many people sling softballs at the milk jug configuration, but he'd never witnessed anyone who could topple the bottom two jugs. At first, he'd thought they were nailed down, but Lucas made a point of demonstrating to the people that this wasn't the case. The trick was that the bottom two jugs were very heavy, unlikely to be knocked down by a mere softball.

Other games were purely skill based. At the top of this list was the rope ladder climb. It was amazing to Amos that a game of that type could be deceptive enough to lure the money out of carnival-goers' pockets. It certainly looked easy, especially when Cain McDonald demonstrated it. The rope ladder climb was very much like the High Striker in that people would be just competitive enough to keep attempting to win, thinking they could learn and build from their previous failures. It was a logical assessment in principle, but it was difficult to achieve within such a compressed time. On some occasions, Amos had witnessed people spending as much as twenty dollars on one game, only to walk away dejected, broke, and empty-handed.

Lastly, there were the sideshows with performances. Amos's favorite was "Swords of Death," Lester Cobb's spectacular feat of swallowing six swords at once. Cobb was a veteran carny, but his physical appearance didn't offer any clue as to his occupation. He was, in fact, quite the physical specimen, and he looked more like a bodybuilder than an operator of a carnival attraction. Lester had become a good friend to Amos, as well as to many others.

Later that evening, before the carnival closed, Amos was there for Lester Cobb's final performance. When he arrived back at the trailer home, Bill was already halfway through a bottle of whiskey. Amos attempted to avoid him, to no avail.

"Hey you," Bill slurred, sitting over in his favorite chair, "it's about time you got your lazy ass back home. I had to close the show all by myself, you little prick."

Amos was careful and responded diplomatically, "I was watching Mr. Cobb's show."

"Mr. Cobb? I don't know why you like hanging out over there with that sword-swallowing freak. I ought to go over there and kick his ass! Let *me* shove a sword down his throat, and we'll see what happens to the fucker. The same goes for that old dumb-ass Dr. Drake as well. What a useless fool! What kind of real doctor works in a fucking carnival anyway?"

"Dr. Drake is a nice man, and Mr. Cobb is nice to me as well. Plus, his show is very good," Amos answered in defense.

"Very good? Shit, why don't he ever come over here and see if he can beat the striker? Hell, anybody with a big mouth can swallow a sword, but it takes a damn real man to sling that sledgehammer hard enough to beat my striker!"

Amos didn't respond; there was no reason to answer Bill on that night—or on most nights, for that matter. Usually, Amos could ignore Bill and wait until he fell asleep in the chair. However, as Amos walked by Bill in hopes of seeking refuge in his bedroom without a conflict, it became obvious that this was not going to be one of the easy nights.

"Where the fuck are you going, boy? Don't you walk away while I'm talkin' to you! That old fucker's bad manners are wearing off on you! Maybe I oughtta shove a damn sword down your throat to teach you a thing or two!"

As Amos kept walking, Bill's verbal bashing continued. Finally, his moment of relief came when he made it to his bedroom and closed the door behind him. Although now more faint, he could still hear Bill ranting until there was a welcomed silence. Amos took a seat on the edge of his bed, waiting and listening. Finally, he heard Bill stand up, and footsteps began to move down the hallway. The sound of the footsteps ceased when Bill reached the bedroom door, and Amos could hear his heavy breathing. Just as he dropped his head into his hands, Bill kicked in the door and it flung open, barely hanging by the bottom hinge.

"You little shit! I was talking to you," Bill slurred. As he approached the bed, he grabbed Amos by his left arm and forced him to his feet. "You stand up when I'm talkin' to ya, boy! Show me some Goddamn respect!"

Amos stood silent.

"Well now, ain't this strange? You're always running off at the mouth, but now you got nothing to say." Bill released his arm and looked at the broken door. "What a fucking mess." With that, he turned back and unleashed a violent backhand across Amos's face. The force knocked Amos back onto the bed.

Amos was hurt, but he didn't show any fear. He just lay there on the bed, bleeding from the nose and staring Bill right in the eyes.

"Wipe that blood off your face," Bill slurred. "I ain't buyin' you no more sheets if you stain those up 'cause of yer bullshit sassing." He half-walked, half-stumbled drunkenly toward the door, but before leaving the room, he turned to Amos for a final remark. "And tomorrow I want you to get your ass up early and fix this door." Bill then made his way back down the hallway and passed out on the couch.

The next morning, Amos arose early and repaired the door, just as he was ordered to do.

CHAPTER 15

AFTERNOONS WITH DR. DRAKE

When Amos turned eleven, the nature of his relationship with Dr. Drake changed. Until then, they had been friendly, but at eleven, Amos's curiosity with understanding deeper subject matter became insatiable, and he sought a closer relationship with the old carnival physician. In a casual conversation, Drake had mentioned his library to Amos, who had become desperate for new reading material since he'd already read every book Bill owned, including a set of old encyclopedias. Lester Cobb had also let him borrow what few books he possessed; Amos literally read everything he could get his hands on.

During the early afternoons, Amos got a break for a few hours from the High Striker. It wasn't an act of charity or thoughtfulness; it seemed like the only time of day when Bill actually wanted to be outside. It was a routine: Most days Bill slept in till noon, ate some lunch, and then came outside to sit in a lounge chair by the High Striker. He always brought tea with him, which he kept in an old plastic gallon jug. He rested the jug on top of a rusty aluminum cooler, in which he stored the ice for his glass.

On a spring day in 1975, Bill's routine was true to form, and Amos took the opportunity to visit Dr. Drake and return one of his medical books. It had taken Amos only three weeks to read the volume, and at precisely 1:10 p.m. on that Monday afternoon, Amos was outside Drake's door with the book in hand.

"Good afternoon, my boy. Come on in," Drake said.

"Good afternoon, Doc," Amos said. Early on, Amos had attempted to call him "Mr. Drake" out of respect, but the man wouldn't hear of it. He requested that Amos simply call him "Doc," just like everyone else.

"I see you have my book. I'm assuming you've already read it."

"Yes, Doc. I finished it. I'd like to discuss it today, if you've got time."

"Sure." Drake turned to walk toward his sitting area with Amos following close behind. "First, a quiz," Drake said, as was his custom. As they sat on the couch together, Drake asked, "How many brain cavities are there?"

"Four. They are called ventricles."

Drake only nodded. "And what are the four divisions of the adult brain?"

"The cerebrum, diencephalon, cerebellum, and the brain stem."

"Very nice. So tell me, what goes on in the cerebrum?"

This time, Amos paused briefly, squinted, and then began to speak as his own cerebrum engaged. "Well, the cerebrum controls speech, thinking, and muscle control."

"Good," Drake said. "Very good! Now, tell me, what's on your mind today?"

"Well, the brain seems to be mysterious. I mean, nobody really understands how it works. Doc, do you think it's possible that people who do bad things can't help it?"

"You mean like a disease?"

"I suppose so, yeah. If I got cancer, that would be something I couldn't really control, right? What if someone's brain is diseased or something and they can't help the things it thinks or tells them to do?"

"You know, before I started my family practice way back when, I toyed with the idea of becoming a psychiatrist, so I took a lot of classes on the mind during medical school. There are people who do suffer afflictions of the mind, just as people suffer afflictions and sickness in other parts of the body. Some people are actually diagnosed as insane, and they are put in institutions for their own safety and the safety of others."

"Yes, I know, I've read about it, but I'm talking about something different. Take people like Adolf Hitler. People think of him as a monster. What if there was something wrong with his brain, something he couldn't control?"

"Well, I know you are not a Nazi apologist, so something else must be going on in that head of yours. What are you getting at?"

"Well..." Amos paused. "Take people like Bill. He's awfully mean, and I just don't think it's natural. He drinks a lot, but don't get me wrong, because he's still mean when he's not drunk. I have to wonder if maybe there is something wrong with his brain."

"You ask really good questions for a youngster, lad. Let me tell you from personal experience that there may be a fine line between being in control and out of control due to circumstances beyond your control, but there definitely is a line nonetheless. You've seen *me* drink, haven't you?"

"Yes, but you're not mean like Bill."

"I may not be mean, but the abuse of alcohol is the major reason I live in a carnival. I used to be a good doctor, but I made many bad decisions. I once had a successful practice, but I lost it all on account of my drinking. Now I'm seventy-two years old, divorced, and live in a carnival. I wouldn't even be here if it weren't for the graces and mercy of an old friend. You see, Amos, we all have to take responsibilities for our decisions. We can't put the blame on other things. Bill is an alcoholic. Some people say that's a kind of disease, and it may be, but Bill *chooses* to drink. He could stop, but he doesn't. Take me, for example. I was once completely sober for over three years, and then I started to drink again. If one can be sober for that long, they can be sober for their entire life, as long as they choose to. I don't blame anyone or anything for the way my life has turned out. Everything is a result of the decisions I've made. Does that make sense?"

"I suppose, but it still makes me wonder."

"Well, that's good. It's part of human nature to think about things. It's just that you tend to think about things a little harder than most, especially for a boy your age. Now, back to Hitler. I believe that man was evil. Perhaps he was insane, but I would still have to hold him responsible for what he did. We are all accountable, Amos—each and every one of us. There is a universal justice, a force that demands it."

"Do you believe in God, Doc?"

"Well, I can't honestly say I don't believe in Him, so by default, I suppose that makes me a believer of sorts. I read something Isaac Newton said while I was in grad school that always stuck with me."

"What was that?"

"In *Principia,* perhaps the greatest math book ever written, he said that the sun, planets, and comets could only come from an intelligent and powerful being. Newton was a pretty smart fellow, so I figure that whatever he believed is a safe bet. What about you?"

"I'm not sure, but it makes sense. I've read Bill's Bible, but it's very confusing. There are some strange stories in there, and from what I've read, God seems to be angry a lot."

"I would have to agree with you on that, Amos, but you have to remember that the Bible is split into two parts, two testaments. In the first part, God seems angry, like what you described, but in the second part, He has much to say about love."

"It's called the New Testament, I think. Yeah, I've read some about love, but there's also a lot of stuff in there about punishment. To me, God still comes across harsh at times."

"That's an interesting perspective. Let me take the viewpoint of a believer, if I may, just for the sake of argument. Try thinking about it another way. If you were God and you put mankind on Earth, how would you handle it? It seems to me you would have to give man free will, or else you would have only created a machine."

"I see what you are saying."

"But what happens if mankind chooses to disobey? Should there be punishment?"

"Probably—or maybe not. Why not just let things happen?"

"Amos, I think it has more to do with justice than punishment. Bad people cannot be left to their own devices, or they would rule the Earth and get away with it. How is that fair to good people? Also, if God just stood by and allowed things happen for a long time, there might eventually be chaos."

"So you think God actually gets involved?" Amos asked.

"I don't know. Maybe He does to keep things from getting out of hand and we just don't know it."

"Well, Doc, it seems to me He could do more to help make it clear so we're not always just stuck guessing with only that confusing book of His for answers."

"You are quite perceptive, Amos, and the truth is, you do not belong in a carnival. I have no idea why you are here. A deep thinker like you should be enrolled in a proper school, where you can learn to use that wonderful brain of yours for the greater good in society. You shouldn't be here living in a trailer with a drunk and hanging out with sword swallowers."

"Thanks. Maybe someday when I'm all grown up, I can leave this place. Maybe I could be a doctor like you."

"I'm sure you would make a fine one, Amos, as long as you don't start drinking!"

"I suppose I could even be a preacher," Amos countered with a smile.

Drake shook his head. "Your sarcasm is uncanny for an eleven-year-old. You are a gifted young man. Don't ever forget that."

"Thanks, Doc."

"Getting back to the brain, Amos, let me tell you a story. When I was a youngster, about your age, my father got sick. By the time I graduated from high school and was ready for college, he was having seizures. He had epilepsy, which is like a storm in the brain. Later, during the 1960s, a man named Roger Sperry carried out studies on split-brain patients. They were able to cure people with certain kinds of epilepsy by cutting off the connection between both sides of the brain. That might have been a cure for my father, but he died shortly after the war when he drowned while fishing. Everyone assumed he'd had a seizure and fallen into the water. Anyway, getting back to our earlier discussion, my father had a disease, but he was not crazy. In fact, he was one of the smartest men I've ever known, yet he went fishing alone, knowing full well of his illness. Did epilepsy affect his good judgment? I think not. Life is all about managing risk, Amos, and sometimes you just have to live and forget the fear. It cost my father his life in the end, but I never blamed him for it. It was his decision, and he took responsibility for it."

"Do you know very much about memory, Doc?"

"Memory? Why do you ask?"

"I've started to forget a lot about my life from back when I was younger. I think about my mother and father, and it bothers me that I can't remember their faces any longer."

"Your mother and father? But I've always assumed that Bill is your father."

"No, and my name isn't really Amos. It's Larry, but it's a long story, and please don't tell Bill I told you that. I shouldn't have brought it up."

"Are you sure you don't want to talk about it? You know I won't tell your secrets to anyone if you don't want me to, Amos…er, Larry."

"Not today, Doc." Amos could feel the tears welling up.

"How about some ice cream? I made some homemade vanilla just last night."

"Sure," Amos answered. "That would be nice."

Dr. Drake opened his freezer and extracted what looked like a gallon-sized aluminum container. "This here's on old family recipe. The secret's in the mix." He popped off the plastic cover and looked down at his creation. "Some people like it soft, when it's first made. I prefer ice cream after a day or so, after a good freeze takes hold." He scooped two nice helpings into a bowl and uttered a familiar invitation when it came to food or drink of any kind, "Come and get it, my boy."

Amos quickly got up and walked over, his eyes dry and bright. The sadness had been lifted by the kindness of a friend and the sweetness of the frozen treat. "Delicious!" Amos remarked as soon as the large spoonful greeted his mouth. "You know, Doc, this reminds me of the section in your book on taste buds. There are thousands of them, and they're made of these cells that die off every couple weeks and then grow back."

"Do you remember what role the brain plays in all that?" Drake questioned, gravitating back toward quiz mode.

"Well, if I remember, there are cranial nerves that connect to the tongue, and it's the vagus nerve, I think, that carries the taste back to the brain."

"Right again."

"It's kinda strange why we like some things and not others. I wonder if that has more to do with the taste buds or if it's mostly the brain?"

"If I recall, Amos, it's more about flavor than taste. Taste is only one factor. Then you have texture—you know, the way it feels on your tongue. Then we add smell, and all of this together gives food a certain flavor that you either like or you don't. So I think it's more to do with the brain after all, since it's the brain that has to process all that information."

"Well, I think I may have just discovered the way to figure out if someone is insane or not," Amos said.

"How?"

"If someone doesn't like your ice cream, then I'd have to say they're nuts!"

Dr. Drake laughed.

During the next few months leading up to his twelfth birthday, Amos read more of Dr. Drake's books, and he was a constant afternoon visitor at Drake's trailer.

✵ ✵ ✵

As July 21 approached, Amos felt depressed, as he did during that time every year. Although he had forgotten much of his former life, his date of birth had somehow made an indelible mark in his memory. It was the only thing that actually connected him to Larry Stevens, that frightened little boy who had been torn away from his family all those years ago just because he'd dropped a Hot Wheels car.

Around 1:00 p.m. on July 21, Bill emerged from the trailer, and the ritual began. It was down the steps, cooler in hand, with a gallon jug of tea sitting on the top. When he made it to his chair, down went the cooler and out came the words, "Get on outta here for a while." There was no *"Good morning"* or *"Happy birthday"*—only the usual command.

At 1:05 p.m., Amos was outside Dr. Drake's trailer door, this time with Bill's Bible in hand. Before he could knock, he heard the invitation to come inside. As soon as the door closed behind him, the chorus began, "Happy birthday to you, happy birthday to you, happy birthday dear Amos, happy birthday to you!" At twelve, it was the first birthday party he could remember, although the words that rang out were somehow familiar. As he kept walking into the small dining area, he saw his two favorite faces, Dr. Drake and Lester Cobb. On the counter was a cake, lit with twelve candles.

"Blow out the candles and make a wish," Drake said.

Amos hesitated only for a moment before he happily complied. He closed his eyes as he blew out the candles. When he opened them, Lester Cobb was standing beside him with an arm around his shoulder.

"Happy birthday, Amos! A young man's twelfth birthday is a big deal," Cobb said with a big smile on his face.

"Thanks, Mr. Cobb."

Dr. Drake handed him a knife. "Why don't you do the honors?"

"Okay." Amos set the Bible on the table. "After our conversation last week, I starting reading this book again and wanted to talk to you about it. It's Bill's, but I'm sure he won't miss it." As Amos cut into the cake, the white icing no longer concealed its identity, and Amos made his approval vocal. "Chocolate! That's my favorite."

After cutting three big slices, they all took a seat at the small, round table in the kitchen, which barely accommodated the three of them.

"This is really nice of you," Amos said. "You are my two best friends." After eating, Amos made his way into the living room. On the coffee table were two presents, neatly wrapped.

"Those are for you, Amos." Lester Cobb pointed to the table. "Go ahead and open 'em."

Amos grabbed the long, rectangular box and tore through the paper, revealing a beautiful sword—the sword Amos was particularly fond of and had asked to hold on several occasions while visiting Cobb's show. "Wow!" Amos said in loud voice. "This is for me?"

"Yep," Cobb answered. "I'm hoping Bill will let you keep it."

"Thank you so much, Mr. Cobb."

Next came another rectangular box, much smaller, wrapped in blue paper. When Amos opened it, he discovered a book, *Huckleberry Finn.*

"I think it's time you read a little more fiction," Drake remarked. "Go ahead! Open it and read the inside cover."

Amos had heard of Samuel Clemens, but he'd never had the opportunity to read any of his works. There, on the inside cover, was an autograph from the author himself. "This is an original signature? A signed copy?" he asked.

"Yes. It was passed on to me from my father, and I thought if anyone would appreciate it, you would."

"From your father? I don't feel right taking it."

"It's yours. After all, I have no children of my own. You can pass it down through your family now."

"Thank you so much, Doc." Tears trickled down his face. In the dark shadow of his otherwise unhappy life, it was the happiest day Amos could ever remember.

CHAPTER 16

THE FALL

It was a cold day in December of 1975. Amos had just finished with his chores. When he entered the trailer home, Bill was on the couch, as usual, with a bottle of whiskey in hand.

"Is all your work done, you worthless sacka shit?"

"Yes, I'm done," Amos said.

"Good. Now sit your ass down. I got something to say." Bill downed another huge gulp of whiskey and then burped grotesquely. "Now you listen here. This carnival is getting to be a drag, don't you think?"

"I don't know," Amos answered.

"You know something, boy? I ain't really lookin' to hear your lame-ass opinion. That was a rhetorical question. Jesus, I can't ever just say a simple Goddamn thing without you running off at the mouth!"

"Sorry."

"Sorry? You're damn right you're sorry. But listen...I ain't interested in a fucking argument tonight, so just sit there and shut up. You got that?"

Amos nodded.

"Like I was saying, this carnival sucks, and what's more, this whole country sucks. These people here are just plain dumb-asses. It's time to head back to America, the home of the brave, away from these sissy Canadian cowards up here." It was the beginnings of yet another drunken rant. In Bill's case, the more he drank as the evening progressed, the more belligerent he became. Most of his statements were utter nonsense; however, this night they seemed woven together with a thread of truth. Bill intended to leave Canada and return to the States.

To Amos, crossing the border was no more significant than moving on to a new town, just another part of carnival life. However, he was fond of Dr. Drake and Lester Cobb and immediately thought about them. Given Bill's state of mind, though, it was a fleeting thought, and Amos stayed focused on Bill's actions. As was the case all other nights, he just wanted to get through it with as little confrontation as possible and move on to the next day. Bill rose to his feet and pointed his finger at Amos. "You know something, boy? I think you're turning into one of these Canadian pussies."

Amos remained seated and calm. He closed his eyes, hoping for the storm to pass. However, lightning struck with a sting as Bill's backhand lash connected solidly with the side of Amos's face.

When the tirade ended, Bill walked back to the couch and sat in silence until he passed out cold.

The next day when Amos awoke, his face hurt. As he rose from bed, he took notice of the dried bloodstains on the pillowcase. When he made it to the bathroom mirror, he examined his reflection and then proceeded to wash his face gingerly. After patting it dry with a towel, he sat on the toilet. It was a Sunday morning, and a noise outside drew Amos to the window. He pulled back the brown towel masquerading as a curtain and saw Bill working on the High Striker.

The bright sunshine was too much to handle, so Amos went back to the bedroom. He lay down in bed, the back of his head resting once again on his bloodstained pillow. He cherished the rare moment of solitude, knowing that at any second, it might abruptly end with Bill initiating a verbal demand. Sometimes as he lay there, he would try to remember life before Bill Konklin, but his pleasant memories were becoming fewer and fewer.

This particular peaceful Sabbath ended when Bill entered the trailer, slamming the door behind him. "Amos!" Bill shouted. After a brief pause, the shout came again. "Amos! Get your lazy ass out of bed."

Amos emerged from his bedroom. "I'm awake."

"Good. I need your help outside on the striker."

"Let me get dressed."

"Jesus! Still lying around in your bedclothes? What the hell? Hurry up and get your ass outside."

Amos knew the routine, and getting dressed in haste had become a skill he had acquired while living with Bill.

Outside, Bill was waiting for him, holding a ladder. "The bottom guide wire connector is broken. We need to detach it at the top."

Amos wasn't fond of heights, and the apex of the striker was some twenty feet in the air, so he couldn't help but approach the task with caution.

"Come on, boy. Get to it!"

Amos didn't respond but walked toward Bill while he leaned the rickety ladder against the vertical shaft and held it steady for Amos's initial step. When he made it to the top, Amos grabbed the wire but was unable to release the pin. "It's too tight," he called down.

"Ah, fuck! Hold on." Bill let go of the ladder and walked over to the loose board. He popped up the board and pushed the lever to relieve the tension on the wire.

Amos was still pushing the wire away with a lot of force, so when the tension slackened, he slipped. He plummeted to the ground, landing on his back, his head receiving the full force of impact against the steel base. And in an instant, everything went black.

CHAPTER 17

AMOS KONKLIN'S NEW LIFE

Amos Konklin opened his eyes; he saw white—just lots and lots of white everywhere. *Where on Earth am I?* Suddenly he knew when a dark-haired man in a white coat with a stethoscope around his neck came into focus. It was a hospital. He shut his eyes tightly, searching for a memory, for any clue of how he'd gotten there, but none came to mind. Everything was blank. Then, as he turned his head, he suddenly realized that something must have happened to him, for the pain was poignant.

"Well, you're awake." The man leaned down and took hold of Amos's left eyelid. He peered at Amos, just inches away, for several seconds.

Amos wanted to say something about the awful breath but figured it best to keep quite while the man had hold of his eye. "How long?"

"It's been three weeks."

"What happened?"

"You fell and hit your head. Consider yourself fortunate."

"Am I...am I all right? Am I going to be okay?"

"I believe the worst is over, though you're going to be very sore for a while."

"Are you my doctor?"

"I am now, but you owe a lot to Dr. Joseph Hartley, the resident on call the day you arrived in the emergency room. You had developed a subdural hematoma. If not for the prompt actions of the people who brought you here, along with Dr. Hartley, you would have died."

"Have I been asleep the whole time, for three whole weeks?"

"You've been in and out, vacillating between a state of awareness and unconsciousness."

"I don't remember a thing."

"We're hoping your memory loss is temporary. You will have to be patient. The healing process will be slow."

"But I...well, I don't even know my name."

"Your name is Amos Konklin."

"Amos Konklin?"

"That's right," came another voice from inside the room.

Amos shifted his gaze and saw someone else emerge from behind the man in white. "Do I know you?" Amos asked as the man stepped closer to the bed.

"Yes you do. I'm Lester Cobb, a friend, and I brought you to the hospital."

"Sorry. I can't remember."

"That's okay. You don't need to worry about that right now."

"How many fingers am I holding up?" the doctor asked.

"Two."

"Good. Now grip my hand as hard as you can."

Amos squeezed.

"Good. What about this?" the doctor asked, grabbing his feet. "Can you feel anything?"

"Ouch. Yes. You're squeezing pretty tight."

"Excellent. Are you hungry?"

"Starving."

"That's a good sign too. I'll tell the nurse and let you two be alone for a while."

Amos watched as the doctor jotted down a few notes on a clipboard, smiled, and then departed the room. "Have you been waiting here very long?" Amos asked the man, who called himself Lester.

"I've been here a while."

"How do I know you?"

"I'll tell you what. Let's go easy on the questions until after you've eaten. Is that okay?"

"Sure," Amos replied as a nurse entered the room.

"I'm so glad to see you awake," she said.

"Thanks," Amos replied.

"I have lunch coming soon."

Lester spoke again. "It's really good to see you awake, Amos. I have a few matters to attend to, but I'll be back after lunch."

"Okay." After lunch Amos felt tired again and closed his eyes. It seemed like only a moment had gone by before he opened them again, but the clock on the wall indicated otherwise: Over three hours had passed.

Sitting in the corner of the room, reading a newspaper, was Lester Cobb.

"You're still here," Amos said.

Lester Cobb put down the paper and rose to his feet. "You're awake again. How was lunch?"

"It was okay. Tuna is not my favorite."

"When I got back, you were asleep again."

"I feel very awake now."

"You know, they're gonna have you walking the halls soon."

"I think I'm ready." Amos paused. "So, you were the one who brought me here?"

"Yes, along with Dr. Drake."

"Who?"

"Dr. Drake, another good friend."

"Where is he?"

"Well, I'm sorry to say that Doc suffered a stroke a couple of weeks ago. I think he took your accident pretty hard. He would be here if he could."

"How do you know me? Are you my family?"

"I know you from the carnival. You lived there with your father, Bill Konklin. We are all carnies—you, me, Bill, and Doc."

"A carnival? Where's my father?"

"I wish I knew. I don't know how to say this, but it seems Bill just up and took off. He left the carnival just after the accident, and nobody has seen him since."

"He just...my father abandoned me?"

"I know this must be overwhelming for you, Amos, but you two weren't exactly close."

"What did I do there, at the carnival?"

"You and Bill ran a sideshow called the High Striker."

"The High Striker?"

"Yes. The point of the game is quite simple. You use a mallet and strike a platform as hard as you can. If you hit it hard enough, it sends a block of metal up a pole twenty feet in the air and rings a bell."

"What about you? What do you do?"

"I'm a sword swallower."

"Wow! For real?"

"It's for real all right. It takes years of practice."

"I can't believe I lived in a carnival. Will I go back there after I get out of here?"

"I've been thinking a lot about that actually. It might be best for you to experience life outside the carnival, to have a normal childhood. I'm Canadian and have some family ties in the country. I've already approached my brother, Herman Cobb, and his wife Shirley about having you live with them. Herman and Shirley have no children, and they are open to the idea."

"This is all so strange."

"I know it has to be hard, Amos, but Herman and Shirley are good people. You will have a good life with them."

Two weeks later, Amos made the transition from the hospital to the small, rural Canadian town and home of Herman and Shirley Cobb. The first few months living in his new home went well, and as autumn approached, Amos nervously awaited the start of the new school year. Herman and Shirley were nice people, but Amos did not exactly feel comfortable sharing all his thoughts and feelings with them, especially his disturbing dreams, which had started soon after he was released from the hospital.

Their frequency and intensity only increased as the summer progressed.

One the eve of the beginning of the new school year, Amos went to bed early in an attempt to get a good night's sleep. At 3:40 a.m., he sat upright in bed, startled and dripping with perspiration. He had a feeling he was being chased and was overcome with an overwhelming sense of dread, a feeling that his life was in danger. In his dreams, there was always this pervasive fog, with Amos recognizing himself standing alone, holding something rather large and heavy in his hand. Then he would take off running in an attempt to find something. However, he never made it. The running continued, on and on, as if he were in a marathon. He felt his body ache, along with a sidesplitting pain that nearly overwhelmed him, but then he'd wake up.

During the subsequent hours, although Amos lay in bed with his eyes closed, he was awake, thinking about what the first day at school would be like. As soon as he slipped away into sleep once again, the alarm clock rang, and it was time to begin a new day. He could smell sausage frying downstairs.

In the kitchen, home of the beckoning aroma, Shirley stood by the stove, holding a spatula in one hand and cup of coffee in the other. "Good morning, Amos," Shirley remarked when she saw him enter.

"Good morning, Shirley," Amos replied.

"Hungry?"

"Yes, ma'am—at least a little, I suppose."

Shirley walked over to the table, picked up a plate, and then headed back toward the stove. "Did you sleep well?"

"Yes." Amos saw no need to openly discuss his sleeping problems or his odd nightmares with the woman, who could do nothing to solve either of them.

"That's good. I hope you're all ready for your first day of school."

"I'm not sure," Amos said, a bit of a more honest response.

"Just do your best and everything will work out."

After breakfast, Amos returned to his room to brush his teeth, put on his shoes, and grab his notebook and school supplies.

On his way out the front door, Shirley was there to bid him farewell, this time holding a brown paper bag. "It's your lunch."

Amos reached out to take it. "Thanks. I'll see you later."

From the Cobb house, it was roughly eighty yards to the nearest bus stop, a common area for Amos and two other kids who lived nearby. At the bus stop was Becky Woods, alone. The Woods family lived a few houses down from the Cobb house, and, unlike Herman and Shirley, they were new to the area.

His first encounter with Becky had been on a warm Saturday in early July. Amos had been outside and had spotted a moving van in front of a nearby vacant house. When he'd first laid eyes on Becky, she had walked around the van to get something out of a car. She'd been dressed in a casual pair of shorts and a t-shirt, and her hair was in a ponytail. After she'd closed the car door, Becky had turned and locked eyes with Amos. She had stood for a moment, smiled, and then offered a friendly wave. To Amos, she was a goddess. He'd felt as though his heart was going to explode right there in his chest. He'd offered a return wave, and then Becky had walked away and vanished behind the van.

They had met formally a week later, when Herman and Shirley had invited the Woods family for a meal and a welcoming to the neighborhood. Amos and Becky had become instant friends. From that day onward, they had been together every day for the remainder of the summer.

Becky smiled when she saw Amos making his way to the bus stop, and he picked up his pace the last thirty yards. "Hey, Becky."

"Good morning, Amos."

"You too. Where's Willie?"

"I don't know. Maybe he overslept or something."

"Is that your lunch?"

"Yeah. Where's yours?"

"I got lunch money. I'm going to try the school food, to see if it's good or not. I wonder what Shirley packed in your bag."

"Don't know. Probably a sandwich. Oh, here comes Willie."

Willie Cupp lived between Amos and Becky and was a lifetime resident of the community. He was wearing a pair of overalls draped over his stocky frame. His hair was black and neatly combed. Willie seemed nice enough to Amos, at least during the summer.

"He'd better hurry up," Becky said, nodding toward the oncoming bus.

When Willie saw the bus, he started jogging and arrived as the bus came to a complete stop.

"You just made it," Amos said as the doors swung open.

The bus driver was a middle-aged woman with shoulder-length brown hair and a pleasant smile. "Good morning, kids."

Becky entered first, followed by Amos and Willie. Their stop was one of the first on the route, and they had their pick of seats. Becky chose a row in the middle and claimed the window seat. Amos sat down beside her in the aisle seat.

In the back of the bus on the same side was a kid who spoke right away. "Look! If it isn't Daddy's little girl and Mama's boy," he said, loud enough to be heard.

When Amos turned to look, he saw the kid frowning at him, wagging his head in a taunting manner and forcing a smirk. Amos raised an eyebrow and stared at him for a few seconds, showing that he was neither humored nor intimidated.

"What are you staring at?" the kid said.

Amos reacted by rolling his eyes and then turned back toward Becky. "Becky, who is that wise guy?"

"I don't know. I'm new around here as well, you know."

"Yeah, I know. Maybe he'll just shut up."

"Maybe. But who cares if he doesn't. Ignore him and he'll go away…like a bug."

When the bus finally reached the final destination, Powers High, Amos and Becky headed off to find homeroom. Powers High School accommodated grades seven through twelve, roughly 800 kids. It was an old school, and Amos had already heard the tales from Herman Cobb, recounting his fond memories of Powers High. From the looks of the outside of the building, Amos reckoned that the last time it had been painted was, perhaps, during the Herman Cobb years. The block building was covered in a faded, thin coat of cream-colored paint, surrounded by several miniature, portable, mobile wooden structures that looked more like cabins for campers than classrooms for the seventh and eighth graders. One of them was their home-room, although it took a detour through the heart of the block building before that discovery was made.

The morning went smoothly for Amos and Becky. Around 12:15 p.m., they made their way to the school cafeteria for lunch. Amos, brown bag in hand, found a place at a long table while Becky waited in line for the lunch that was being served up by the kitchen staff. By the time she made it to the table, Amos was patiently waiting for her.

"You coulda started without me, you know."

"No problem," Amos said, peeking into the paper sack.

"What you got in there anyway?"

"Looks like a sandwich." Amos retrieved the ham and cheese sandwich and then commented on Becky's lunch. "Hey, that looks pretty decent."

"Yeah. It smells kinda good," Becky said, staring down at her meatloaf and mashed potatoes.

"What was your last school like?" Amos asked.

"Well, it was nice and all, but there were a lot more kids."

"Did you have many friends there?"

"I had some...actually one good one named Marsha."

"Do you miss her?"

"Yeah."

"Do you stay in touch?"

"Well, I wrote her three letters this summer, but she only wrote me once."

"Maybe she's been busy."

"Maybe."

"I wish I could remember more about my friends. Lester Cobb is the only person who really knows anything about my past."

"Have you thought about visiting him?"

"You mean at the carnival?"

Becky nodded. "Yeah."

"Not really. They keep moving all the time. They're far away right now, according to Shirley."

"Maybe you could stop by the next time they come back to town."

"I've thought about it, but I'm not sure. It just feels... strange."

"Do you ever remember anything at all?"

"Nope. Maybe my dad wasn't such a good person, so it's good I don't remember."

"So who's this Lester Cobb anyway? Was he your dad's friend or something?"

"I don't think so. From what I can tell, the other carnies didn't like my dad very much. Besides, he just took off and abandoned me after I got hurt, you know. I don't think a good dad would do something like that."

Becky responded with a concerned look for a moment and then tried to change the subject to something more pleasant. "Well, I think living in a carnival would be neat."

"I really can't say. Don't remember a thing about it. Anyway, how is the meatloaf?"

"Not bad. These mashed potatoes taste fake, like those flakes that come out of a box. I used to like my mom's mashed potatoes. She used real potatoes, milk, and sour cream," Becky said with a reflective, pained look on her face.

Amos did not pry. He knew her mother's death was somewhat of a sore spot and that life with her stepmother wasn't that great, and there wasn't any use pouring salt in open wounds. All things considered, it was easier to discuss food. "Sounds like Shirley's as well. We had chicken and mashed potatoes this past weekend. Good stuff," Amos replied quickly.

"I wonder what our teachers are gonna be like this afternoon," Becky said.

"Math and history, right?"

"Yeah, that sounds right."

"I don't look forward to seeing that moron from the bus again. He gets on my nerves already, and I don't even know him."

"He does seem like a jerk, that's for sure."

"Just stay away from him, Becky."

"I plan to."

"Let me know if he messes with you, and I'll take care of it."

"Hmm. Are you offering to be my bodyguard or something?"

"Not really, but I'm not going to stand by and let anyone pick on you."

"You're a good friend, Amos. Really. I'm glad we met."

After he devoured his sandwich, Amos excused himself to use the bathroom while Becky nibbled away at the remainder of her cafeteria meatloaf. It was a short walk to the facilities, just out the cafeteria door and down the hallway. There was a hazy fog in the bathroom, courtesy of a thick cigarette smoke hanging in the air. Amos didn't see anyone, but he noticed both stalls were in use. He walked to the sink, briefly looked at himself in the mirror, and then found a wall to lean on while he waited for an opening. A few seconds later he heard a flush, and a shaggy-haired kid emerged with an unlit cigarette hanging out of his mouth.

He looked at Amos with a scowl, as if Amos's very existence was an annoyance. "What are you looking at, faggot?"

Amos detached himself from the wall, stared him down, and silently walked past him into the stall. In that instant, he imagined himself kicking the door open and slapping that cigarette out of the kid's sassy mouth. Instead, he took a seat on the porcelain throne and buried his head in his hands.

About that time, the toilet flushed in the adjacent stall; the bathroom door opened and closed.

Amos continued to sit, waiting for the second occupant to leave, longing for some solitude.

By the time Amos returned to the cafeteria, Becky had finished eating and was placing her tray on the rack.

In the rear of the room, Amos again spotted the kid from the bus sitting at a booth, engaged in animated conversation. It seemed as though he was everywhere, and Amos felt annoyed by the sight of him.

"Hey," Becky said as she met him at the door. "Ready to go?"

Amos nodded, and they left together to find their afternoon math class.

The first school day ended with World History, Room 206, a portable classroom hosted by one Mrs. Henry. From there, it was on to the bus to complete the roundtrip home. Amos and Becky gravitated to the same seat they had chosen in the morning and, once again, their bully took the back seat. This time, however, he sat on the other side of the aisle. Unlike the morning, it was a hassle-free ride home. When the bus arrived at their stop, Amos, Becky, and Willie got off, and Willie said his goodbyes. Amos looked back at the bus and saw the mouthy kid staring him down through the window.

When he flipped Amos a finger, Amos didn't hesitate to return the gesture. As the bus pulled away, Amos stood there, his hand in the air, staring at the back window of the bus until it disappeared from sight.

"Amos, are you okay?" Becky asked.

"I'm fine." Amos dropped his hand and his protruded middle finger and turned toward Becky.

"What's up with the finger?"

"Just giving that kid a taste of his own medicine."

"Who?"

"You know...that jerk on the bus."

"His name is Trent."

"Trent?"

"Yep, Trent Givens. I remember from roll call this morning."

"Do you mind if I still refer to him as the jerk on the bus?"

"No, I guess not," she said with a laugh. "What did he do this time?"

"He flipped me the finger through the back window. I was just returning the favor."

"You aren't afraid of anything, are you?"

"I wouldn't say that, but I'm sure not afraid of Trent Givens."

"Do you want to get together later?"

"I'm not sure. We do have some homework, and I need to check with Shirley first. She may have some chores for me to do."

"Okay. Well, I'll see you tomorrow then."

"See ya, Becky."

Back at the Cobb house, Shirley was in the kitchen. Amos went up to his room to drop off his books and then returned downstairs. "Hi, Shirley."

"Oh, hi, Amos. How was your first day?"

"It was good."

"Well, tell me about it. Do you like your teachers?"

"Yes, they all seem nice enough."

"And Becky? Do you two have classes together?"

"Actually, we have every class together."

"That's great! She's such a wonderful girl."

"Yes, ma'am, Becky is great. What are you cooking tonight?"

"Fried chicken. It's Herman's favorite, you know. That oughtta lure him home on time tonight!"

"Can I help?"

"Well, let's see. You could take that bag of garbage out to the garage, for starters."

Amos grabbed the bag and left the kitchen through a side door that led to the large three-car garage. Herman Cobb was a handyman, and the last carport was entirely taken over by his tools; in fact, Amos imagined the man must have owned about every kind of tool there was. Out back, behind the garage, were several large drums where Amos deposited the garbage. Every two weeks, Herman took a trip to the county dump, and Amos had gone along for the ride a couple of times.

When Amos returned, Shirley stood at the sink washing potatoes. "I'm back," he declared, ready for his next assignment.

"Good. Now you can help me peel these potatoes." Shirley lifted a large pail from the sink and set the potatoes on the kitchen table. "Just take a seat in the chair, and you can peel them over this box."

Amos took the small paring knife from Shirley and grabbed a potato from the top of the heap. His first cut was deep, releasing more potato than peel. On the second potato, it got easier and the peels fell into the empty cardboard box that had once been home to bottles of Herman's beer.

"How are you doing with those potatoes, Amos?"

"Good. I think I'm getting the hang of it now."

"Do you have any homework?"

"Yeah, just a little reading."

"Well, you should get started with that after you finish with the potatoes. It will be a while before dinner is ready, and I'll call you."

"Okay. I will."

"I have a lot of fond memories of Powers High School, you know."

"You do?"

"Yes. I've lived here my entire life, and Herman and I went to school together. In fact, that was where we met. We were best friends right away, quite like you and Becky."

"That's neat." After pausing a moment to rid a particularly lumpy potato of a particularly stubborn knot, he asked, "Shirley, I have a question about Lester, if you don't mind."

"Okay. What do you want to know?"

"How did he end up working in the carnival, swallowing swords?"

"Well, I can't say I know all the details. Lester is much older than Herman, and I do know he didn't have a very good relationship with their father. Herman wasn't very close to his father either, and he was young when Lester left home. I think Lester was only eighteen when he joined the carnival."

"I still wonder how he ended up swallowing swords. It's a weird kind of hobby if you ask me—not something somebody just does for no reason."

"Lester told me once that when he first joined the carnival, he worked at a sideshow for sword swallower, somewhat of a mentor for him, I suppose."

"That sounds really cool. Do you know when the carnival will be back in this area? I was thinking about visiting Lester to see if it might help me remember anything."

"I haven't heard from Lester for a while, but I'm sure he'll contact us when he's back in town. Have you been thinking about this a lot lately?"

"Yes. It's really frustrating. It's as if my life began when I woke up in the hospital, and I feel like I don't know who I am. Besides, I'd like to talk to Lester about my dad. Maybe he can help me fill in some of the blanks."

"Hang in there, Amos. I'm sure your memory will return someday."

"Thanks, Shirley. I really do appreciate you and Herman letting me live here."

"You are most welcome, Amos. You are a delight to have in the house, especially since we cannot have children of our own. It is our pleasure."

After Amos finished with the potatoes, he headed upstairs to his room. The house was a traditional colonial style, with three bedrooms upstairs. Amos had taken over one of the spare bedrooms, and the other one had been converted into a sewing room for Shirley. His room was spacious, accommodating two freestanding bookcases and a large desk under the window. The floor was hardwood, with a couple of throw rugs that had been sewn by Shirley. The bed was an antique that had been handed down to Shirley from her grandmother. There was a painting on each wall; Amos was particularly drawn to the one hanging behind his bed, artwork depicting what appeared to be either a carnival or a circus. Although Amos had had no decorative input in his accommodations, he felt comfortable nonetheless.

When Herman arrived home at 5:30, Amos made his way down the staircase.

"Hello, Amos. I was just about to call you," Herman said.

"Hi, Herman. I heard a car door and figured it was you."

"Yep. The smell of Shirley's chicken had me speeding to get here! Let's eat!" he said, rubbing his belly.

"Sounds good to me."

Amos and Herman each took a seat, and Shirley entered with the platter of fried chicken. "I hope you two are hungry."

"I know I am!" Herman answered.

"Amos helped me peel the potatoes."

"He did? Well, it looks like he did a good job."

"Thanks," Amos said.

"I heard from Lester today."

"You did?" Amos responded, surprised at the seemingly coincidental timing.

"Why, Amos and I were just talking about Lester earlier this afternoon. What's the news?"

"He just called to see how we were all doing. He actually remembered this was Amos's first day at school. Lester always has had a great memory."

"I wish I did," Amos responded.

Herman smiled a reassuring smile and went on, "Lester said the carnival will be heading back this way in early October."

"Really? I'd love to go," Amos replied. "I want to have a look around and see if anything—or anyone—is familiar to me. Maybe it will help me remember something."

"I'll talk to Lester, and we'll make plans to get together."

After Amos polished off a breast, a drumstick, and a good helping of mashed potatoes and gravy, he helped clear the table and then headed back to his room. During supper, he had been relatively quiet, preoccupied with seeing Lester Cobb again and spending time at the carnival. When he got back to his room, he tried to take his mind off that for a while by reading a chapter ahead in his science book.

At 9:30, Shirley made her usual goodnight rounds. Amos was allowed to stay up until 10:00, but he was tired and ready to turn in for the evening.

At 3:27 a.m., Amos awoke from his usual nightmare. Each time it happened, he checked the alarm clock. He began to notice a pattern: He always seemed to awake between between 3:00 and 4:00 a.m. Amos wiped the perspiration off his brow and got up to use the bathroom. He tried to be as quiet as possible, but the creaky old wooden floor wouldn't cooperate, especially out in the upstairs hallway. Back in his room, he walked over to look out his window. It was a clear September evening, and the stars were bright. At that moment, he thought of his own insignificance. There he was, a teen in a small Canadian town, peering out into the vastness of the universe, with no real understanding of himself, much less the meaning of life—if there even was one. The feeling was so intense that he felt like screaming, until he imagined the loud sound and a panicked Herman and Shirley. When the thought left his mind, he went back to bed, where he lay staring up at the ceiling for a while before finally shutting his eyes.

CHAPTER 18

CARNY TIME AGAIN

Time passed quickly, and by early October, Amos had adjusted well to the routine of school. He had also been anticipating the arrival of the carnival, which was about sixty miles away, outside one of the larger nearby towns. During the week leading up to the carnival, Amos and Becky spoke of it often. Now that the day had finally arrived, he was as excited as he was anxious. After lunch, Herman led the way to the garage, and they all loaded up in Shirley's station wagon. Amos and Becky took the back seat.

The path leading up to the carnival was a dirt road, off a two-lane highway. It looked like a large track of empty farmland to Amos. When they arrived, they were waved on by the parking attendants, who were trying to maintain some semblance of organization. It had rained the day before, leaving mud puddles and sludge patches in its wake.

The old station wagon struggled through a couple of slippery spots and slipped in next to a large truck.

"We're here!" Herman announced, as all four of the car doors opened and then shut in rapid succession.

"Let's walk on this side," Shirley said, pointing away from the mud puddles.

At the front gate, three separate lines of people had formed. There was a buzz of excitement: people talking, children laughing, and the sounds of the carnival filling the air. At the cashier, Herman paid for all four tickets. They all entered through a turnstile, getting a hand stamp in the process. As Amos stood still for a moment, absorbing the energy from the surroundings, he felt a fleeting sense of déjà vu. It almost felt like home, yet Amos recognized nothing familiar.

"Now, kids, there are a lot of people here. Let's try to stay together. If anyone gets separated for any reason, come back to the entrance and wait here for the others."

"Okay, Shirley," Amos answered, overwhelmed by another sense of déjà vu, as if he'd heard those same warnings before, from another loving female voice, back when he was a little child.

"I think we should just walk around until we find Lester's show," Herman said in a loud voice, trying to speak over the commotion.

Herman and Shirley walked in front, with Amos and Becky lagging behind a few steps. Up ahead, they could see the "Swords of Death" sign. Lester's show had already begun. The entrance to the tent was roped off, and a crowd of people was gathered inside, ooh-ing and ah-ing at what their eyes beheld.

"Sounds like Lester is hard at work," Herman said, hearing the reaction of the people within.

"Do you think we could just go in?" Shirley asked. "I don't see anyone standing guard."

"I think we should wait," Herman replied. "The shows don't last too long."

Amos looked up to read the advertisements. The billboards were custom art, depicting Lester Cobb swallowing swords. On one side, mounted to a pole, a loudspeaker extolled the death-defying acts of Lester Cobb in a running sound bite loop: "Lester Cobb, the greatest sword swallower on Earth! Step inside and see Lester perform feats that defy human ability. Lester Cobb, known the world over, will swallow, before your very eyes, six swords at one time. Ladies and gentlemen, prepare to be amazed, astounded, and mesmerized. Prepare to see something you will never forget! The amazing Lester Cobb will defy death in front of your very eyes!...Lester Cobb, the greatest sword swallower on Earth! Step inside..."

"Wow! That sounds pretty dramatic," Amos said, as the tape recording began to repeat.

Herman smiled. "Guess what. That's Lester's voice! I think he recorded that a long time ago, but it must do the trick and draw people in, because he's been using the same one for all these years."

About that time, thunderous applause came from inside the tent, and people began to exit.

"I guess the show is over already," Shirley remarked.

After the crowd was gone, Herman poked his head inside.

Lester emerged from the side of the stage and caught sight of his brother. "Come on in, you guys!" he said. Waving, Lester stepped down and moved to shake hands with Herman. Next, he gave Shirley a hug and then turned to his old friend. "Amos! How are you, son?"

"I'm doing fine."

Lester put his arm around Amos. "It really is good to see you."

"You too. This is my friend Becky."

"Hello there, Becky. It's nice to meet ya. We can always use more pretty faces around here, what with all of us freaks running about!" Lester extended his hand for a shake.

"How'd your show go? Sounded like everyone was enjoying your act," Herman asked.

"Yeah, it was good."

"Do you still run the show all by yourself?" Shirley asked.

"Yep, and it keeps me busy. Of course, I do miss Amos. He used to drop by and help me once in a while. It can get lonely, ya know."

Amos smiled, pleased that Lester thought so fondly of him, but he was sad that he had no recollection of the fun times they'd spent together.

"When is your next show?" Herman asked.

"In about twenty minutes or so. I assume you'll be staying to watch?"

"Of course," Herman replied. "But twenty minutes? That's not much of a break."

"I generally do three shows close together, then take a break for a couple of hours."

While Herman and Lester continued to talk, Amos walked up and examined the stage closely, hoping to see something that might jog his memory. The stage was really quite plain, not the usual flamboyant carnival fanfare. There was a backdrop with some strange-looking artwork, and in the center sat a stool and a cylindrical can.

"You can hop up there and have a look around if you'd like, Amos. Heaven knows you've had plenty of walks around my set before."

Amos took advantage of Lester's offer and stepped up on the stage. The first thing he did was check out the swords. The cylindrical can was actually a sword rack, with a dozen slots, each occupied with a unique blade. From there, Amos moved toward the back of the stage and examined the mural. Truly, it was eerie-looking artwork: a man with horns standing in the midst of angelic creatures. The horned man's head was tilted back, and his mouth was agape, revealing the dark pit of his throat. His unusually long arms were stretched upward, as if beseeching some heavenly force to help him with his feat. At the top of the mural was a sword, enveloped in an array of light and fire, descending in the direction of the man's open mouth. Amos sensed that he was seeing something familiar. Something drew him toward the art, yet his brain would not cooperate in summoning up the memories. There were no flashbacks, no distinct remembrances or moments of clarity; there was only a feeling. After his exploration, Amos decided to rejoin the rest of the family, who had all made their way toward the tent entrance—all except for Becky, who had patiently waited at the stage for Amos.

"Amos, Mr. Cobb's next show is going to start in a few minutes. They're headed back outside. Mr. Cobb said we could wait right here by the stage," Becky said.

Amos joined Becky front and center. Within a few minutes, people started coming into the tent, including Herman and Shirley. As Amos stood there, he was again smacked with a strong sensation of déjà vu, as though he had once stood in the very spot he now occupied.

Following the show, Lester visited with Herman and Shirley for a while before he and Amos departed from the group. "You were very good friends with the gentleman I'm going to take you to visit," Lester explained. "His name is Dr. Drake, but most people around here just call him Doc."

"I remember you telling me about him in the hospital that day."

"Oh yeah, that's right. After your accident, poor ol' Doc had a pretty serious stroke. He was in another hospital for a while, and I'm sad to say he hasn't ever fully recovered."

"I wish I could remember him," Amos replied.

"That's okay. Doc, of all people, understands because he's a doctor, after all. He'll be glad to see you either way. He's had a hard time getting around since the stroke. He took care of everyone else around here for a long time, and now everyone is pitching in to take care of Doc."

Amos followed Lester to the entrance of a small trailer.

Lester knocked on the thin door. "Hey, Doc, it's Lester. I'm coming in…and I've got a visitor here that you're gonna wanna see!"

Inside, an elderly gentleman sat in a recliner.

"Hey, Doc! It's good to see you sitting up tonight. Here he is, just like I promised." Lester motioned for Amos to step forward.

"Hi there," Amos said in as friendly a tone as he could muster.

"Well, hello there, my boy! It's so, so good to see you. I've really missed you." Doc leaned forward, offering an invitation for a hug.

"Good to see you too, sir," Amos replied, hugging him back.

"What's with this sir business? It's Doc!"

"Sorry. It's good to see you, Doc."

"Well, I'm going to run a quick errand, so I'll leave you two alone to catch up." Lester turned back toward the door.

"Amos, my boy, sit for a spell. You know, you and I used to be good friends."

"That's what Mr. Cobb told me. I'm sorry, sir…er, Doc, but I just can't remember."

"No need to apologize. I understand. I'm a doctor after all."

Amos smiled.

"So why don't you tell me about your life?"

"Well, I live with Herman and Shirley Cobb now. I get to go to school with my good friend Becky, and she's in all my classes."

"I'm glad you're in school. Said all along that's where a bright boy like you needed to be. I'll bet you are doing well."

"Yeah, so far. Actually, I can't believe how easy it's been, considering they tell me I'd never been in a normal school before."

"That doesn't surprise me at all. You used to read my medical books, you know."

"Your medical books?"

"Oh yes! You couldn't get enough of them. You see that book there on the coffee table? I got it out when I heard you'd be paying me a visit. It's a book on the brain. I think it was one of your favorites."

"Really?" Amos bent forward to take a closer look.

"Go 'head. You can pick it up."

"The brain, huh? And why was I so interested in that?" Amos thumbed through a few pages.

"You seemed to be interested in knowing why people think the way they do. Anyway, tell me, have you made any new friends?"

"Well, like I said, there's Becky. She's actually with me tonight."

"Ah, yes. You did mention her, didn't you? Damn this stroke, makin' me forget all sorts of things. Good for you, though, Amos. Good for you! Friends are important. Has Lester told you very much about your life here, before the accident?"

"Well, he mentioned that I lived with my father Bill Konklin, who ran a sideshow or a game of some kind, the High Striker."

"You don't remember any of that?"

"No, sir. I'm afraid I don't. I wish I could remember."

"Perhaps it will all come back to you someday."

"Maybe, but the doctors couldn't make any promises. But tell me about you. How are you doing after your stroke?"

"To be honest, my health is not very good. On top of that stroke I suffered just after your…well, your accident, I have heart problems as well. It's difficult for me to move or even breathe these days, and I do forget things now and again."

"I'm sorry, Doc."

"It's okay. I've lived a good life, and meeting people like you has made it all worthwhile."

It was a compliment for which Amos had no suitable response, so he remained quiet.

Dr. Drake continued, "Amos, I need to tell you something I've never told anyone else. Actually, it's something you told me once."

"Me?"

"Yes. You told me back then that your name is not really Amos Konklin at all and that Bill Konklin is not your father."

"I said that?"

"Yes. It was a brief conversation, and you didn't go into details. You seemed uneasy about it and asked me not to tell anyone."

"Hmm. That's a shocker. I'm not sure what to say." Amos sat for a moment, trying to absorb the revelation, and then asked, "So...did I mention my real name or anything else about my past?"

"You told me your biological parents named you Larry."

"Larry? That's it? No last name?"

"Nope. Just Larry."

"I still don't know what to say," Amos repeated.

"I hope this doesn't upset you. I just thought—well, considering the circumstances—that you'd want to know. Besides, I don't know how much longer I'm going to be around."

"I'm so sorry, Doc, but thanks for telling me. I do appreciate it, and maybe it will help me remember who I am."

"You're most welcome, my boy."

In spite of the fact that their prior bond had melted away in the ocean of Amos's amnesia, another bond had formed between the two during that short visit. Amos felt comfortable around Doc, and vice versa, and the conversation flowed easily until Lester Cobb appeared in the doorway.

"I'm back!" announced Lester. "I hope you two have had a chance to do some catching up," he said.

"We sure did, Lester. We really did," Doc replied.

"I don't mean to break up your happy reunion, Doc, but I need to get Amos back to Herman and Shirley."

"I understand, Lester. Thanks for bringing my old friend by to see me."

Amos stood and extended his hand to Dr. Drake. "I've really enjoyed talking to you. Thanks very much."

"You take good care of yourself, my boy," Doc replied, choking back his emotion.

"I will," Amos said.

After connecting again with Herman, Shirley, and Becky, Amos told Lester goodbye and thanked him again for facilitating his most meaningful and comforting visit with Dr. Drake.

From "Swords of Death," it was on to the other carnival sights. Finally, Amos caught sight of a large mechanical object, quite like the one from his dream the night before. He rushed over to take a closer look, Becky right on his heels, and he found a game in progress; a tall, skinny man, perhaps thirty years old, was holding a mallet with both hands firmly gripping the handle.

The carny spoke, "Step right up, ladies and gentlemen. It's two swings for fifty cents or five swings for a dollar. All you gotta do is strike the platform hard enough to ring that bell at the top. Simple enough, eh? It's the High Striker, a game of skill and strength."

Amos was mesmerized as the tall man made five attempts at ringing the bell but fell short each time. Lester had told Amos about the High Striker, but his descriptions had fallen short of the reality.

"Amos, isn't that the game you and your dad used to be in charge of?"

"Yes, Becky. I think so."

"I've seen it before. I went to a carnival once with my older brother and watched him play it. He's a big, strong guy, but he didn't win."

"Just like that last guy. Let's see what happens with the next person in line," Amos said, referring to a man in front of what now appeared to be a short line of three or four people. He was a large fellow, upwards of 300 pounds.

"Yeah, he's a big fella, way bigger than my brother. Maybe he has a chance," Becky said.

The man placed fifty cents in the carny's hand.

"He must be pretty confident that he'll win, Becky. He only paid for two swings."

The man selected the largest, heaviest mallet and stood back a couple of feet from the platform. He lifted the mallet with both arms behind his head and grunted as he swung. The results were disastrous: The block on the cable only rose about halfway and then fell back to the ground. He swung again with an even louder grunt, to no avail.

"Does this bring back any memories?"

"I'm not sure. I mean, I don't remember anything specific. I just have this feeling…you know, like I've been here before."

"I think I understand," Becky said.

"Amos, what do you think?" Shirley and Herman had caught up. "Are you gonna give it a try?"

"No. I think I already know the outcome."

They stood and watched as the next four people in line played the striker, and all walked away in defeat.

"Would anyone like to get something to eat?" Shirley asked.

Everyone agreed, although Amos was a bit reluctant. He followed the group to a nearby food kiosk, all the while gazing back at the action going on at the High Striker.

After getting hot dogs, they walked on to check out the other sights of the carnival. Toward the end of the evening, they made a final stop back at the High Striker and then went to say goodbye to Lester Cobb.

The trip home was quiet. Amos had looked forward to the day for so long, and it was already over. He had some reflecting to do.

CHAPTER 19

CHANGES

The following years in Canada passed quickly for Amos. One Saturday morning in late July, following Amos's seventeenth birthday, Becky stopped by the Cobb house as Amos was out in the front yard, trimming the hedge. She waved at him, and he stopped what he was doing.

"Hey there!"

"Hi, Becky."

"What are you up to today?"

"Just doing a little yard work for Herman and Shirley. What about you?"

"That's what I wanted to talk to you about. Trent has invited me to a party at his parents' cabin."

"Great." Amos rolled his eyes.

"You disapprove, of course."

"I can't believe you actually like hanging out with that asshole."

"God, Amos. You are so harsh. Trent's not so bad if you'd just give him a chance."

"Me? No, I get it, Becky. He's a pretty boy, to die for, and you just can't resist."

"That's not fair! You really don't know him. People can change, Amos, and you're holding stuff against him from years ago."

"It's fair, all right. Look, you can do whatever you want. I just can't believe you are so gullible."

"You've always been my best friend, Amos, but lately, you've really been difficult."

"Lately?"

"Well, mostly this past year. You know how I know people can change? Because you have, and it's been for the worse. I mean, you're the same, but you are so much more hard-headed now and less forgiving. I know your dreams have been tormenting you. You've been having those awful nightmares for years, and it's about time you talk to someone about them besides me. I'm not a shrink, Amos. I'm just your friend."

"A shrink? What are you saying? You think I'm crazy?"

"I didn't say that, but I think you do need help. Everyone does sometimes. It's not a sign of weakness to ask for it. Besides, you don't even confide in Herman and Shirley."

"Why should I? I don't want to lay this stuff on them. What good would that do anyway? They're nice people. They don't need to know everything that goes on in my head. It's not their responsibility to deal with my baggage."

"Amos, the things you tell me are pretty intense. I think it's starting to affect your judgment, bleeding over into our friendship. Look, I need space. I need to be able to choose my own friends without having to ask for your approval. Can you understand that?"

"I understand, Becky. Like I said, you can do whatever you want."

"See what I mean? It's always the same sarcastic crap with you. I stopped by today just to talk. I don't even know why I bother. I shouldn't even have to tell you where I'm going. I'm not even sure why I'm here. The lines are blurring for me when it comes to us, Amos. You've always been my best friend, and I feel like I need to tell you everything, but I'm starting to realize I can't tell you anything."

"Well, Becky, maybe you shouldn't. Seriously, you should feel free to do what you want without including me in any decisions." Amos turned his back and walked toward the open garage without another word.

"Amos!" Becky shouted.

He never turned back to answer.

CHAPTER 20

TURNING POINT

Early that afternoon, the infamous Trent Givens stopped by Becky's house to pick her up in the Mustang convertible he'd been given for his seventeenth birthday. He had arrived just in time to take Becky's mind off Amos, and Becky found him to be a welcome diversion. He opened the car door for her like a perfect gentleman, and they took off toward the cabin.

It was a beautiful, sunny afternoon, a perfect day for a drive. Becky enjoyed the quiet ride along the shady back roads, her hair blowing in the wind. The hour-long trip passed quickly.

Becky had just closed her eyes and was settling into a daydream when Trent turned off onto a side road—a dirt road with a barely visible sign revealing it to be Givens Lane. The road was bumpy and stretched for a half-mile into the woods, terminating by the side of a cabin. "This is it," Trent said. Then he got out of the car and walked behind it to pop the trunk, where he'd stored a large cooler.

"Need any help?" Becky asked, still sitting in the front seat.

"Naw. I got it. It's just a cooler."

"A cooler full of what?"

"All kinds of stuff—food, beer, snacks…you know, all the stuff we need for a proper party."

"Did you say beer?"

"Sure did."

"And just how did you manage that?"

"I've got my ways."

"You know it's illegal, Trent."

"Relax, Becky. Geez. We're just here to have a good time. No one is going to get wasted or anything like that. We're just gonna hang out and have some fun, like kids are supposed to."

The cabin was an old wooden structure, part log and pine siding. It looked weathered, with moss covering the tin roof and green mold creeping from the ground upward along the sides. In the back was a metal swing set, old and rusty.

"Did you play on those swings when you were young or something?" Becky asked as she finally got out of the car and walked toward the cabin.

"Yeah. We used to come out here a lot when I was a kid. This cabin was built by my grandpa a long time ago, and he left it to my dad when he died."

"Do your parents still come out here?"

"Sometimes, but not so much anymore." Trent grunted as he heaved the heavy cooler from the trunk. "Make way," he said as he ran by Becky toward the front porch, holding on tightly. "Damn. This thing's heavier than I thought," he said, welcoming the relief of the front steps.

"I asked if you needed any help."

"Naw, I got it. Just a couple more steps." He lifted and grunted again, and when he made it to the porch, he found a bench and set the monstrosity down. "That oughtta do it."

The front porch ran all along the front side of the cabin, and there was a porch swing on the left side, nearest to the car.

Trent dug into his pocket and pulled out a key chain. After fumbling around for a few seconds, he isolated a key and placed it in the lock on the door. "Come on." Trent motioned to Becky to join him inside.

"You go ahead." Becky took a detour to the porch swing. She sat cautiously, taking notice of the rusted chains attached to the porch ceiling by some even rustier fixtures. "I wanna stay out here and enjoy the fresh air for a minute, if you don't mind."

"Uh, okay," Trent said before he went inside. Minutes later, he emerged from the cabin. "Hey. Comfortable?"

"Yes. It's such a pretty day."

"Well, I'm gonna go back inside and take care of a few things. Feel free to join me anytime." Trent lifted the cooler from the bench with a grunt.

Becky stared out at the lake for a few seconds and then closed her eyes, gently rocking back and forth in the swing. She could hear the sounds from inside the cabin as Trent moved about, but they soon faded into the background as she drifted into a peaceful afternoon nap. It felt like her eyes had only been closed for a moment before she was awakened by the sound of a car door slamming shut. Startled awake, she noticed Wayne Albright and Amanda Stone from school.

About that time, Trent came out of the cabin. "So you're awake, I see. You fell asleep for a while."

"How long?" she asked, yawning and stretching.

"I'd say about thirty minutes or so."

"Wow. It feels like I just shut my eyes."

"Well, it was a while. I figured I'd leave you alone and let you sleep."

"Dude, how are you?" Wayne said to Trent as he made his way toward the cabin. He was seventeen, very good looking, and the captain of the football team. "Oh, hey, Becky," he said before Trent could respond.

"Hi, Wayne," Becky replied.

"Dude, what's up?" Trent shouted from the porch.

By that time, Amanda was out of the car. She was also seventeen, a cheerleader, and in every high school club imaginable. She and Becky were not exactly the best of friends, but they did find occasion to socialize during the Future Business Leaders of Canada activity after school, the FBLC. Amanda joined Becky on the swings while Wayne and Trent walked down toward the lake and started tossing a football back and forth. During the next hour, four more couples arrived. All the girls settled onto the porch while the boys opted for football.

Becky had never considered herself the popular type, so she felt a bit out of place among four cheerleaders and the class president. Most of her years in school had been spent hanging out with Amos Konklin, who was more of a loner. Although Amos was not popular, he didn't exactly fit the nerdy criteria either. He was the smartest kid in school, but he possessed his own unique place among the student body. He wasn't picked on; rather, people just left him alone. Becky assumed he'd established that reputation early on, after a couple of fights during his first year in junior high. In each case, although not the initiator, he was the finisher, taking the fight to the public square at school and handily whooping his opponents. With Amos by her side, the other students generally left her alone. However, now she was in Trent's world, immersed in everything that went along with that level of popularity among the clique-infested high school culture.

Around 4:00 p.m., the boys wrapped up their football game and joined the girls at the cabin. Trent broke out the cooler, and beer began to flow freely. Once everyone had a drink in hand, Trent went behind the cabin and pulled around a barbecue grill, placing it by the front porch stairs.

"There he is, my man. The chef!"

Trent smiled at Billy Pressman. "That's right, dude. Get ready for burgers, cooked in the traditional Givens style. I'm gonna use my old man's method."

"And what method is that?" Wayne asked.

"Gentlemen, the secret is to slow cook these puppies to perfection!"

"Ooh," came the simultaneous, sarcastic response from the five boys.

"That's right, boys. Ooh is right!"

Becky watched the entire scene, listening intently to the dialogue. It seemed life was simple for the guys, all about football and grilling out. *Is it possible,* she thought, *that there could actually be some perceivable difference in a hamburger cooked by Trent versus someone else?* It was silly to her, and she was amused. She found it fascinating that the boys could compete in jest, since the girls adopted a different model of interaction. In that estrogen-fueled group, a girl never really knew where she stood, and a catfight could break out at any minute over the simplest of things.

Around 5:00 p.m., the grilling was complete. Trent was noticeably proud of his accomplishment, enthusiastically inviting everyone to grab a burger.

"Dude, gimme one of those," Wayne said, ignoring any protocol as to who should be first in line.

"Whatever happened to ladies first?" Amanda piped in.

A roar of laughter ensued after Wayne excused himself with a loud, "Well, excuse me!"

"I'm just kidding, Wayne. Go ahead. I'm sure there are more than enough to go around."

"All right then," Wayne replied.

After Wayne grabbed the first burger, the boys quickly jumped up into single file, each one taking their turn.

Back at the porch, Trent had set up a small table with all the fixings. Wayne threw on a slice of cheddar, followed by ketchup, mustard, and mayonnaise. In his first huge bite, he managed to devour nearly one-third of the massive sandwich. "Dang! This *is* awesome. Nice job, dude."

"I'm glad you like it," Trent replied, gratified by the compliment.

After the boys were finished, the girls made their way off the porch—all except for Becky, who lingered on the swing.

"Are you coming, Becky?" Trent asked.

"I'll be down in a few minutes."

"Hey, I'll tell ya what. Tell me what you like, and I'll bring it to you."

"Oh, how sweet," Janet remarked sarcastically, rolling her eyes. Janet Jamison was a cheerleader and very popular.

Becky didn't know her very well, but from her experience, it seemed that most of Janet's remarks were more often sardonic than not.

"That's right, Janet. I'm sweet as hell, ain't I?" Trent joked.

"I'll take just a little ketchup, nothing else," Becky replied meekly.

"What about cheese?"

"Sure. A slice of cheese would be fine."

A couple minutes later, after a brief stop for some cheese and ketchup, Trent walked over to the porch swing. "Here you go." He extended a burger plate to Becky. "You want a beer or anything?"

"Um…you got any Coke in that cooler of yours?"

"Yep."

"I'll have one of those, if you don't mind."

"Coming right up, milady."

Around 6:00 p.m., after everyone had finished eating their fill of Givens special recipe burgers, the boys started a drinking contest. Trent brought out a bottle of whiskey from his father's stock in the cabin pantry, along with a shot glass. The trick was to gun a shot of whiskey, followed by an entire bottle of beer. By the end of the contest, the whiskey was empty, shared amongst Trent, Wayne, and Tommy.

"Dude, I concede," Tommy said.

"What about you, Wayne?"

"Man, I'm done too."

"You guys are gonna pussy out already? Well, I guess that makes me the winner!" Trent walked over and gave Tommy a mild shove.

"Who you calling a pussy?" Tommy replied with an air of irritation.

"You!" Trent responded, followed by an obnoxious cackle.

"I fucking hate it when you're drunk, dude! You're such a dumb-ass, and you say all that dumb shit."

"Listen, Tommy, I ain't fucking drunk."

"Sure, Trent."

"Don't be such a smart-ass, Tommy. I saw you down about half that bottle yourself."

"Yeah, but I can hold my liquor. You, on the other hand, are a lightweight."

"Oh, I see. You're Tommy the great, the big man who can hold his liquor! What the fuck does that mean anyway? Hold your liquor? That's about the stupidest thing I've ever heard. You ain't seen me puking mine up, have you? I still say you're a pussy, a quitter, and you know as well as I do that I can drink your ass under the table any day."

"You know, Trent, you're a real asshole."

"Hey, Tommy," Wayne intervened, "don't take it personally. Just forget about it, man. For me? Just forget about it."

"Hey, Wayne," Trent said, "don't go pampering that pussy."

As Becky looked on, it became obvious to her that the mood had quickly disintegrated, revealing that dark, obnoxious side of Trent that she remembered from junior high, the one Amos always warned her about. Unfortunately, the alcohol only intensified his jerk tendencies, and she thought it was time to intervene. "Hey, you guys, calm down." Becky hurried down the front porch stairs and grabbed Trent's hand. "Trent, please calm down, okay? You've all been drinking, and it's probably best to just sit down and stop arguing right now. I don't think anyone here wants to see a fight. We're all friends, remember?"

"Amen to that," Amanda stated in agreement.

"Whatever," Trent said, shoving Becky's arm away as if he couldn't stand the touch of her.

The atmosphere remained quiet for a minute before Wayne attempted to break the silence and the tension by changing the subject. "Did you guys hear the latest news about Coach Carlson?"

As Tommy began a request to hear more details, Trent drowned him out by raising his voice. "We don't wanna hear about Coach Carlson. Who wants to listen to fucking gossip? You guys wanna hear a story? How 'bout this one? A guy invites his friends to a cabin party, and they turn into a bunch of drunk assholes, so he tells them he wants all of them gone. Right now! Just fucking leave! I don't want you assholes here!"

"Okay, dude. You don't gotta ask me twice. I'm outta here." Tommy motioned to Amy with a nod. "Come on. Let's go."

"Good!" Trent shouted as the three other couples followed their lead. No further words were exchanged as the so-called friends got into the cars and left.

Wayne and Amanda lingered for a few minutes to make sure all was well. Wayne was Trent's best friend, and he didn't seem alarmed by the behavior. He had remained calm, and Becky thought that perhaps he had seen the crass behavior before and had learned to ignore it.

Amanda leaned over toward Becky and whispered quietly, "Why don't you leave with Wayne and me? Since Wayne is a bit toasted, I'll drive and drop you off at your house. Trent should stay here tonight and sleep it off. He'll be okay tomorrow."

"Hey, what are you two whispering about?" Trent slurred, his tone remaining obnoxious.

"Amanda, I'll be fine," Becky replied. "You guys just go. I'll make sure Trent gets home."

"But if you take him in his car to his house, how will you get home from there? He sure as hell can't drive you."

"I'll figure that out. Maybe I can drop him off and keep the car at my house tonight."

"Are you sure?"

"Yeah, I'm sure."

Wayne was attempting to have a rational conversation with Trent, but Trent was drunk far beyond the point of cooperation.

Amanda interrupted, "Wayne, let's go. Becky will make sure Trent gets home safe."

"Okay, cool. Give me just a minute, and I'll meet you at the car."

Amanda looked at Becky and gave her an unexpected hug.

Becky was surprised by the gesture but welcomed it nonetheless. Once they broke their awkward embrace, she made her way back to the top of the front porch stairs and sat down. She watched as Wayne and Amanda got into their car.

Amanda backed up toward the swing set, and as she turned the car to move forward, she gave Becky a final wave.

Becky kept staring at the car until the taillights faded into the evening dusk.

Trent was standing by the barbeque grill with a beer in his hand, looking off toward the lake. When he turned to look at Becky, there was a cold stare in his eyes. It was frightening. He walked toward her rapidly, in silence, and when he reached the top of the front porch stairs, he grabbed her by the arm and jerked her toward the front door.

"What are you doing, Trent? Let go of me!" Becky's appeal quickly turned to desperation as his fingers dug deeply into her arm. It was an unknown feeling, like what Becky had imagined it would feel like to be the victim of a crocodile, caught in its powerful jaws. As she fell forward, her nails dug into the wooden porch, but her resistance was overcome by Trent as she slid through the door and into the foyer. "Trent, what are you doing?"

Trent remained silent, answering her only with his cruel actions.

Thoughts and images raced through Becky's brain. *Is he going to beat me, kill me, rape me—or all of them? Oh God! What have I gotten myself into? I should have listened to Amos!*

His forceful manhandling continued, and he dragged her toward the center of the cabin, where he finally let go of her arm and pounced on her like a cat, hovering.

With both of her arms pinned to the floor, all Becky could think of was to spit in his face.

"Bitch!" Trent responded with a reciprocal action, then struck her with the back of his hand. He reached down and tore her shirt open.

"Why? Trent, why are you doing this to me?" Becky screamed.

"Because I can!"

"Stop it, Trent, you bastard! Get your hands off me!"

"I might be a bastard, but you're still a bitch...and a prude!" He grabbed at her bra, pulling it up toward her face, revealing her breasts.

Becky continued to squirm. *My God, he's really going to hurt me. Amos was right. Why didn't I listen to him?*

When Trent rose up on his knees to unzip his pants, Becky freed herself momentarily. As she crawled away, Trent grabbed her leg and pulled her back close enough for a slap to the face, which stunned her. He unfastened her pants roughly, and after a couple of strong tugs, her naked frame lay on the floor of the cabin, exposed and vulnerable. In a last attempt to break free, she hit him as hard as she could with both arms to the chest. It was futile, however, as he pinned her arms back to the floor and lay on her. She felt the full force of his weight as he penetrated her and then thrust violently. The pain was excruciating, but within a few seconds, it was over. He rolled off her and onto his back.

Becky felt helpless and defeated for a moment, but in the next, she was overcome with rage. She quickly stood, pulled up her pants, and kicked him in the groin with all the force she could summon, causing him to shriek in pain and roll over on his side. This was her moment, and she seized the opportunity while he lay vulnerable. She grabbed a lamp from a nearby coffee table and swung it at full force into the left side of his head. When she raised it up in preparation for another blow, she noticed he was already unconscious. Sobbing and hysterical, she dropped the lamp to the floor, then stood for a few seconds, looking down at his motionless body. The time that passed felt like an eternity, and then, in shock, she dropped to the floor, wiping away the tears with her trembling hands. She wondered if he was dead but dismissed those thoughts in order to focus on getting away as quickly as possible. With trembling hands, she found his car keys in his front pocket. It was a surreal moment; the unbelievable had just happened.

Trent opened his eyes and called her name, yet he appeared to remain immobilized. It was a confirmation that he was still alive and a threat, so she ran out of the cabin, not looking back until she reached the car. It had been a nice day with a nightmare ending, and all she could think of was getting home.

During the following week, Becky found herself avoiding Amos as much as possible. She had told no one about the incident, but Amos was growing suspicious. He asked her about the mark on her face, but she had dismissed it as an accident.

Trent, on the other hand, had not attempted to speak with Becky at all. He didn't even seem vaguely interested in whether or not she had told anyone, even the police. *Perhaps he's too embarrassed,* Becky thought, *or maybe he feels guilty and is waiting for it all to come out.* In any case, he used Wayne as his intermediary. He and Amanda had stopped by Becky's house the next day to pick up Trent's car.

Becky assumed her attacker had lied to them—and everyone—about what had happened, but she didn't really care. All she wanted was some way to remove the burden and to somehow forget, but the emotions lingered for another couple of weeks, until she was unable to hold it inside any longer. The one person she could tell, she felt, was her dear friend Amos.

☆ ☆ ☆

Approximately one month later, in September of 1980, Trent Givens was murdered. It was big news at Powers High School. The topic dominated the senior class that was now missing one of its own during their final year in high school together.

For a fleeting moment, Becky thought of it as justice served, but the reality of the news of Trent's mangled body hit her hard. She suspected Amos, for it seemed to be too much of a coincidence. At the same time, however, she doubted Amos could kill anyone, especially so brutally. The rumors surfaced that Trent's skull had been crushed, most likely bludgeoned with a blunt object. Becky felt guilty, like she was carrying a cement block in her backpack. Nevertheless, she never broached the subject with Amos. Instead, during the month of October, she discovered she was pregnant and promptly dropped out of school. She subsequently became reclusive, and when Thanksgiving arrived, her family moved away.

CHAPTER 21

AMOS KONKLIN'S DIARY, THE FIRST KILL

August 20, 1980

Becky broke the news to me yesterday. She told me about her trip to Trent's cabin and that he raped her. I was furious but kept calm for her sake. Last night I had another dream, but this time it was about Trent Givens. In the dream, I killed him. When I awoke this morning, I realized I am going to kill him for real. I went to the store with Shirley and bought this journal. I've titled it, A Diary of My First Killing, by Amos Konklin. *It's a fitting title, I think, because it demonstrates my commitment to carry out the act. Starting today, I'll keep a detailed account. It may be a stupid idea to record everything in this book, but I'm gonna do it anyway. I want to have an accurate account of what happens. Well…till tomorrow…*

August 21, 1980

    I awoke at 3:30 a.m. from one of my dreams. My pillowcase was wet from sweat. My heart was pounding. I wonder if these dreams will ever end. Am I crazy? Is it from my injury, the blow to my head? In my dreams, I'm carrying a hammer—not an ordinary hammer, but a sledgehammer. I also saw Trent Givens in my dream this time, and I was smashing his head with it. It reminds me of the High Striker, except it's not a game this time.

August 22, 1980

    I saw Becky today. She's still upset about what happened. She has sworn me to secrecy, and I promised I won't ever tell anyone. I wonder if writing about it is breaking my promise. I don't think so, since I'm not deliberately telling anyone. She just wants to forget about everything and get on with her life. I know she is relieved to get the truth off her chest, if only to me. I think we may be getting closer as friends again. We were such good friends for such a long time. I don't understand why we grew apart this last year. I suppose she blames me. Maybe I said too many things that freaked her out, talking about all my crazy dreams and not remembering who I was back then. But I shouldn't have to pretend, especially in front of my best friend, right? So I have no regrets. In the future, though, I've decided I'm not going to burden Becky with so much of what is going on in my head. I'm not going to tell her what I've got planned for Trent. I know the sledgehammer from my dreams is a sign. I think practicing with Herman's old sledge out in the garage will do just fine.

August 23, 1980

    Today I did some yard work for Herman and Shirley. It was nice to be outside. It gave me some time to focus and think about how I'm going to kill Trent. I never realized that mowing the grass could be such a profound experience. I literally forgot about the job at hand, and my mind just ran free. I imagined a lot of scenarios, a lot of ways I might kill him. When I put the lawnmower back in the garage, I grabbed Herman's sledgehammer that he always leans over in the corner, near all his tools. It looks worn, like it's seen a lot of use. I took it outside behind the garage for a few swings. It's a bit heavy, but it felt natural in my hands. I placed a pecan on the ground and took a good swing at it, and it split right open. It made this popping sound when it cracked. I imagine cracking a skull would make a popping sound like that, only louder.

August 25, 1980

I awoke with a sore throat this morning. Shirley has the flu, so I'm sure she made me sick. God, I hate sore throats.

August 29, 1980

I'm feeling a little better today. I had some of Shirley's homemade chicken noodle soup, and I think it helped. It tasted great anyway, and it was nice of her to make it since she's not feeling so great herself yet. She's a great cook.

August 30, 1980

I'm feeling a lot better. I think I'm over the worst.

August 31, 1980   .

My sore throat is pretty much gone today, thank God. My nose is still stuffy, but I'd rather have a stuffy nose than a runny one. Shirley seems to be back to her old self. I suppose that's a good sign for me. It's good to get my energy back.

September 1, 1980

Becky stopped by to see me today. I told her to stay away while I'm sick so I don't pass it on to her, but I guess she thinks I'm no longer contagious. She didn't stay very long, and she seemed to be in good spirits. She never talks about the incident at the cabin anymore. I guess she wants to put it behind her, maybe pretend it never happened. But it did happen, and unlike me, she hasn't had the luxury of forgetting. I know what that bastard did to her is going to affect her forever, for the rest of her life. People like Trent Givens do bad things and get away with them all the time. It pisses me off. Isn't there any justice in this world? He raped her, for God's sake, and I just know the asshole will do it to some other innocent girl one day unless someone stops him. So I'm not leaving that to chance. I'm going to end it, to put him out of the world's misery.

September 2, 1980

A new month has begun. A week from now, I'll be back at school. I've decided to wait until school starts before I kill Trent. I don't want to act too quickly or make Becky suspicious. I still need to figure out a good way to get him alone. The last thing I need are witnesses, though I'm sure most people would consider getting rid of him a favor.

September 3, 1980

Shirley went shopping today and was out of the house for a while. I'm glad, because that gave me a chance to take some practice swings with Herman's sledgehammer. I'm getting better at it. Hey, maybe I can beat a High Striker someday. Who knows?

September 4, 1980

Becky and I took a long walk today. It was so nice to see her again, kinda like old times. We have such good discussions about things. She still won't talk about Trent though. I never bring up the subject because it seems like it will only upset her.

September 5, 1980

I woke up at 3:45 a.m. this morning. The nightmare was intense this time. I was carrying the sledgehammer, but it got too heavy since I was trying to catch someone who was running away from me. After I dropped it, I was overcome with this weird sense of dread because I felt vulnerable. I think it was some kind of sign. Maybe my dreams are telling me the sledgehammer is a heavy burden, but I have to carry it anyway.

September 6, 1980

Shirley took me school shopping today. I bought a couple pairs of jeans and some nice shirts. Afterward, we got all my school supplies. I can't believe school will be starting in two days. I'm looking forward to my senior year. I don't really care much about my classmates—except Becky, of course—but I do enjoy learning new things. I'm taking all advanced classes.

September 7, 1980

Herman grilled some steaks, and Shirley made potato salad and a blueberry cobbler to go with it. It was excellent.

September 8, 1980

Today was the first day of school. I saw Trent, but I didn't make any eye contact. He is as popular as ever, and that makes me sick to my stomach, knowing what he did. What a fake! And why are people so easily fooled? They're like stupid sheep, following him around. It's hard to understand why some kids are so popular, especially when they are so average—or so far below it.

September 9, 1980

I have decided on a date. September 20 will be the perfect day for Trent's life to end, courtesy of me. That's Herman and Shirley's anniversary, and they are taking a weekend trip for some alone time. I've been told by Gary White, who happens to be in the know, that Trent visits his cabin every weekend. I also found out from Gary where it is located. I'm going to stake it out and look for an opportunity for some much-needed alone time of my own—some alone time with Trent Givens.

September 11, 1980

The first week of school is almost over. I like all my classes pretty well, though some of them seem pointless.

September 12, 1980

I heard from Lester Cobb today. He sends me letters every few months to keep in touch. He has always been a good friend—even before I remember, apparently.

September 13, 1980

I went to church with Herman and Shirley today. We sang this hymn that is stuck in my head, probably because it seems so fitting: "High on His holy seat…He bears the righteous sway… His foes beneath His feat…Shall sink and die away…" *It was written by Charles Wesley, in 1746, according to the hymnal. Boy, that was a long time ago, but it still seems to fit somehow. I'm not sure I believe in God. If He does exist, I wonder what He will think of me after I kill Trent. With all that talk of smiting* enemies and so on, I'm sure He'll understand. And if He doesn't, oh well.

September 14, 1980

For some reason, I wanted to read the Bible today. I didn't have much homework, so I spent some time in my namesake, the Book of Amos. It's strange reading a book of the Bible with my name at the top of every page. It has nine chapters, and it's really kinda difficult to understand, even though I usually understand most things I read.

September 15, 1980

I did some more Bible reading today, but I've decided to give up on the Book of Amos for now. I'm focused on writing my own book, The Journal of Amos Konklin. If anyone ever reads my diary, I'm sure it will be much easier to understand than God's version of an Amos book. Oh, and I've decided that if God does exist, I'm sure He demands justice.

September 17, 1980

We had a nice supper tonight. Shirley made chicken and dumplings. Boy, that woman can do such amazing things with chicken! Herman and Shirley talked about their upcoming week-end vacation. They seemed excited. I sure hope they have a good time. If anybody deserves it, they do. They work hard and take good care of me and each other.

September 19, 1980

Herman and Shirley left earlier tonight. They are celebrating their anniversary and will be out of town until Sunday, so I guess tomorrow is my big day—and Trent's last.

September 21, 1980

   Well, I did it. I killed Trent Givens yesterday, or early today, I suppose, depending on the exact time of death. I didn't sleep very well Friday night. I woke around 3:15 a.m. and couldn't go back to sleep. I just lay in bed thinking, like I do sometimes. Around 6:00 a.m., I got up, took a shower, and then ate a bowl of cereal. After breakfast, I went out into the garage and grabbed Herman's sledgehammer from the place where I'd left it. It felt natural in my hands, and I practiced pounding on some stumps outside that I was sure were as thick as Trent's stupid head. I got the keys to Herman's truck from his secret hiding place in the garage and drove out to Trent's cabin. After I found the right road, I decided to drive past and park the truck back in the woods, off a different road. It was about a half-mile walk from there. It was isolated, and I'm pretty sure no one saw me or even noticed.

   I wanted to scout things out first, so I left the sledgehammer tucked behind the front seat. The walk was nice. I assumed I'd be nervous about the whole thing, but on the contrary, I felt quite calm. Maybe that's because I've been writing about it and thinking about it for so long. My heart was pounding, but that was due to pure adrenaline. When I found the cabin, I sat a good distance away. I found a pretty nice hiding spot where I was sure no one could see me. I waited for what seemed like an eternity before Trent finally showed up. He'd made me wait too long, so I was even more compelled to go through with it—like I needed another reason to be pissed off at him. Anyway, as I waited to see what would happen, a few more cars arrived. I recognized some of the kids from school. Once their stupid party was underway, I wondered how my plan was going to work out. I wasn't sure how to get Trent alone, so all I could do was wait. You have to have patience for things like this, for important things. The worst part about waiting was the stupid mosquitoes. Those things nearly ate me alive, and I've still got little red bites all over me, itching like crazy.

Around dusk, the party was in full swing, so I headed back to the truck. I needed to stretch my legs, and I was starting to get hungry. I can't believe I didn't think about bringing something to eat. I guess I thought it would all be over more quickly than that, so I didn't figure I'd need a snack. I admit now that it was a miscalculation.

I got back to my hiding spot at just about dark, the hammer in hand. A few minutes later, everyone started to leave. Brenda Pressman hung around, and she and Trent went back into the cabin. Around 11:00 p.m., I was getting tired and thought about whether to give up or go inside and kill both of them. Fortunately, about ten minutes later, Brenda walked outside under the porch light, had a quick smoke, and then left.

At 11:50 p.m., I made my move. I was sure he'd be passed out after all those beers I'd seen him guzzle. Plus, I think I saw him drinking whiskey or something too. I left my hiding spot and started walking toward the cabin, walked right up onto the porch. I was fully exposed in the light, but no one was watching. I knew he was inside asleep. The door opened easily, and the creaking sound it made was drowned out by those loud snores coming from the bedroom. Trent was out cold, just like I suspected. In that moment, standing there gazing around the cabin, I thought about Becky. I was standing right there, right in the cruel place where that nasty son of a bitch had hurt her. The snores led me right to the bedroom, and there the monster was, drunk off his ass, all stretched out, completely naked, with his disgusting, shriveled prick catching the moonlight.

It was an unbelievable feeling. I felt a powerful rush of energy, but I was calm. Without hesitating very long, I walked over to the bed and swung as hard as I could. I'll never forget the sound.

His head popped like a watermelon. I mean, it was instant. It is peculiar, I suppose, just how much can happen within a few seconds of time. Trent went from snoring to one final gasp to not breathing at all before another moment passed. He was dead. I had killed him, and I wasn't a bit sorry about it. I am still not sorry. After all, he had it coming.

When I got home, I washed the sledgehammer under the garden hose behind the garage. I then wiped down Herman's truck just in case there might have been some blood on my clothes. It's such an old, dirty truck, though, that it probably wouldn't have mattered, but it's better to be safe than sorry. When I came back inside, I washed my clothes and took a long, hot shower. I slept like a baby. When I woke up today, I felt great. Why wouldn't I? I've done Becky—and probably the world at large—a favor. I simply took out the garbage. What's not to feel great about?

CHAPTER 22

THE JOURNAL OF AMOS KONKLIN REVEALED

January 28, 2019 was a wet, cold, windy day in New York City. Peter Wild, a reporter at the *Times*, stepped out onto the street and flagged down a taxi. He was on his way to the Metropolitan Detention Center in Brooklyn, the MDC, at the request of Amos Konklin. The Konklin case had been the news item of late 2018, and now, at the beginning of the New Year, Wild was still right in the thick of it. Amos Konklin was being temporarily held at the detention center in Brooklyn, awaiting trial for a double homicide. Much of the news surrounding the case had already leaked into tabloid exaggerations and speculations, with the all too familiar puns hailing Dr. Konklin, noted neurosurgeon, as "The Skull Cracker."

Although Wild had already written three columns about the case, he was not sure why Konklin had requested to see him. It was an unusual arrangement because Konklin had requested a private session with him. There were to be no cameras or recordings—only the two men talking. Konklin's lawyer had advised against it, but the authorities were in favor of the meeting, hoping it might somehow convince Konklin to open up, to ultimately confess enough that they could bring the trial to a swift conclusion, with a guilty verdict. It was Wild's first experience interviewing someone who was already widely believed to be guilty of murder. The interview would likely lead to greater fame for him as a member of the press, so, although he was nervous about the whole thing, he welcomed the opportunity. Truly, for a reporter, it was a dream interview.

The taxi stopped outside of the MDC; Wild handed the driver the cash and got out of the cab, with only his briefcase in hand. He made his way through security and up to the second floor. The north wall outside the elevator held a sign with an arrow pointing left, toward the Administration Office. Wild followed the labyrinth of hallways and cubicles and doorways around another left and then a right turn, until he saw the large sign hanging on the Administration Office door.

He checked in with the attendant and was directed to a nearby conference room. Waiting to greet him were District Attorney James Seymour and Police Lieutenant Tom Wallace.

The D.A. was a middle-aged man of average height, with a receding hairline. Wild had seen pictures of him, but it was his first time to meet Seymour in person.

"Mr. Wild, how are you?" Seymour said, reaching out to shake the reporter's hand.

"I'm good."

"This is Lieutenant Wallace." Seymour pointed back toward his very tall companion.

"Hello, Mr. Wild. I'm Tom Wallace. I'm a big fan of your column." The lieutenant gripped Wild's hand as soon as Seymour had relinquished control.

"Thank you. It's nice to meet you."

Seymour and Wallace walked back toward the small rectangular table.

"Have a seat, Mr. Wild." Seymour gestured toward the chair nearest the door, and then he got right to the point, stating, "I hope you're here for the right reasons. We want to bring this monster to justice."

"I know Dr. Konklin requested to see me, but as to why I'm really here, I think we both know it's really because the public wants to hear the true story."

"Fair enough," Seymour said. "I'm sure you are eager to find out the truth of his involvement. I know we are."

"I just want you to know that I plan on abiding by all of Dr. Konklin's conditions. What is said in that room will remain confidential, between Dr. Konklin and me, unless he agrees otherwise. I hope you are okay with that, because that's how I understood the arrangement, and that is what I have agreed to."

"I guess I can't ask for anything more than that, Mr. Wild, although I believe you would no doubt feel morally obligated to reveal any information that might be critical to closing this case."

"Critical? And who decides what is critical?" Wild asked.

Seymour smiled, but just as he was about to speak, Lieutenant Wallace interrupted, "Hey, we all believe in innocent until proven guilty. We are not asking you to break your oath or your reporter code. However, our allegiance is to the people, the victims, and their families. I'm sorry, Mr. Wild, but all things considered, a killer's rights do not overshadow theirs. We're talking about murder here, brutal at that."

"I understand that, Lieutenant," Wild replied. "I'll have to wait and see what happens and then make a judgment call."

"The primary reason we wanted to meet was to assure you that nothing will be filmed or recorded," Seymour reassured, though he didn't sound so reassuring. "Mr. Wild, before you go in there, do you have any further questions for us? We want to make sure you are 100 percent comfortable with this interview."

"I don't think I have any questions," Wild said. "I'm ready to get on with it."

At that, they all rose and left the conference room. Seymour took the lead, followed by Wallace and Wild. The trio remained quiet as they walked along the hallway and then down a staircase that led to the basement. Looking up, Wild noticed a sign that indicated they had arrived at the detention center holding area. Another hallway brought them to the door of Room B32, where an armed guard stood at the entrance.

"This is it," Seymour said, standing outside the door.

When Wild entered, he saw Dr. Amos Konklin sitting in the corner of the room in an uncomfortable metal folding chair. He had cuffs on his hands, and his feet were chained to a hook on the adjacent wall, fastened to the shackles between his ankles. He was wearing the official detention clothing; ironically, Wild noted, the ensemble resembled a surgeon's scrubs, only prison orange instead of hospital green. "Hello," Wild said, initiating the conversation.

"Hi," Amos responded.

"I guess this is my seat." Wild pointed to the empty chair.

"If it's anything like this one, I can tell you it's not very comfortable. Nevertheless, I suppose it beats standing."

"I'll give it a try." Wild sat. "Yeah, I see what you mean."

Amos acknowledged with a smile, but he did not speak.

"So, Dr. Konklin, I have to say I'm puzzled as to why you wanted to see me."

"I've always been a big fan of mysteries. What about you?"

"I suppose I do like a good mystery."

"Well, believe it or not, they let us read in this place, and that's one thing I love to do. I must say, I've followed your columns closely. I suppose that should not come as a surprise, considering I seem to be your favorite topic to write about. Seems you do like a good mystery as much as I do."

"Well, I've tried to be fair and stick to the facts."

"Yes, and that's exactly why I invited you here."

"Because I was fair, or because you have some additional facts to offer?"

"A little bit of both, I suppose. It's a long story, as most stories really are. I noticed in your columns that you didn't write about my pre-college years."

"I must say, your life before college is a mystery," Wild commented with a crooked smile. "We know you lived in

Canada, but we didn't pursue that any further. We focused on the absolute facts…you know, Harvard Medical School and then practice as a surgeon. You seemed to have it all—a beautiful wife, a successful career. You were a contributor to the community, an upstanding citizen. So, Doctor, you must understand why people are in shock. It was a bit of an unexpected blow."

Ignoring his play on words, Amos responded, "Yes, it is completely understandable. My life is quite contradictory. I'm now fifty-five years old, sitting in a detention center, awaiting trial for two murders. I would love to tell you a story—my story—but that all depends, Mr. Wild, on how much effort you are willing to make in order to hear it."

"So, am I to presume it will require more than me sitting in this chair and listening?"

"Oh yes, much more. Nothing worthwhile should ever come easy, in my opinion."

"I'm all ears. Tell me what you want me to do, Dr. Konklin."

"I'm not going to tell you the story today, because we have to start at the beginning, and that part I've already written down. I have a journal I would like you to read. I need you to read it first before telling anyone about it. Afterward, I'd like to speak with you again. Then we'll take it from there."

"Okay," Wild replied, eager to hear more.

"Do you have a piece of paper and a pen?"

"Yes." Wild opened his briefcase.

"On Highway 19, just south of Umatilla, Florida, there is a storage facility called Citrus Storage. You can get to it from Mill Street. Go after hours—I think they close at 7:00 most days, unless they've changed that—and enter the security code at the gate. The security number is actually the telephone number of Citrus Storage. I forget it, but it is posted on the gate. Go to Unit 18 and enter the pass code that corresponds to 'Konklin' on the door pad. I forget the actual numbers, but you're a smart man, Mr. Wild, and I'm sure you can figure out that little riddle. Inside the storage unit, you'll find an antique desk. Open the drawer, and you will find a key to a safety deposit box at the United Southern Bank in Umatilla. I have already arranged with the bank to allow entrance to anyone other than myself who has the key and the password."

"Password?"

"Yes. It's 'soma.' You'll still need to sign your name, of course."

"Is that all, Dr. Konklin?"

"For now, Mr. Wild. Does the assignment interest you?"

"Most definitely."

"Well, good, but I wouldn't wait too long if I were you, considering what's going on in my life at present. As they say, time is of the essence."

"All right. In that case, perhaps I should get going."

"I think that's a good idea."

Wild put the notes back in his briefcase and walked to the door. He looked back at Amos, nodded his head, and left the room like a man on a mission.

In the hallway, he was greeted by Seymour and Wallace, who lingered, discussing the case.

"I'm done," Wild said flatly, offering them no explanation or information.

"What? Already? That's it? You were only in there for five minutes," Seymour replied in utter disbelief, looking at his watch.

"Well, he didn't have much to say."

"Really? Well, what did he say, if I may ask?"

"You know that's confidential, Mr. Seymour. He does want to speak with me again later. Perhaps then he will have more to tell me, something I feel comfortable sharing with you."

"Did he say when he wants to see you again?" Wallace asked.

"No. I think we should wait a day or so and see what happens. By the way, can you gentlemen show me how to get out of here? This place is confusing as hell, even with all the signs. I don't know how you guys find your way around."

Wallace smirked. "Sure, follow us." He took the lead all the way back to the front entrance.

Once he was on the street, Wild turned and waved goodbye, then hailed a taxi. "Take me to JFK…quick."

✿ ✿ ✿

At 6:18 p.m. on January 28, 2019, Delta Flight 1712 arrived at Orlando International Airport. Peter Wild was carrying only a briefcase, so he made his way swiftly through the airport without having to get any luggage.

By 6:40 p.m., he was outside the airport, looking for a taxi again, and he quickly flagged one down. "I'd like to head toward Umatilla. Do you know where that is?" Wild asked the driver.

"Yeah, it's 'bout sixty miles from here. I can be there in seventy-five minutes, maybe ninety. You know, traffic dictates, man."

"Ninety minutes? That'll be fine if that's what it takes," Wild replied, looking down at his watch; it was 6:45 p.m. "Let's go. I'm headed for Citrus Storage on Mill Street."

The driver entered the information into his GPS.

As the taxicab pulled out of the airport, Wild leaned his head over on the side of the door, looking out the back window. He was tired; it had been a long day. He closed his eyes in an attempt to see if a nap were possible, but the excitement of the day rendered that an undoable feat. For the time being, he was content to rest and let the words of Amos Konklin play over in his mind. The moment was surreal. Twelve hours earlier, when he'd awakened in his apartment in New York, he'd had no idea that by dusk he would be in Florida at the request of Amos Konklin.

Once the taxi was cruising along the interstate, Wild found himself at ease with the rhythm of the car. It was so different from the stop-and-go of downtown New York, and somewhere along the way, he lost track of time.

His trancelike state of mind was interrupted around 8:10 p.m., when the cab driver spoke. "This here's Highway 19, man. Should be 'bout ten mo' minutes."

"Hey, where are all the orange trees?" Wild asked, taking notice of the surroundings.

The cab driver smiled. "Not many 'round here no mo'."

"I see," Wild replied. "Where are we anyway?"

"This here's Eustis. Umatilla next."

"Eustis? I've never heard of that before. Odd name for a city."

The conversation stopped until the driver turned a corner and headed toward Umatilla. "This be the last stretch. City limits are up there 'bout a mile."

On the right was a small lake, followed by a plot of pine trees.

"Mill Street coming up. You said Citrus Storage, right?" the driver asked.

"Yep, Citrus Storage, off of Mill Street."

"Yeah, okay." The driver applied his foot to the brakes in response to the GPS indicator. He signaled, made a right turn, drove a block, and turned into the area in front of the gate.

Wild looked out and saw the sign for Citrus Storage. Underneath was the phone number, 352-669-2651. "This is it," Wild said quietly. He looked at his watch, which read 8:19 p.m. "You are four minutes late."

"Huh?" the driver asked.

"Remember, you said ninety minutes. Actually, it's been ninety-four," Wild replied with a smile.

"You gonna cut me some slack, man?"

"Yep, it's close enough." Wild opened the door. "Can you wait here another ten minutes or so? I need to quickly get something inside, and then I'd like you to drop me off at the nearest motel."

"I be right here, mista," the driver replied.

Peter Wild was now standing at the gate Amos Konklin had described to him earlier that morning. It was dark, and no one else was there. Wild walked up to the security gate and confidently entered the phone number from the sign. The gate opened immediately, and Wild walked briskly through. There were several rows of units. Since Unit 18 was a low number, Wild correctly guessed it was down the first row. When he arrived, he realized the storage unit looked quite like a garage door with a small beige key-pad. Wild entered the numbers corresponding to the name "Konklin" on the keypad.

Again, just like the front gate, Unit 18 opened, reveal-ing a spacious storage unit occupied by only a few items. In the center stood an antique desk, just as Konklin had said. Wild approached with nervous excitement. When he pulled open the top drawer, there lay a safety deposit key alone in the drawer. He was pleased with himself for being able to follow Konklin's accurate instructions.

When he got back to the car, the driver was standing outside taking a stretch. "All done?" he asked.

"Yes. Is there a place to stay the night in town?"

"I'm sure we can find one, man."

The taxi headed north on Highway 19. Within a couple of miles, they found a motel.

"How 'bout this place?"

"I think it will do just fine." Wild reached into his pocket to pay the fare and then some. "Here, take this card and add 30 percent."

"Thanks, man." The driver took Wild's Visa, and, after a quick swipe, returned it to him.

"Oh, one last thing. Can you wait here a couple more minutes, just in case they don't have a vacancy?"

"Sure thing, man."

After he'd secured a room, Wild walked outdoors to tell his faithful cabbie it was okay to be on his way.

"Thanks again, mista. Take it easy. Hope you get to see some orange trees 'fore ya head back to wherever you from, man."

Wild smiled. "Thanks. You take it easy too."

✵ ✵ ✵

The next morning, Wild awoke, took a shower, and put the same clothes back on. He was eager to get to the bank as soon as it opened, so he had arranged another taxi for 8:50 a.m.

At exactly 9:01 a.m., he entered the bank. It was unusually quiet, he thought, assuming he was either early or Umatilla was one of those very small, sleepy towns that ran on its own schedule. There were two tellers and no lines, so Wild chose the better-looking of the two women.

"May I help you, sir?"

"Yes, ma'am. I'd like to get into Safety Deposit Box 148. My signature is not on file, but I do have the key, and there are special instructions given that should allow a password in lieu of a signature on file."

"Just a minute," she said.

"The box should belong to Amos Konklin," Wild volunteered.

"Oh yes, I see it right here. Can you write the password down for me?" She pushed him a piece of paper and a pen.

"Sure." Wild wrote "*soma*" and slid the paper back.

"Okay. I'll need to see a photo I.D., and I need you to sign your name on this card as well."

"Sure thing," Wild said as he eagerly complied.

"Okay. It looks like everything is in order. Follow me."

Minutes later, the box was opened. It contained only a leather-bound book. Wild made a quick check, and inside the cover were words alluding to a diary by Amos Konklin. "Mission accomplished."

Outside, the taxi was waiting.

He got back into the car and told the driver, "Orlando International Airport." Then he sat back in his seat, took a deep breath, and exhaled in relief. His curiosity was running high, and he took another opportunity to carefully survey the title of the book. Then, he began to read at once the opening words to *A Diary of My First Killing, by Amos Konklin.*

By the time the taxi arrived at Orlando International, Wild had read the journal twice. It was a remarkable, telling account, and Wild was fascinated. Considering that Amos Konklin had committed his first murder at such a young age, Wild at once considered that this might have been only the start of a lifetime of bloodshed, culminating with Dave Garth and Lois Winston. Only Dr. Konklin knew the answers, and Wild was anxious to discover the facts.

CHAPTER 23

ANOTHER INTERVIEW WITH DR. AMOS KONKLIN

On the evening of January 29, 2019, Peter Wild was back in his New York home. The trip was over, and now it was time to begin preparing for his interview. From the airport, he called the D.A.'s office and arranged a second meeting with Dr. Konklin to be held the next day, on January 30. Wild spent several hours that evening taking notes, making sure he was prepared to ask all the right questions.

The next morning, he arrived promptly at the MDC in Brooklyn at 9:00 a.m. It was his second visit in as many days, and he followed the same path inside he had taken two days prior. However, this time there was to be no meeting with Seymour and Wallace. Wild proceeded to the detention holding area, Room B32. He was greeted this time by an MDC staff member who was expecting him, and after showing his credentials, he was allowed inside the room.

Sitting in the same corner of the room in a hard folding chair was Dr. Amos Konklin, dressed in the same orange garb and shackles, as if he'd never left. Wild proceeded to sit in the vacant chair, this time without asking.

"Good morning, Dr. Konklin," he said.

"Mr. Wild," Amos answered. "I got your message. How was your trip?"

"It was good."

"So I assume you found my journal?"

"Yes." The room was quiet a few seconds, and then Wild spoke up, after clearing his throat. "Dr. Konklin, I must say, it was quite a read."

"In what way?"

"Well…" Wild paused for a moment. "Maybe I should rephrase that. What I meant to say is that it was not what I expected. I mean, I had no idea what I would find."

"I'm sure it was unexpected," Amos said, staring at Wild. "I suppose some of it even came as a bit of a shock."

"Do you mind if I ask a few questions and take notes?"

"Not at all."

"Did you actually write the journal in 1980? I mean, was it an actual diary of your life as you lived it as a teen-ager, or did you write it later on?"

"I wrote it in 1980. It was a day-to-day journal, an account of how things unfolded during that time. I'm curious why you would ask such a question."

"Well, if I may, the title is, uh…" Wild bent to take the journal from his briefcase. He opened it and continued, "It's titled *A Diary of My First Killing, by Amos Konklin*. It sounds like a historical retelling, if you know what I mean.

Unless, of course, you knew when you wrote it that other killings would follow."

"I see," Amos said. "I suppose when I wrote it that way, I didn't give it much thought. The words just came naturally to me. In hindsight, I suppose it did turn out to be prophetic, in some respect, albeit I can't say that was intentional when I titled it that way."

"Because of Dave Garth and Lois Winston?"

"Yes…and others."

"Others?"

"Yes, there have been others."

"How many?"

"Is that really important?"

"I think it could be, but let me ask another question about the journal. I understand what Trent Givens did to your friend Becky Woods was despicable, but what made you think it was right, acceptable, to take the law into your own hands?"

"I'm disappointed in you, Mr. Wild. It seemed to me that you would be beyond asking such cliché questions. I was young, Becky was my friend, rape is a crime, and I believed people like Trent Givens deserved to die for their crimes. It's really rather simple and begs no explanation, if you think about it."

"Yes, he raped a young woman, Dr. Konklin, a friend of yours, but you killed a young man. Is that not a crime as well?"

"I suppose that depends on the judge and jury. You see through a filter, Mr. Wild, a perspective of the modern legal age."

"Is there another lens? You seem to suggest my view is somehow blurred."

"Have you ever read the Bible, Mr. Wild?"

"I've read it and consider myself a somewhat religious man," Wild replied.

"Then surely you know the Bible has much to say about capital punishment. It certainly presents a perspective that is noteworthy to consider."

"Forgive me, Dr. Konklin, but we live by the laws of this country, not by the laws of the Bible. Do you have some kind of newfound belief or something?"

"I'm not sure I follow."

"Well, the reason I ask is because in your journal, you mentioned the Bible, but you spoke of how difficult it was to understand. In fact, if I recall, you even questioned the existence of God."

"I was seventeen, young and ignorant. Earlier, you asked whether my killing Trent Givens was a crime or not. I'm not sure if that was a rhetorical question, but let me attempt to answer in any case. Let's set aside the topic of God and the Bible for a while and talk about something you seem more interested in, the laws of this country, as you put it."

"Okay."

"What is your political affiliation, Mr. Wild? Are you a Liberal, Conservative, a Democrat perhaps, a Republican, maybe an Independent?"

"I'm a registered Democrat."

"Have you ever read anything on classical liberal thought?"

"Some."

"Have you ever heard of Murray Rothbard?"

"Yes. He was a popular Libertarian, I believe."

"I guess you could use that word, although I think Rothbard was more of a classical Liberal. He had much to say about the anatomy of The State, that entity whose laws you claim we are supposed to be following. In one of his writings, he quotes Franz Oppenheimer, a famous German sociologist, who said, *'The State is a social institution forced by a victorious group of men on a defeated group, with the sole purpose of regulating the dominion of the victorious group on the defeated group, and whose dominion has no other purpose than the economic exploitation of the vanquished by the victors.'* In other words, Mr. Wild, as Rothbard so eloquently stated, *'The State is not born of a social contract, it has always been born in conquest and exploitation. The State provides a legal, orderly, systematic channel for the predation of private property, thus freedom is anterior to The State.'"

"And your point, Dr. Konklin?"

"I find it fascinating that people are so willing to relinquish their power of thought and free will and hand it over to something that is, in and of itself, counterproductive to their own best interests, something that exists for the purpose of exploitation, something inherently evil—a necessary evil, in fact, quoting the famous American Thomas Paine, although I'm not quite sure I believe in the necessity part. If I kill a man, Mr. Wild, you think it is morally wrong, but if The State, in its infinite wisdom, gave me the power to do so, you would be willing to accept my actions and absolve me of my crime. Albert Jay Nock wrote, *'The State claims and exercises the monopoly of crime. It forbids private murder, but itself organizes murder on a colossal scale.'* I'm on trial for murder, for taking lives, yet if I'm found guilty, The State will sentence me to death. It will take my life for taking lives, all the while sending young men and women to countries around the world to carry out more murders, to kill those who it considers its enemies. Ironic, isn't it? So, I ask you, what is more rational? To put faith in The State or to put faith in God?"

"I'm no philosopher, Doctor, but I'm listening."

"Let's just say I threw in my lot with God."

"I don't believe that is, in and of itself, irrational, Dr. Konklin, but that doesn't mean God condones your actions. What you did was deliberate and calculated."

"You claim to be a religious man, Mr. Wild, so let me ask you how you reconcile your faith with certain Biblical commands. In Leviticus 20:10, it says a man who commits adultery with another man's wife should be put to death, along with the adulteress. That seems to be quite deliberate and calculated, and it fits Dave Garth and Lois Winston, wouldn't you say?"

"Dr. Konklin, I'm happy to leave Biblical interpretation up to the scholars."

"Let me guess. You're a Catholic man, aren't you?

"Yes, I am Catholic."

"That makes perfect sense. Once again, you are content with relinquishing your freedom of thought and expression to another central, State-like authority, only this time it's a religious one instead."

Wild crossed his legs and paused for a moment. "Dr. Konklin, I'm not sure there are very many people who take the liberty to murder adulterers because of a passage in the Old Testament. Besides, no one really knows whether all that really came from God or not."

"Mr. Wild, the existence of God and the authorship of the Bible are independent. I view the Bible merely as an access point. However, the passage in Leviticus is consistent with my understanding of God, based upon my own personal experience. There is a bigger point here, a context of universal significance. See, some of the Levitical law given to the Israelites in the Old Testament was given to enforce respect for people and their rights. If you violated the rights of another, you forfeited your own. It was a system that demanded justice. I didn't fully understand this when I executed Trent Givens, for I was merely acting on my own instincts, but when I was in college, my perspective changed."

"How so?"

Amos Konklin leaned his head back and briefly looked up toward the ceiling before he spoke. "It was on the eve of July 28, 1984, one week after I turned twenty-one. I was alone in my dorm room at college, taking classes over the summer, when I gave the Bible's Book of Amos another try. Before reading the book that bears my name, though, I decided to try and put it in context, if possible. I opened the Bible to the preceding book of Joel. There, stretched out on my bed, under the subtopic *'The Day of the Lord,'* I read Joel 2:28 which says, *'And afterward, I will pour out my Spirit on all people, You sons and daughters will prophesy, your old men will dream dreams, your young men will see visions.'* I have to tell you Mr. Wild, I was fascinated that God communicated by means of visions and dreams. As I read the book of Amos once again, I began to sense that God is very personal. God spoke through the prophet Amos as if it were one man talking to another man. He reveals himself as a righteous God, one that punishes men for their crimes. The Amos of the Bible was an ordinary man prior to becoming a prophet, but God called him out and spoke to him, asking *'What do you see, Amos?'* to which Amos replied, *'A basket of fruit,'* to which God replied, *'The time is ripe…The songs in the temple will turn to wailing. Many, many bodies flung everywhere. Silence!'*"

As Wild looked intently at Amos, he saw him close his eyes, as if he were reliving the experience. The room fell silent, and Wild just sat, waiting for Amos to speak.

The short break in conversation seemed like an eternity, and then Amos opened his eyes once again, staring directly at Wild. "That night, as I lay on my dormitory bed, it occurred to me that God was asking me what I saw and heard in my dreams. The answer was simple. I had seen a sledgehammer and a command to exact vengeance. I heard God's reply, *'Surely, I will never forget what they have done,'* in Joel 8:7. That night, I realized my dreams had meaning. I knew that bearing the name of Amos is not a mere coincidence. I knew my life apart from the carnival happened for a reason. From that night forward, when I discovered injustices for which there were no accounting, my dreams grew more intense, and I saw myself carrying out the acts of vengeance against the guilty parties. My dreams were a reflection of the court of supreme justice. I was acting as God's avenger."

"What do you mean, your life apart from the carnival?" Wild asked, hesitant to immediately challenge Amos's claims of being God's executioner.

"Before I went to live with Herman and Shirley Cobb in Canada as a teen in 1976, I traveled in a carnival with a man named Bill Konklin. I don't remember anything about that life, though, and I've never been able to put all the pieces together. You see, I was injured. I fell and hit my head and suffered memory loss and awoke in a Canadian hospital. I had been friends with a man named Lester Cobb at the carnival, a sword swallower, and Lester told me about my life prior to the accident."

"What happened to Bill Konklin?"

"He left after the accident. He abandoned me."

"Was he your father?"

"I think he may have passed himself off as such, but I don't think he really was."

"Why would you say that?"

"It's something someone told me a long time ago."

"What about your mother?"

"I have no recollection of my mother either. According to Lester Cobb, there was no mother in the picture when I lived in the carnival with Bill Konklin. I'm like Melchizedek."

"Who?"

"Melchizedek. He is mentioned in the Bible as a King of Salem in the Old Testament. In the New Testament, Jesus is referred to as a king or priest in the order of Melchizedek."

"I'm not sure I follow the connection."

"Well, in the book of Hebrews, Jesus is referred to as a priest perpetually, because like Melchizedek, he was father-less and motherless, without genealogy."

"Oh. I see the connection now. You feel the same, like a person without genealogy, in a sense, due to the obscurity surrounding the identity and whereabouts of your biological parents."

Amos didn't respond.

"I must say, Dr. Konklin, you seem to reference the Bible often. Do you feel that's necessary to defend your argument or make your case?"

"Like I said earlier, I consider the book an access point to the mind of God, albeit not an exclusive one. I suppose my affinity for it is subconsciously linked to its cultural significance. The historical accounts of divine intervention, of God's one-on-one interactions with humans is profound, whether it's Moses on Mount Sinai or Paul on the road to Damascus. These stories are interesting to read, but there is nothing quite like a personal experience. I believe such experiences are prevalent. They are just not documented, in the Bible anyway."

"Surely you understand why some people would not consider such personal experiences as credible."

"Of course, but I'm a spiritual man. I can understand a physical man, but I realize that a physical man will not be able to understand me. Moreover, he is unable to judge me because he does not understand spiritual things."

Wild scratched his chin. "Another Biblical reference?"

"Yes. First Corinthians 2:15 says, *'The spiritual man makes judgments about all things, but he himself is not subject to any man's judgment.'*"

"So you don't believe your actions should be judged by others?"

"I know my actions will be judged, but such judgments are meaningless to God."

"But why you, Dr. Konklin?"

"Why *not* me? I suppose you are missing a bigger point here, Mr. Wild. Your question insinuates that there is something special about me. On the contrary, I consider myself only one of many."

"Are you really suggesting that God uses many people like yourself as modern-day executioners?"

"I don't have a definitive answer for that, but I think it would be presumptuous of me to assume I have some exclusive privilege. Why is it so hard to believe that God intervenes? In fact, if He hasn't, it's likely we would have self-destructed already. What God does is keep the balance. He systematically eliminates bad from the world in order to prevent a total breakdown of society. It happens, whether or not people recognize or appreciate it. As far as execution is concerned, two-thirds of the states have the death penalty, and a recent Gallup poll indicates that nearly 60 percent of the population favors capital punishment for certain crimes."

"Well, Dr. Konklin, capital punishment is still controversial nonetheless. Even more, state executions after people have been judged in a trial by their peers is completely different from a solo avenger."

"It is different. However, The State can make mistakes. God, on the other hand, does not."

"I remember reading your reference to the High Striker in your journal," Wild said, attempting to steer the conversation in a different direction. "I did some research. I assume it's the game where you use a sledgehammer to strike a platform, sort of a test of strength."

"Yes."

"Was Bill Konklin in charge of that game at the carnival?"

"Yes."

"Do you believe there is any significance to you having been raised in a carnival environment?"

"Yes. I believe it was part of God's plan, though I'm not yet sure of the reason."

"If this Bill Konklin was not your father, how do you suppose you came to live with him?"

"That is a question only Bill Konklin could have answered. A few years ago, I tried to find him. I turned up a few leads, including a carnival circuit that had employed a man by that name. However, I came to find that he was deceased. It would have been interesting to know my real name. I have part of the clue, but last names are the key."

"Are you saying you know your real first name?"

"I'm saying it's probable that I do. Perhaps I'll tell you…when I'm ready, if I ever am."

"Do you mind?" Wild rose from his seat. "I need to stretch for a moment."

"By all means."

"My lower back gives me a fit sometimes." Wild walked across the room and then returned to the hard chair. "So then, getting back to the topic of Trent Givens from your diary, I find it interesting that you killed him with a sledgehammer, the instrument of the High Striker game. Is that what you used to kill Dave Garth and Lois Winston?"

"Yes, so the sledgehammer is obviously significant, isn't it? It's inextricably linked to my past. It's a part of who I am and what I represent. It's an unusual instrument for executions because it's heavy and burdensome to carry, not an elegant weapon by any means. The sledge is really a symbol of the heavy responsibility I carried upon my shoulders as God's avenger. But, Mr. Wild, it's the game itself that's the real metaphor. You see, God is the High Striker, and I'm simply a participant in His plan."

"God is the High Striker? Is that another Biblical reference?"

"Not directly, but there is a passage that says, '*He will strike the Earth with the rod of his mouth; with the breath of his lips he will slay the wicked.*'"

"I see. To be blunt, Dr. Konklin, have you considered the possibility that you may be insane?"

"If I were insane, I'm not sure I would possess the intellect to accurately address your questions. Of course, that's the conclusion most people would reach, I understand. My story does sound fantastic, even delusional, I'm sure. However, many of the men who formed the cornerstone of the Christian faith, which you seem to hold in regard, also made grandiose statements about their own personal experiences. Remember the Apostle Paul's journey to Damascus, claiming divine intervention with Jesus who blinded him and spoke to him? That story is not doubted by believers and has since come to represent a significant event in the course of human history, an instance when God decided to use a man who did more for the spread of Christianity than any other. In fact, the Bible is full of accounts of divine intervention, and many men over time have been participants in the grand revelation of God."

"The Bible is a closed book, Dr. Konklin. It's been written. Those stories are in there for a reason, I suppose, but I have no reason to believe God is writing another book in which you—or any of us—are to be mentioned by name."

"Perhaps not, Mr. Wild. I can only attempt to relate to you what I experienced. When I was twenty-one years old, I had an experience so profound that it's nearly impossible to describe in words, and since that time, my dreams have been an ongoing confirmation of that initial experience. There are people in this world who must be brought to justice, and God is very active in making that happen. Of that I am certain. Don't forget, everything I'm telling you has Biblical precedence. For example, in the book of Joshua, it tells of those whom Joshua smote with the edge of his sword. Samson slaughtered the Philistines as an agent of God. Even the Apostle Paul describes sinners in Romans

1:32 as those deserving of death. It seems pretty clear to me."

"Is it possible that your head injury affected your brain in some way that makes it difficult for you to separate fiction from reality? You speak a lot about your dreams. Do you concede that it may be possible that your dreams are a side effect of your injury rather than some mystical, supernatural phenomenon?"

"I am a neurosurgeon. The brain is my specialty. As a man of science, I entertain all the possibilities, but there is only one truth."

"Why did you become a neurosurgeon, if I may ask?" Wild responded, attempting to change the focus of the conversation.

"According to Lester Cobb, when I was in the carnival, I was friends with a man named Dr. Drake. I have no recollection of him, although I did meet him when I was younger, following the accident. Cobb said I spent a lot of time with the old doctor, discussing science and medicine. Perhaps I retained this fascination in my subconscious. Who knows? I do remember always being drawn toward science, and when I started medical school, there was no doubt I was choosing the path I was destined to follow."

"I know the path you chose enabled you to help many people, Dr. Konklin. Do you think that perhaps your good works are a compensation of sorts?"

"Compensation for what? For bad works? That's where you are mistaken, Mr. Wild. I consider my acts of vengeance to be good works, complementary to my surgical practice."

"I'm not sure you'll be able to convince a jury of that."

"I'm not concerned about convincing a jury. I'm telling my story. People can believe whatever they wish. It doesn't change the facts. The truth is a constant."

"So can you explain how it all works, this whole dream process?"

"Let me just say my dreams are more like nightmares. It's not something I would wish upon anyone, but since I can't change it, I've grown to accept it."

"Do you see the faces of people you are going to kill?"

"Yes."

"Are they people you have already met, or are these visions?"

"Both. Sometimes the dreams begin before I actually meet someone, and then when I do, I make the connection. At first, it was strange, I must admit. It wasn't that way with Trent Givens, though, nor with Garth and Lois Winston, but it was with the others."

"Would you care to elaborate on that, Dr. Konklin?"

Wild watched Amos close his eyes once again. He took a deep breath, and the room fell silent for several seconds before Amos finally spoke. "After I completed my undergraduate degree in Canada, I was accepted to graduate school at Harvard. It was there that I met Craig Clemens for the first time. Craig, President of the Student Government, was quite popular. About a week before our first encounter, I began having dreams about a man who was killing people, innocent people. I kept seeing his face over and over, but it wasn't familiar to me. However, the day I met Craig Clemens, I met the man from my dreams. It was the first time I had distinctly seen a person in my dreams that I had yet to meet in person."

"Did you kill Craig Clemens?"

"Yes. I executed a man who was a murderer of innocent people."

"Was there any proof of his guilt?"

"Yes, my dreams, which are proof enough for me. However, during that time in Boston, many young women were being killed by someone believed to be a serial killer. Incidentally, when I executed Clemens, the serial killings ceased."

"Perhaps it was coincidence."

"Providence, Mr. Wild."

"When did this happen?"

"January, 1986."

"After Clemens, you always saw the faces of people in your dreams before you met them?"

"That is correct."

"And you always used a sledgehammer?"

"Yes."

"How did you conceal it?"

"In a case. On appearance, the case looked like something for a musical instrument."

"Okay. Who was next?"

"The next execution occurred in the summer of 1987."

"About eighteen months later?"

"Yes. The person's name was Ralph Hanes. I took a break from graduate school during the summer and went on a road trip into New Hampshire. In fact, I planned to drive across all of the New England states, and I especially wanted to go up to Mount Washington in northern New Hampshire."

"Were you alone?"

"Yes. During the trip, my dreams started, and they were graphic. Hanes was a real creep, quite fond of little boys."

"You saw his face clearly in your dreams?"

"Yes. Hanes moved around a lot in order to stay under the radar. When I met him in New Hampshire, he was camping up around Mount Washington."

"How did you meet him?"

"Out in the woods. He had pitched a tent, and I actually met him down beside a little creek. I recognized him right away."

"Were there any doubts about your recognition of him?"

"No. I never went out with the intent to find the people I dreamt about. It just happened, and when it did, I knew it."

"I assume you traveled with your sledgehammer."

"Yes."

"So you met him at the creek. Then what?"

"He told me approximately where he was camped. I waited until that night and found his tent. It was convenient, really. When I approached, he was snoring loudly, and his head was leaning against the wall of the tent. From the outside, I could see the bulge, and it was a clean stroke. It was justice."

"If he actually was a pedophile, Dr. Konklin, perhaps he did receive justice. However, even if I were sure about someone's guilt, I would leave it to the authorities in charge to bring about justice."

"Spoken like a true man of The State. However, in this case, The State wasn't exactly doing such a good job."

"I never claimed the system is perfect, Dr. Konklin, but it is our system. Those are the rules."

"Man's rules."

"Yes, that's right, and we are men, are we not?"

"We are indeed, Mr. Wild."

Wild leaned forward and pressed down on the small of his back. "So how long until the next execution?"

"It was the next summer."

"Another road trip?"

"Yes."

"Where to this time?"

"Out west, into Arizona."

"Did the summer executions become a pattern?"

"Yes, until I graduated from medical school."

"Then what?"

"Well, I moved to Detroit for a residency at a hospital. The executions became more frequent. Detroit is a big city, and there was more work to do there."

"How long was your residency?"

"Five years."

"How many executions during that time?"

"Twenty-three."

"Do you remember the details of each one?"

"Yes."

"Including their names?"

"Yes."

"Does any one execution or person stand out in your mind?"

"Not really, although it was during that residency that I first executed a woman. Her name was Shelia Jackson. She was sixty-two years old. She poisoned her husband when she was sixty, after forty years of marriage."

"Where did you execute her?"

"In her home."

"How did you manage to meet so many people? Weren't you really busy during residency?"

"Yes, extremely busy. However, I didn't spend all my time at the hospital, although I did meet some of the people from my dreams there."

"How did you know where to execute them? Like that woman, Shelia Jackson, for instance. You said you killed her in her own home?"

"Much depended upon the content of my dreams. In the case of Shelia Jackson, I saw her in a coffee shop and recognized her from my dreams."

"What's the purpose of it all, Dr. Konklin? I mean, why would God act in such a manner? Is this His M.O. for the rest of eternity?"

"Are you questioning God, Mr. Wild?"

"Actually, I'm questioning you. Your story is so fantastic. If God really is intervening, why not do it on a large scale? Why the onesie-twosie stuff? Why not the most evil people, you know, like mass murderers? Even more, why not just execute all bad people at once and get it over with? That's what all the preachers say is going to happen anyway."

"I think the idea of utopia is overstated. If God did destroy all the wicked, that wouldn't solve the problem. The people who are left would always have a choice to do good or to do evil. The concept of freedom of choice is universal. If not, you would have a robotic society. As I said earlier, God intervenes as necessary to maintain order and balance."

"Dr. Konklin, as strange as it may sound, you sound both insane and convincing at the same time. You seem to have an answer for everything. However, I think most people would place you either in the crazy camp or the evil camp."

"It would not be the first time that important things go unappreciated. However, I received enough adulation from my career as a surgeon."

"While we are on the subject of your career, I assume the executions continued after you moved to New York?"

"Yes."

"And during all that time, you practiced medicine here?"

"Yes."

"So Dave Garth and Lois Winston were different, I assume?"

"In what way?"

"I mean, you knew them before you dreamt about them."

"Yes, that case was different. I had many dreams leading up to the night when I executed them, but I never saw the faces of Lois and Garth. Don't get me wrong…they were deserving of death, but I don't know if they were part of God's immediate plan. I was on my own with them."

"Do you believe that to be why you were caught and arrested?"

"Yes. I had grown weary from it all."

"So, after all of those years and all the executions, God abandoned you?"

"I'm not sure *abandoned* is the most appropriate word."

"What then?"

"I don't feel abandoned. Perhaps I didn't have His protection, but we will have to wait and see what happens. Maybe God has something else planned for me. In the meantime, Mr. Wild, you are my biographer."

"Getting back to your dreams, Dr. Konklin, do they occur every night?"

"Yes."

"So, do you keep dreaming over and over about the executions until they occur?"

"I think I need to clarify something. I don't always dream about executions. I also dream about things related to my work as a surgeon. I dream about my patients and their diseases. The dreams are quite vivid, and I see anatomical details."

"Are you saying your dreams assist you in your medical practice?"

"Yes."

"If that is the case, why do you consider them to be nightmares?"

"Well, I dream about the diseases. I see people dying, and I'm the only one who can save them, but there is always some kind of obstacle, something in my way. It's an intense experience."

"So you believe those to be visions from God as well?"

"Yes, of course, but I've always considered them a blessing and a curse at the same time. I feel the need to save people, Mr. Wild, and there is a lot of pressure associated with that. Ask any doctor, and I am sure he or she would tell you the same."

"So you play the role of both savior and destroyer?"

"I suppose that's one way of putting it."

As the room grew silent again, a guard entered. "Time is up today, Mr. Wild."

"Already? Can I have a few more minutes?"

"I'm sorry, sir, but there are rules."

"Right." Wild stood up and walked toward the door. "Dr. Konklin, I'd like to arrange time for another interview."

"Please call me by my first name, Mr. Wild." Amos paused briefly and added, "Actually, before I forget, I have something else I want to tell you. A few weeks ago, Shirley Cobb died, and I received something she wanted me to have—a Bible. I was told in a letter that Lester Cobb had sent it to her before he died, and he'd told her it was mine. I don't know why she kept it so long. Anyway, it's here at the MDC, but since they won't give it to me, I'd like you to have it."

"Why me?"

"It seems like the right thing to do. I've already given my consent. All you have to do is ask for it."

"Okay. Till next time, Dr. Konklin."

"My first name, please, Mr. Wild. We are beyond the point of titles."

"Okay then. Till next time, Amos."

"Or Larry, if you would like."

Wild was puzzled for a moment, and as he left the room, he turned for one final look at Amos Konklin, then raised his hand in a goodbye gesture.

Amos nodded, and the interview was officially over.

From there, Wild made his way through the halls of the MDC until he found the Administration Office, in search of Amos Konklin's Bible.

CHAPTER 24

AMOS, ENOCH, AND MR. STEVENS

The morning following the interview, Peter Wild was awakened early by the ringing of his phone, the police department calling to inform him of an urgent matter at the MDC, requesting his immediate presence. When he arrived, he was escorted to a familiar room; it was another meeting with Lieutenant Wallace, yet the D.A. was absent this time.

"Mr. Wild, let me get right to the point. Amos Konklin is dead."

"Dead!? How is that possible? I mean, I'm really stunned. What happened? He's been in custody all this time, hasn't he? How could he—"

"That's what we are trying to figure out. You interviewed him yesterday. Did he mention anything we might need to know about?"

"He told me many things, but he said nothing that would indicate his impending death, I can assure you. I'm just as surprised as you. Can you shed more light on the details?"

"He was found in his cell, lying in his bed. There were no indications of suicide. All outward appearances would suggest natural causes. Of course, we're not sure about the cause, but there was nothing suspicious. Also, he left a note for you."

"A note?"

"Yes. It's evidence, so make sure it stays in the plastic bag." Wallace pointed toward the table.

Wild sat in yet another uncomfortable folding chair and slid the plastic bag toward him so he could read the note:

"Dear Mr. Wild:

I enjoyed our interview. However, I wanted to personally inform you that I will not be available for another. It appears as though my work is finished.

Regards,

Amos Konklin

Genesis 5:24"

"This is it?"

"That's all, Mr. Wild. Does any of it mean anything to you?"

"Not really."

"What's the Bible verse all about? Genesis something or other?"

"I don't know, Lieutenant."

"Well, if anything comes to mind, do let me know. Thanks for coming, but I have to get going. Looks like it's going to be a very busy day. No offense, but I'm gonna have my hands full keeping the press leeches under control on this one. They'll be swarming the place as soon as word gets out, I'm sure."

"I understand."

As the MDC was busy due to the death of Amos Konklin, Peter Wild returned toward home with Konklin's note referencing Genesis 5:24 playing over in his head. He had traveled to a storage facility in Florida, obtained a secret journal from a bank vault, and sat in a detention center interviewing Konklin. Now the storyteller was dead, and Wild again found himself a pawn in an unfolding drama. For the moment, at least he was in a familiar place. He took the elevator up to the sixth floor, standing beneath that horrid fluorescent light only briefly, as he had so often. When the doors opened, he turned left, and from there it was only a few paces to Apartment 615. Once inside, he wasted no time. He went into his study and searched a top shelf, looking for the copy of Konklin's Bible that he had placed there the night before. There, in the first few pages, he found the reference at Genesis 5:24: *"Enoch walked with God; and he was not, for God took him away."*

Wild smiled wryly and let out a singular chuckle. He had sat with Konklin, interviewing him, listening to what he thought was the rhetoric of a brilliant but delusional man. Now that man was gone. Then, Wild entertained something irrational for a moment. He wondered whether Konklin had actually been taken by God.

"This is crazy."

Wild then sat and happened to open the Bible to the inside front cover. There, his eye caught three notable entries. The first was the name Isaac Newton. Directly underneath was the name Nikola Tesla. However, the third entry appeared to be a combination of two names: Larry Stevens, followed by a forward slash and then the name Amos Konklin. At the very bottom was the inscription, *"Property of Hugh Konklin."*

He sat for a minute, staring at the names, and then remembered what Amos Konklin had told him during the interview. The name Larry suddenly hit him like a ton of bricks, and Wild had a hunch. *If Bill Konklin was not his father, then his last name was not really Konklin. Maybe it was…Stevens?*

He immediately connected with his old friend Dan Evers on the police force. The mission was to discover any information on the name Larry Stevens. As the day unfolded over several discussions with Evers, it finally became obvious to Wild what he was looking for. He then requested that Evers focus on any police information about a child named Larry Stevens, including missing children, particularly during the late 1960s and early 1970s.

Peter Wild was awakened by his telephone the next morning, and he found himself on the couch in his study. The clock read 9:02 a.m. as he stumbled over to his desk. "Yeah, this is Peter," he said, answering the phone on the sixth ring.

"Peter, Dan here. I think I have some information for you."

"Uh…okay."

"Did I wake you? Sounds like it."

"Oh, that's all right. I fell asleep on the couch and overslept."

"Well, I ran that name, Larry Stevens, through multiple databases last night, and I got a match. There was a missing persons report filed on a six-year-old kid named Larry Stevens in Centerville, Minnesota, on May 28, 1970."

"Six years old in 1970? That would put his birthday in 1963 or 1964," Wild muttered. "Konklin was born in 1963."

"Konklin? What are you talking about, Peter?"

"Never mind, Dan. I'm just talking to myself. Go on. Do you have anything else?"

"Well, the report was filed by William and Wanda Stevens, at 800 Trowell Avenue, Centerville, Minnesota. From the notes in the file, it looks like William Stevens owned a shoe store there."

"Anything else?"

"Not really, except that the case was never solved. They never found the kid."

"Are the Stevenses alive, and do they by any chance still live in Centerville?"

"I can find out for ya. I'll call you later."

"Thanks, Dan. I owe you one."

"No problem."

Wild set the phone down and leaned back in his leather chair. "Wow, Peter. This is one crazy fucking story you got your hands on!"

✢ ✢ ✢

Later that evening, Wild arrived at the Minneapolis-St. Paul International Airport, and from there it was on to Centerville. Before leaving New York, Wild had received a follow-up call from Evers, confirming that William Stevens still lived at 800 Trowell Avenue. It was another whirlwind trip, another small town motel for the night.

The next morning around 10:00 a.m., Wild arrived at 800 Trowell Avenue, the address of an old colonial with chipping, faded white paint and a noticeably weather-beaten roof. It appeared in need of repair, yet it blended well, given the surroundings. The taxi waited while Wild walked to the front door and rang the bell.

A few seconds later, a woman opened the door.

"I'm looking for William Stevens."

"This is his home. I'm Rosemary, his nurse."

"May I see him?"

"Are you a friend of the family?"

"No, not really. Actually, I'm a journalist. My name is Peter Wild. I flew in from New York yesterday and was wondering if I could ask Mr. Stevens a few questions."

"Well, this is unexpected. Come inside. I'm sure he'll be glad to see ya. Mr. Stevens doesn't get many visitors these days."

Inside, there was an immediate sense of familiarity, a distinctive musty smell. *The stench of old age,* he thought, as it reminded him of the visits to his parents' home in Wisconsin.

"Mr. Stevens is out on the back porch. He likes to sit there after breakfast."

"Isn't it a bit chilly for that?"

"The back porch is closed in, and there are heaters."

Wild followed Rosemary as they navigated through the living room. *It's amazing how much stuff some people can pack into a room*, he thought, as they finally made their way into the kitchen. Through the glass door in the back of the kitchen, Wild caught sight of old man sitting in a chair, coughing.

Rosemary opened the door and held it for Wild.

"Thank you, Rosemary."

"Mr. Stevens," Rosemary said loudly.

"Yeah? What is it?"

"Mr. Stevens, this here is Mr. Wild. He came from New York to pay you a visit."

"I don't know nobody from New York."

"Mr. Stevens, uh, hi. I'm Peter." Wild held out his hand for a shake.

Stevens lifted his trembling hand, wiped his nose, and then extended it to Wild.

As Wild gripped his cold, damp, hand, he could feel the fragility, as if he could literally crush the old man's bones with a firm shake. "It's nice to meet you, sir."

"She says you're from New York?"

"Yes, sir. May I have a few minutes of your time? I'd like to talk about your son Larry."

"My son?" His dull eyes brightened at once. "My Larry? Go ahead and sit down, mister. Tell me what brings you all the way from the Big Apple."

"I got some stuff to do inside. I'll let you two talk for a while. If you need anything, Mr. Wild, please give a holler."

"Thanks."

After Rosemary returned to the kitchen, the old man asked bluntly, "Now, what do ya wanna know about Larry? They never found him, ya know. All those years of lookin', turnin' every stone over again and again, and they never found my boy."

"I know, sir, and I'm sorry. I'm doing some stories about missing people, and your son is on my list."

"Why Larry?"

"Well, I'm a Midwestern boy myself. I grew up in Wisconsin. I'm doing a story on Midwestern boys who went missing in the sixties." Wild hoped his fabrication would keep the man interested enough to keep talking.

"The sixties, eh? Well, my Larry went missing in 1970. Went off to school one mornin', and we never saw him again. Nearly sent his mama to an early death."

"Well, sir, 1970 counts as well," Wild quickly responded. "Does the name Amos Konklin mean anything to you?

"Who?"

"Amos Konklin."

"Is that another boy who went missing?"

"Uh…yes, sir. Just wondering. Never mind that. Let's get back to your son."

Wild looked on as the old man turned his head away, his eyes gazing through the large porch window into the back yard. It was a contemplative stare, as if he were looking into the past. Just as Wild was about to ask another question, the old man spoke up, repeating, "They never found Larry, ya know. It was a mighty crazy time around here when it all happened. It was so unexpected, you see. We had just come back from a trip down into Iowa. I'd never seen the kids so happy. It nearly killed Wanda, my wife. She's dead now. Maybe she's in heaven. I'd like to think my Larry is there with her, keepin' her company till I get there."

"Can you tell me more about what happened to your son?"

"Like I told ya and like I told them cops, he went to school that day but never made it back home. Things like that just didn't happen back then—not like they do now with all them crazies runnin' about and all those perverts goin' after little kids they find on them damn computers."

"I understand, sir. Were there ever any suspects?"

"Suspects? Heavens no! Larry just vanished. We did everything we could to find him, but nothing ever turned up. You never give up hope, but sometimes you just gotta accept things."

"Can you tell me more about him?"

"I reckon Larry was just about the closest thing to a genius there was around here. Smart boy, I tell you."

"Must have been good genes," Wild said, hoping the compliment would be meaningful.

The old man started to speak and then sat silent again for a few more seconds. Finally, he turned toward Wild, looking him directly in the eyes. "Well, here's the thing. It may have been on account of genes, but they weren't my genes, to be sure."

Surprised, Wild asked, "What do you mean, sir?"

"Well, let's just say those gifts ran on Wanda's side of the family."

"Oh, I see."

"I'm just an ordinary fellow who sold shoes to the locals, that's all. Larry woulda been a lot more than that."

"Well, I'm sure Larry did get a lot of good things from you, sir." The old man just frowned without responding, so Wild quickly followed with another question. "When was Larry born?"

"Back on July 21, 1963. I never forgot his birthday. In all those years while he was gone, I remembered him every July 21, and it tore my heart in two not to be watching my boy blow out his candles." Then, the old man freely offered additional information before Wild could respond. "This may sound strange, but after Wanda passed, I took some of Larry's hair that she kept in a brush, all sealed away. She kept all his stuff you know—every last bit of it. Like I was saying, I took his hair and had a DNA test done, after I found out they could do that kind of fancy stuff."

"What for?"

"I don't know. I was curious, I suppose. I wanted to know more about my son. Them scientists will send you a profile of the person based on the DNA. I guess I wanted to know what kind of man he would have become, if he'd had a chance to."

Wild noticed tears in the old man's eyes but continued on, "Did you use the DNA Online Institute?"

"That sounds like the place. How did you know?"

"I do a fair share of investigative reporting and just happen to know about them."

"I don't know what else you wanna know, mister, but I'm getting tired of talking now." It was the old man's way of saying he wanted Wild to leave, as politely as he could.

"Actually, that's all I needed to know, Mr. Stevens. You've been quite helpful." Wild rose from his seat.

About that time, Rosemary opened the door. "You two finished talking?"

"Yes," Wild replied. "Thanks again, Mr. Stevens." Wild followed Rosemary through the kitchen and then back through the living room maze of clutter. Outside the front door, he spotted the taxi, and he turned to Rosemary. "Thanks again. Tell Mr. Stevens I enjoyed our chat."

"Will do," she said.

✵ ✵ ✵

During his flight back to New York, Wild leaned his head against the cabin window, looking out at the vastness. It was difficult to comprehend all that had happened, all he had seen and heard in the span of a few short days. *What am I supposed to write about? Seems I've got all the makings of a masterpiece of investigative reporting, but how would I begin the saga? Do I report only about the two murders the world is aware of or reveal the destruction of life that spanned nearly forty years? Will it be the heartfelt story of a kidnapped child that ended badly? The story of a brilliant surgeon and a psychotic serial killer, or the tale of a delusional man claiming to be God's avenger? Do I make him out to be some modern-day Enoch, a man whisked away by God for his faithful service?* Wild allowed his mind to entertain all the possibilities for a moment, and then he drifted off to sleep.

He was awakened when the plane landed, and then shut his eyes again until the airplane made its way to the gate. When the lights came on in the cabin, he noticed there was a text message from the D.A.'s office: *"Konklin's death appears to have been from natural causes."*

When Wild pressed the delete key, he started to think again about his adventure and what he might eventually write about. One thing he was sure of: The story of Amos Konklin was still unfolding, even after his death. *The world will just have to wait.*

CHAPTER 25

WILD'S ARTICLE

The following article by Peter Wild appeared in *The New York Times* on July 21, 2020.

"In late 2018, I wrote a series of three articles on the Amos Konklin case. For those of you who may not be familiar with the details, in the autumn of 2018, Dr. Amos Konklin was arrested for the murders of Dave Garth and Lois Winston at the Old Wilderness Campground, located about an hour outside the city. Mr. Garth was a fellow physician of Konklin's, and Ms. Winston had been a friend. Konklin was incarcerated at the MDC awaiting trial when he died unexpectedly on the eve of January 30, 2019, later determined to be from natural causes. Although The New York Times published an article on his death, it was not written by me. Now, a year and a half later, I'm prepared to finish my series on Konklin. Why the long delay? Allow me to explain...

"On January 28, 2019, Amos Konklin invited me to meet with him at the MDC. Konklin had read my articles covering the murders, which were no doubt the catalyst prompting his invitation. During that brief initial meeting, Konklin asked me to go on a quest. The next day, on January 29, 2019, I was in Florida acquiring Konklin's diary, which he had stored in a safety deposit box. In that diary, Konklin chronicled events that happened in August and September of 1980. These events culminated in a self-described 'first killing' of a young man in Canada, a killing committed by Konklin, while he was still in high school.

"I met with Konklin again on January 30. He revealed that he had executed numerous people since 1980, culminating with Dave Garth and Lois Winston at the Old Wilderness Campground. According to Konklin, those executions were carried out as part of a divine plan. As fantastic as it may sound, Konklin believed his victims were deserving of death. Moreover, according to Konklin, he received dreams from God disclosing the identity of those who were to be executed. On the surface, this story appears to fit the classic serial killer mold, with an added touch of insanity mixed with delusion. However, following my interview with Konklin, I did not immediately reach the conclusion that he was insane—or evil. On the contrary, I found Konklin to be brilliant, articulate, and even convincing at times. My instincts told me there was more to this story.

"Throughout the interview, it became apparent that Konklin was obsessed with the Bible. He quoted it often, using it as a reference to make his arguments. Toward the end of the interview, Konklin gave me a gift, an apropos one, given our conversation. That gift, a Bible, was an artifact from his childhood that had been mailed to him by the woman who had raised him from the time he was twelve years old. Prior to that, Amos Konklin had lived with a man named Bill Konklin, believed to be his father, *in a traveling carnival. At age twelve, though, Amos Konklin suffered an accident and a head injury that resulted in a lengthy hospitalization and a loss of memory. Bill Konklin disappeared, so following the boy's recovery, Amos Konklin moved into the home of a Canadian family, where he lived until he graduated high school.*

"The day following his death, I discovered some interesting entries written inside the front cover of the Bible—the names Isaac Newton, Nikola Tesla, and Larry Stevens/Amos Konklin. It seemed an odd mix of names, but it was the name Larry Stevens that stood out at first. Playing on a reporter's hunch, I soon discovered that Amos Konklin's real name was Larry Stevens.

"The road to this discovery began when, on the third day after Konklin's death, I visited an elderly gentleman named William Stevens of Centerville, Minnesota, whose son, Larry Stevens, had disappeared in May of 1970 when Larry was just six years old. During our conversation, Mr. Stevens told me of a DNA profile test he had requested by submitting samples of his missing son's hair, taken from a hairbrush his saddened mother had kept as a memento of her little boy gone missing. When I returned to New York, I had a friend at the police department follow up with the DNA Online Institute record of that hair sample from Larry Stevens, the one Mr. William Stevens had requested. That sample was cross-matched with a DNA sample from Amos Konklin, and the DNA was identical. As I relate these facts now, it should be appreciated that they were unknown to Konklin himself.

"Although I have given an outline of this story, it would be difficult for me to effectively articulate all I heard, learned, and experienced in that short span of a week in the winter of 2019. Let me just say I felt writing an article about Konklin at the time of his death would have been premature and a disservice. Therefore, I declined. Then, about a month later, there was another unexpected

occurrence. A man named Paul Thomas, serving a life sentence for rape, confessed in a memoir that he and another teen named Trent Givens had raped and murdered a young woman in Canada in 1979. Thomas stated in his memoir that Givens was later murdered, which he considered, in his own words, to be 'poetic justice.' I immediately recalled what Konklin had told me during his interview—that Trent Givens had actually raped a young woman who was a close friend of his and that the Givens execution was justice. At the time, I did not know whether or not to believe him. Even so, I told Konklin that if Givens was guilty of rape, he should have been delivered to the authorities. Now, not only was there an independent story lending some support to Konklin's claim that he had executed Givens, but it was also believable that Trent Givens was a criminal, a rapist, who, at least in the minds of those who believe in capital punishment, would have been deserving of death.

"After I read the Thomas memoir, I began an investigation that lasted more than a year. While Konklin had confessed to numerous executions, he only revealed the names of six of his victims, the latter two being Dave Garth and Lois Winston. Since Konklin had stated that Garth and Winston were not divinely identified for execution, I focused my investigation on the three other names besides Trent Givens. To make a long story short, I concluded my investigation believing there was strong circumstantial evidence to support Konklin's claims about his other named victims. Why was this discovery important? Well, my intentions were not in any way aimed at justifying Konklin's crimes. Rather, I was curious about whether these were innocent victims or people who also had blood on their hands. I concluded my investigation believing these people were not innocent men and women. To say these four people, including Trent Givens, are a good statistical sample representative of all of Konklin's alleged victims is certainly debatable. However,

the information cannot simply be ignored. For me, the question became: How did Konklin know about these people? If they were truly criminals, as I believe the evidence suggests, was it just co-incidence? I must admit that one could play the devil's advocate and suggest that Konklin was more of a vigilante who took justice into his own hands rather than a serial killer, yet such activism would require somehow attaining information about these people. Although this is a possibility, the things I found that led me to my conclusions were, for the most part, not part of an easily accessible public record. Rather, they came as a result of hard, unrelenting investigation.

"Additionally, one of the things I had to reconcile was Konklin's personal testimony of his haunting dreams and night-mares. According to him, these experiences were intense. I had no reason to dismiss his explanations, yet I needed more information and confirmation. About six months after his death, his widow, Cynthia Konklin, agreed to an interview. Although she was un-aware of her husband's other alleged executions (the ones he re-vealed only to me), she did corroborate his story of the dreams. She described them as nightmares that persisted throughout their married life. While I have no way of knowing what Konklin saw or experienced in his dreams, I cannot easily discount his personal testimony. I have no reason to doubt that he believed what he was telling me.

"Finally, there was the manner of Konklin's death. What most people don't know is that Konklin left me a note on the eve of his death. While one might think of it as a suicide note, the manner of his death is actually quite mysterious. According to the coroner's report, Konklin died in his sleep, from natural causes. The difficult question to answer is: How did he know, as he insinuated in his note, that he was about to die? That note read:

'Dear Mr. Wild:

I enjoyed our interview. However, I wanted to personally inform you that I will not be available for another. It
appears as though my work is finished.

Regards,
Amos Konklin
Genesis 5:24'

"The Bible verse Konklin referenced, Genesis 5:24, says:
'Enoch walked with God; and he was not, for God took
him away.'

"As time passed, I began thinking about the other two names
written on the inside cover of Konklin's Bible. Although I don't
know who put them there, I thought it may have been for good
reason. Isaac Newton was certainly familiar, while Nikola Tesla
was a name I had only heard a few times.

"Isaac Newton is well known for his contributions to math
and science. His book, Mathematical Principles of Natural
Philosophy, is regarded by some as the most important science
book ever written. In addition to calculus, Newton discovered
gravity and described the three laws of motion. Newton was also
an astronomer, revealed secrets about light and color, and built the
first telescope. He is regarded by many scholars as one of the most
influential people in human history and the most brilliant scientist
who ever lived. A less well-known fact about Newton is that he
was a theologian, and his writings on religious topics dwarfed his
writings on science, consisting of millions of words.

"Nikola Tesla was an electrical and mechanical engineer
whose contributions are numerous, including that of the alternating
electrical current system that powers the modern world. However,
Tesla was eccentric. Hence, the name Thomas Edison became more

prominent, although it would be debatable to suggest Edison's intellect was superior. In fact, Tesla was an original thinker, ahead of his time. For example, Tesla had described the concept of radio ten years prior to Marconi, although Marconi is credited as the inventor. In 1943, the courts found Marconi's patents to be invalid due to Tesla's previous descriptions. Among his other achievements were the AC motor, fluorescent lights, wireless communications, robotics, the hydroelectric plant at Niagara Falls, logic gates, radar, and X-rays. It was said that Tesla had a photographic memory and possessed the ability to memorize entire books. Tesla was not as outspoken about Newton on religious matters, yet he seemed to share the same fascination with God and the Bible.

"It is not my intent to use Newton and Tesla as a case for belief in God. Throughout history, there have been many brilliant men and women who were believers and many others who were not. Instead, as a reporter, I cannot escape the facts of this case. Yet, of these two names, it's the reference to Tesla that is the most fascinating, for what I soon discovered about him led me right back to Konklin in a way I could have never predicted. What I found most enlightening was Tesla's autobiography, which he wrote in 1919 at the age of 63 years. Below are some interesting excerpts:

'There was another and still more important reason for my late awakening. In my boyhood, I suffered from a peculiar affliction due to the appearance of images, often accompanied by strong flashes of light, which marred the sight of real objects and interfered with my thoughts and actions. They were pictures of things and scenes which I had really seen, never of those imagined. When a word was spoken to me, the image of the object it designated would present itself vividly to my vision, and sometimes I was quite unable to distinguish whether what I saw was tangible or not. This caused me great discomfort and anxiety.

None of the students of psychology or physiology whom I have consulted could ever explain satisfactorily these phenomena. They seem to have been unique, although I was probably predisposed as my brother experienced a similar trouble. The theory I have formulated is that the images were the result of a reflex action from the brain on the retina under great excitation. They certainly were not hallucinations such as are produced in diseased and anguished minds, for in other respects I was normal and composed. To give an idea of my distress, suppose I had witnessed a funeral or some such nerve-wracking spectacle. Inevitably, in the stillness of night, a vivid picture of the scene would thrust itself before my eyes and persist despite all my efforts to banish it... This I did constantly until I was about seventeen, when my thoughts turned seriously to invention. Then I observed to my delight that I could visualize with the greatest facility. I needed no models, drawings, or experiments. I could picture them all as real in my mind. Thus, I have been led unconsciously to evolve what I consider a new method of materializing inventive concepts and ideas, which is radically opposite to the purely experimental and is in my opinion ever so much more expeditious and efficient. The moment one constructs a device to carry into practice a crude idea, he finds himself unavoidably engrossed with the details of the apparatus. As he goes on improving and reconstructing, his force of concentration diminishes, and he loses sight of the great underlying principle. Results may be obtained but always at the sacrifice of quality.

'My method is different. I do not rush into actual work. When I get an idea, I start at once building it up in my imagination. I change the construction, make improvements, and operate the device in my mind. It is absolutely immaterial to me whether I run my turbine in thought or test it in my shop. I even note if it is out of balance. There is no difference whatever; the results are the same. In this way, I am able to rapidly develop and perfect a conception without touching anything. When I have gone so far as to embody in the invention every possible improvement I can think of and see no fault anywhere, I put into concrete form this final product of my brain. Invariably, my device works as I conceived that it should, and the experiment comes out exactly as I planned it. In twenty years, there has not been a single exception. Why should it be otherwise? Engineering, electrical and mechanical, is positive in results. There is scarcely a subject that cannot be examined beforehand, from the available theoretical and practical data. The carrying out into practice of a crude idea, as is being generally done, is, I hold, nothing but a waste of energy, money, and time.

'My early affliction had, however, another compensation. The incessant mental exertion developed my powers of observation and enabled me to discover a truth of great importance. I had noted that the appearance of images was always preceded by actual visions of scenes under peculiar and generally very exceptional conditions, and I was impelled on each occasion to locate the original impulse. After a while, this effort grew to be almost automatic, and I gained great facility in connecting cause and effect. Soon I became aware, to my surprise, that every thought I conceived was suggested by an external impression. Not only this but all my actions were prompted in a similar way. In the course of time, it became perfectly evident to me that I was merely an automaton endowed with power of movement, responding to the stimuli of the sense organs and thinking and acting accordingly.

'At this time, as at many other times in the past, my thoughts turned toward my mother's teaching. The gift of mental power comes from God, Divine Being, and if we concentrate our minds on that truth, we become in tune with this great power. My mother had taught me to seek all truth in the Bible; therefore, I devoted the next few months to the study of this work.'

"*After I read those words, I thought about Konklin, his dreams, and his obsession with God. Obviously, Konklin was not alone, so I began to wonder about Tesla's self-described* 'affliction.' *What would be a rational explanation for his experiences? Did he suffer from a mental disorder? Rather than an isolated biological anomaly, Tesla claimed his brother* 'experienced a similar trouble.' *Unfortunately, little is known about Tesla's parents or his ancestors, but it would be interesting to know if the explanation lay in some inherited genetic traits. While Tesla alludes to a divine connection, his words were not as direct and specific as Konklin's. Moreover, Tesla never used his gifts to bring vengeance or execute people. He was an inventor. While one cannot prove Tesla's claims about the* 'appearance of images,' *his productivity is beyond question. His contributions as an inventor are enormous and undeniable.*

"*But Tesla's words do invoke thought and conjecture about the possibilities of divine gifts that are otherwise dismissed by most. For many days following my reading of his autobiography, I kept thinking about the words:* 'In the course of time, it became perfectly evident to me that I was merely an automaton endowed with power of movement, responding to the stimuli of the sense organs and thinking and acting accordingly,' *contemplating their implication. It suggested to me that Tesla may have been able to access or tap into something that is elusive to most of us. Again, I thought of*

Konklin, but Konklin the surgeon instead. Amos Konklin was called 'Dr. Golden Hands' and revealed in our interview that his visions did not constrain him simply to the role of God's executioner. On the contrary, he often dreamt of his patients and their diseases, and he claimed his uncanny successes as a surgeon were derived from these experiences rather than what would typically be described as intuition or good fortune.

"For me, there were striking parallels between what Konklin described and Tesla's words, 'I had noted that the appearance of images was always preceded by actual visions of scenes under peculiar and generally very exceptional conditions.' *Nevertheless, I must concede, as a reporter, that my objectivity could be questioned. Konklin was highly intelligent, having scored 178 on at least one IQ test taken during college, so it is possible that he told a grandiose story and nothing more. Yet, like Tesla the inventor, Konklin's accomplishments as a surgeon are well known and documented.*

"But it's the visions and tales of executions with divine backing that stretch the imagination of what can be believed as true. Is it possible that God not only exists, but that He is intimately involved in human affairs, so much so that He carries out His will through the actions of men like Konklin? Was there some force that maneuvered Larry Stevens from Centerville, Minnesota, to become a kidnapped child living in a carnival? Did his experiences in the carnival shape the personality of the man he was to become, or would there have been a Dr. Larry Stevens, noted neurosurgeon and serial killer? And what of the High Striker carnival sideshow hammer, the instrument Konklin used to commit his executions? Is there a particular reason for such a brutish, blunt weapon, or is it arbitrary, simply a manifestation of a man's psychosis? Having considered the evidence, I have to admit that I don't know the answers. I can only try to keep an open mind to the possibilities.

"Before I bring this topic to a close, I want to share one final set of facts, for the story of Konklin and Tesla is intertwined beyond a notation in a Bible and words about visions and God. Nikola Tesla arrived in Colorado Springs in May of 1899, constructed a lab, and carried out mysterious experiments there until January of 1900. He created a large Tesla coil to conduct what he referred to as 'wireless telegraphy tests.' During these experiments, he transferred energy to receiving devices without wires, and inhabitants of nearby towns described sparks coming up from the ground and across their shoes. He was able to light 200 lamps without wires from 25 miles away. Interestingly enough, Margaret Ann Harrison was born in Colorado Springs in 1899. She later married a farmer and moved to Iowa, where she gave birth to a daughter named Wanda, later the mother of Larry Stevens—yes, the same Larry Stevens known to us as Amos Konklin.

"I hope this article has been well worth the wait and not a cause for identifying me as a kook or a sympathizer. My purpose here is to share this story, as incredible as it all may sound. I leave it to my audience to decide for yourselves. As Amos Konklin once said to me, 'People can believe whatever they wish. It doesn't change the facts. The truth is a constant.'"

www.ingramcontent.com/pod-product-compliance
Lightning Source LLC
Chambersburg PA
CBHW070220260626
47160CB00002B/615